THE HIDDEN YEARS

THE HIDDEN YEARS

A novel about Jesus

by

Neil Boyd

Carmel, New York 10512

Originally published 1984 by Hodder and Stoughton, 47 Bedford Square, London, England.

ISBN 0-89622-318-3
Library of Congress Catalog Card Number 86-50903

'How Jesus spent the greater part of his life is a mystery.
Not one word has been recorded about it.
Some scholars regard this as the most provoking
problem in history, while others believe it to be an
intentional mystery.'
H.V. Morton, *In the Steps of the Master.*

Chapter 1

The sun dipped into the Great Sea like the beak of a predatory bird and suddenly the day was at its close.

The Man put down his tools with a sigh, removed his leather apron and brushed himself free of wood-shavings and sawdust. Leaving his workshop that opened on to the narrow street he slowly made his way through the stirring village. It was a village that had no pattern to it. The houses came first, long before anyone could remember, and the paths through the houses, in the course of time, became streets.

According to custom, he greeted everyone as he walked. Old men stood against a wall like shadows talking. Lads with slings which they released at unsuspecting sparrows imagined they were King David demolishing Goliath. Little girls with bare legs so caked with mud that they looked like the barks of trees were hopping and tossing pebbles in squares traced in the dust.

The Man greeted his fellow tradesmen as they too prepared to close down for the evening. There were onion-sellers, makers of carpets and sheepskin coats, sellers of poultry and nomads' beads, leather-makers, pastry-makers, potters, vendors of spices and candles and wickerwork.

Many a boy was leading a man, his blind father or grandfather, who insisted on a stroll now that the air had cooled. Outside a limestone house, a woman was seated on the ground with a mortar and pestle grinding corn into flour.

The Man loved this part of the day best. At dusk, every shape of the white-stoned village stood out, distinct, magnified, and the general sense of relief at the sun's going down was palpable. Smoke ascended. Smells of cooking filled the air, mingling with, then overcoming the thick daylight odours of asses and camels and the stench of animals' dung. The flies continued to be a pest but already they were sizzling less noisily than before and no longer settled in black patches on children's faces. It was possible, for the first time since dawn, to open the eyes wide without being bothered by sunlight or blinded by midges and flies.

He pressed a couple of coins into the hollow of a blind man's hand near the village well. Women had gathered there with buckets and pitchers of all shapes and sizes. Some of the buckets were his own handiwork; he wished there were more of them.

He nodded respectfully to the chattering women, saying nothing. One or two of the marriageable ones, more languorous than the rest, turned their gaze coyly away until he was past. They hoped, all the same, he had noticed how fat, brawny and delectable they were.

The son of Mary was tall, straight, handsome, with a spring in his step. He had a high forehead and big candid eyes, though he was somewhat shy. He had a reputation for being a hard and honest worker. His voice was powerful but used softly, suggesting hidden reserves. His smile was open, it cancelled out ill-will in others. His laughter was never hurtful. He was liked by everyone.

Higher up the southern slope the Man walked, his sandals slapping the packed-mud path, past fields of yellow and rose-coloured flax spiked by scarlet poppies, past hillocks of myrtle, arbutus and holly-oak, past the caves in which he had played as a boy. Until, slightly out of breath, he was up to the rim of the cup in which his village lay.

A breeze was blowing out of the north-east, wafting cedar and pinewood. The Book was right to say that God spoke to the first Man in the cool of the evening breeze. No touch was more gentle or considerate in this land of fire. The breeze filled a man like the Spirit of God, made him feel free and alive.

The sky was empty. Not a wisp of cloud had appeared

8

that day or for thirty days before it. But here in Galilee, high above sea-level, it was nearly always cool at evening. Whenever he had left his village – never for more than a few days at a time – he always returned with a sense of relief because he cherished this wind on the tops of the hills.

In a few minutes he had reached the spot he liked best. A rocky knoll from which he had a clear view of this land that meant so much to him. A holy land. The land of his fathers.

In the still clear light, he could see every copse and wood and moorland tract, every farm building and hamlet around. The dwellings were of wattle and whitewash, built next to slender cypresses. There were stone-tiered olive groves in plenty, vineyards, sparsely planted fig-trees and, in level places, fields of corn.

The summer corn was bleached white by the sun, and the heavy bearded heads proclaimed it was time for harvest.

He heard or imagined he heard the crickets living up to their name, *zarzur*, in the white fields, strident, noisy as a swarm of bees. The wind caused the dry stalks not to rustle but to hiss in response. And over the fields, the ravens wheeled, honking and croaking, like so many good-tempered angels of death reluctant to disturb the serenity of night.

But the Man looked beyond the boundaries of his village, and wherever he looked he was filled with quiet exultation.

To the north was Mount Hermon, the snow still packed in its deep gullies in spite of the heat. From Hermon's three fountain-heads, as every Jewish child was taught, the Jordan, the land's only abundant river, begins. That river flows south into the Lake of Galilee and then from it, down through a great gash in the earth's crust, to the Salt Sea.

To the east, the mountains, lit up by the setting sun, were turning a bruised purple and, hidden in the mists that foretold a hot tomorrow, was the Jordan valley.

Below him, close by, was the great plain of Esdraelon, a Joseph's coat of golds, browns, yellows, greens, all

9

melting in twilight.

To the south-east was Tabor, the table-mountain, the mount of the broken cone, rising 2,500 feet, sheer out of the plain. He had climbed it often, right to the summit where grew oaks that bore enormous acorns, and carob-trees and irises coloured purple and white. Lately he had climbed it for a better view of this mountainous land and for the peace he experienced there, up a scarcely marked track, scattering lizards and the occasional porcupine. It was years ago on Tabor – Joseph had taken him for an outing soon after Passover – that he had a child's unrepeatable moment of glory: he heard his first nightingale.

Farther south, beyond Esdraelon, stood out the mountains of Samaria. It was a sad stretch of land, conjuring up some of Israel's greatest memories, yet now in schism from the traditional Jewish faith.

To the west, the black bulk of Mount Carmel, fertile, wooded, with pasturage for many horses, ending in a sharp cliff that plunged into the sea.

That way, the way of the setting sun, lay Greece and Rome whose armies had enslaved his people, He did not linger on them. Instead, he slowly wheeled round to his right as though he were in the synagogue holding up the scroll of the Law to show it to the entire world.

He finally came to rest facing Jerusalem. For beyond Samaria, seventy-five miles south of where he stood, was Judaea and the City of David.

He was proud of the capital, proud of its noble Temple and the unrivalled place it held in the history of his people. Yet lately, on his few visits, it had troubled him, too.

He pictured to himself the harsh unfeeling landscape with its scentless scrub, its few springs and few refreshing fountains, the sky skin-tight over the bare terrain, the hills under the sun like a gigantic animal whose bones have been picked clean by vultures, the shelves and crags and dried-up gullies, the eroded rocks – all this was daunting to a Galilean like himself, raised in a greener, gentler corner of the world.

Jerusalem disturbed him for other reasons, but he did

not ponder them that night.

Such was the scope of the land he took in, in one slow circle. It was not that the land belonged to his people, his people belonged to the land. Such was the eternal will of God.

Other nations might overrun them, tax them, make censuses to number them as if they were sheep or goats, issue them with coins bearing an emperor's head or pagan images, it made no difference. They belonged to this land, they always would. And they had no king but God.

The light was fading fast. The Man could just make out below him a boy leading a flock of sheep. From that distance, they resembled grey stones moving.

He tugged his mantle over his eyes and settled down with his legs under him on the warm soil. Soon he began rocking to and fro. He did not hear a pair of foxes screaming their rivalry in the valley below him, nor the little owl in an olive-grove already giving out a low wailing note as if it were conducting a private funeral.

His breathing became quieter, his pulse slowed down and in his perpetual rocking only one word came to his lips over and over: 'Abba.'

The stars appeared, uncountable, winking over the hills, and a big clean moon sailed by. He noticed none of this. There was for him no time and space, no outwards and inwards.

Only this rocking motion and, like a soft moan borne on the wind, the one word Abba, my Father.

Chapter 2

The Man came to with the first glint of sunrise, saying instinctively, *'Hear, O Israel, the Lord our God, the Lord is one.'*

11

The traditional prayer with which he cracked the eggshell of the morning.

His clothes were drenched with dew, his teeth began chattering and he discovered he was hungry.

He stood up and stretched himself. He filled his lungs and the earth smelled as fresh as a new loaf.

Down the dark slopes cocks were crisply crowing and asses braying. Farther away, tethered camels were burbling and snorting defiance at the prospect of another day's toil.

The Man allowed himself a last glance round at Hermon and Tabor, mountains which, the Psalmist said, exult in the name of the Lord. Then with brisk strides he descended to his home at the eastern edge of the village.

The dreamy morning scene was familiar to him. He hailed shepherds, piping and calling in a strange musical tone to their long-eared sheep, as they led them to pasture. Beasts were lowing in the fields like women in labour. There was a business-like quality about the flight and chirruping of birds. Lower down, mangy dogs with torn ears stretched themselves and shook out the fleas. In the streets, children were fast asleep shivering, a few branches, or, if they were lucky, a pair of sandals serving as a pillow. Later that day, they would crowd out his workshop, begging him to teach them how to use wood; and he would guide their hands as, long ago, Joseph had guided his. In the market-place, peasants were yawning and rubbing their eyes as they waited hopefully to be hired for a day in the fields.

He arrived at his house, a limestone addition to a rock cave. His mother had somehow trained a caper-plant known as hyssop, rooted in stones, to shade the front of the house like a cloak. With its sprays of thorns, its tassels and edible buds, it seemed to be growing out of the wall.

He did not enter at once. He could hear inside the querulous tones of old Anna, a pious widow – the most avoidable sort, as the Rabbi Ezra put it – who had come to his mother for a good grouse.

Mary was generous by nature. Her open-heartedness extended even to the chickens. Jesus often said to her, 'If

I was as well fed as your chickens I would lay eggs myself.'

Mary was a good listener. 'That way,' she said, 'people think they're important. And they *are* important, every one.'

At present, she was evidently listening attentively to bird-eyed, balding Anna who always wore her late husband's sheepskin coat as a shawl, winter and summer.

Jesus had no scruples about leaving his mother to do good in her own way. He preferred to watch swallows swoop over the village, then, with time still on his hands, to examine the cucumber beds and the vegetables which his mother was always encouraging to grow bigger and bigger. The cabbages and turnips obliged. The onions, she said, were hard of hearing.

Mary was marvellously content. She spread contentment. What was her secret?

Jesus had often asked himself that. His conclusion was, she lived fully in each moment.

'There's too much joy in this moment,' she always said, 'to want it to pass on.'

This may even have explained why she was reckoned the best grape-picker in the district. She went slowly, methodically, *contentedly*, along the vines, never missing one grape. Never eating one, either.

'Tomorrow's bread has no taste for me,' was another favourite dictum of hers. 'Today's is sweet enough.'

Tomorrow was as distant for her as a hundred years hence. If you look to the future, try to live in it, you only cheat yourself of the present. 'I'm only a poor woman,' she remarked, with a rare touch of irony, 'so I have to make do with today. When I don't like it, I mend it or sew a patch on it, but I can't afford to give it away or swap it for tomorrow. Who knows, there may not be a today waiting for me next sun-up.'

In addition, she was a mother. For mothers, tomorrow comes soon enough. Too soon. She didn't want to hurry anything along when today passes far too quickly already.

He was thinking this while Anna was complaining that

13

her rent was being doubled by the owner, who had recently become a member of the Jerusalem Sanhedrin.

'He needs extra money for his plumage,' Mary managed to slip in.

'What am I to do?' Anna concluded, in a kind of wail. 'Soon I'll have no place to light a fire.'

'Never you mind,' Mary said. 'God will look after you.' It was always 'God's will' or 'God willing' with her.

'But what about that swine of a landlord?'

'He'll get his deserts, don't worry about that, Anna. God is on the slave's side, isn't he always? The idle rich won't have it their way for ever.'

Jesus paused in his inspection of the disobedient onion patch to smile at his mother's limitless faith.

'They've had it their way for a long time,' Anna protested.

'Too long, I grant you, Anna dear, but not for ever,' Mary insisted. 'The poor will have their day. God will see to that. He'll wipe away the tears of us that cry and make the greedy howl. Doesn't the Book say, He'll hurl the mighty from their thrones?'

'You reckon so?' Anna was dubious, like a peasant who knows that only rents, taxes, yesterday and today are certain, with a big question against the rest of today.

'Can't you see it?' Mary said, with a lift of the voice. 'The rich coming trembling to the gate of heaven and the blessed God crying, "Off with you, you heathen," and sending them packing without a penny or a piece of pork.'

It was strange how Jesus's gentle, attentive, tolerant mother was famed in the village for her verbal assaults on the rich and powerful of the earth. Many a time someone grabbed him in the street to whisper, 'Your mother would have made a great prophet, Jesus. She could outcurse Jeremiah if she tried.'

'I'm glad I came,' Anna said. 'You cheer us all up, Mary, you do.'

Mary was evidently loading the sad old lady with gifts, for Anna was chanting, 'God bless you for that. May you see your children's children. May your sweet, darling first-born be like the Messiah to you. Ah, he's a grand lad and no mistake, the image of his father before him.'

14

To earn *that*, Mary must have given her the pumpkin.

'We widows have to stick together,' Mary returned.

An understatement. She held that anyone in need belonged to her household. Hers was the shy gallantry of womankind, the more gallant for never being observed.

'Anyway, Anna dear, it's been lovely having you.'

Mary's 'dishonesties' were always true on a higher plane.

Out skipped Anna, smiling, replete with bread, wine, dried figs, raisins, lentils, beans and yes, their last pumpkin.

Jesus, taking care to avoid Anna's gaze, exchanged 'Peace' with her and, bowing his head, went through the curtain of woven goats' hair that shaded the entrance and kept out the flies.

Mary, plump and motherly, with the beginnings of arthritis showing in the knuckles of her right hand, clasped him to her. She hardly came up to his chest.

'Your sweet, darling first-born's home,' he said, mimicking Anna as he was forced to present himself for morning inspection.

'About time too,' she said. Her small nostrils flared, her grey eyes sparkled like water in the sun. 'Just look at you, soaked to the skin again. Out of those clothes!'

'After breakfast,' he pleaded, without conviction.

'This minute, you hear.'

Jesus, his eyes adjusting to the dark interior, shrugged helplessly. He went into the shrouded second half of the house where a freshly laundered tunic was spread out for him.

'Tired?' she called out.

'Not a bit,' he replied. He really felt fresher than if he had slept the night through.

'What were you doing out there?'

'Waiting,' he said.

'I should think so.' Mary said it sternly to mask the immemorial anxiety of a mother who knows she is doomed to lose her son one day.

Sons are like turtles. She always said it, especially at weddings. Year after year they stay around the house so you take them for granted. One morning, you look for

15

them and they've gone.

'You're still only an apprentice, don't forget that.'

When he was washed and changed, he sat down to a simple meal: barley bread – the bread of the poor, it was called locally – dried figs, a hard-boiled egg, a cup of goat's milk. Mary ignored his tongue-in-cheek request for a slice of pumpkin.

'It's a wonder,' he said, 'you didn't give *me* away when I was a baby.'

'I wish I had. Sometimes.' She laughed a girlish laugh. 'Now eat your food slowly as your father taught you.'

She had extinguished the oil lamp which gave at best a weak pool of yellow light. The cloying smell was still in the air. She had, as usual, been to the well before sun-up, for the pitchers were full to the brim.

She fussed over him, drying his hair and gleaming black beard with a towel, so he found it hard to get food inside him.

'Leave me be, woman,' he said, playfully tapping her freckled hand. 'How am I expected to eat with you pulling my hair out?'

She took no notice, simply told him that Rabbi Ezra the wood-cutter had called earlier. 'He wanted to know where you were.'

'You said?'

'About God's business.'

'What did he want?'

The Rabbi wanted him to go with him to the woods. He had marked out some trees but needed someone strong to fell them for him.

Jesus said he would go. He loved Ezra dearly. Though he suspected that today Ezra wanted more from him than help in chopping down trees.

This was one request it was not in Jesus's power to grant.

16

Chapter 3

Rabbi Ezra was seated astride a log on the edge of the wood. A jot of a man with large, fleshy ears, he had the beak and voice of a crow. His eyes were like coal or, rather, one eye was, because the second was always half-closed in a kind of wink. A narrow chin, cleft like a wishbone, was filled out by a scraggy goat-like beard.

The Rabbi was not in a cheerful mood. He had come across a group of children from the village. They had caught a wood-pigeon, shelled its eyes out with a knife and tied it to the bough of a tree to attract other pigeons by its struggles. Ezra had released the bird and chased them off.

'Go before I send bears on you,' he had croaked. The children, who had learned their scripture from him, called out, 'Go home, Baldie,' but retreated none the less, taking their blind bird with them.

The Rabbi settled down, his temper soothed by the prospect of working the day through with his favourite pupil. Jesus had been mischievous enough as a boy and hard to deal with at times but never cruel.

The old man recalled how, twenty years before, he had formed his first children's class, his 'little Sanhedrin', he called it. He told the parents the Torah was the Book of the Child.

'Send them all along,' he had proclaimed, with all the fervour of a late beginner. 'No child is too young to learn God's Law.'

On the very first day, Joseph the carpenter appeared.

He was an astoundingly quiet man, with a voice as soft as dust. The joke in the village was that at the creation, after working non-stop for six days, God needed a rest.

Then it came to him that he had forgotten to make himself a bed. So, to save time and trouble, he breathed on a tiny twig from an olive-tree and turned it into Joseph the carpenter. It was he who made the bed. This was why Joseph never hurried at anything or raised his voice. Because he was made on the Great Sabbath.

Joseph brought to the class this little fellow aged four, with bright almond-shaped eyes and hair black and smooth as a raven's with specks of sawdust in it. Ezra could still see the child's thick upper lids, the long lashes, the keen narrow face. He was wearing a brown tunic a bit too big for him, with the left cuff crusted where he wiped his nose. And, yes, the thumb of his left hand was black and swollen. Joseph whispered, in explanation, 'He hit the wrong nail, Rabbi.'

Why, he wondered, should an old man remember such details after all these years?

Jesus was far and away his best pupil. To begin with, the rest were always to some degree afraid of Ezra. Jesus had no fear. Or perhaps his only fear was not to learn.

The boy was so wise. Once, long ago, Ezra had said to Mary, 'That one was born with a big white beard.' His mother had simply smiled and said, 'You noticed, Rabbi.'

His affection for the boy stemmed from when he had told his pupils a story about the great and gentle Pharisee, Hillel. Ezra had once met and talked with Hillel for a whole hour. That was thirty-five years before.

Hillel had said to him, 'Tell your boys, if only they study Torah long enough, the Romans will leave our land. But never mind, let the heathen steal our Temple, our priests, our olive-groves – provided they leave us two things. First, Shechinah, God's glory and, second, our children.'

Ezra now told the famous story with relish.

Someone interested in the Jewish faith, he said, mischievously informed Hillel that he would convert if only the Rabbi could teach him the whole Torah while standing on one leg. 'That's easy,' Hillel said, standing on one leg like a beanpole. 'What you hate when done to you, don't do to anyone else. This is the whole Torah. The rest is commentary.'

18

Jesus had listened to this story. Too well had he listened.

There was another pupil, a wild one called Nebat. He had stretched the Rabbi's patience beyond Job's when Ezra stooped down to Nebat, at his feet, and slapped him noisily but not painfully on the cheek.

Little Jesus was astonished. He went up to the seated Rabbi, stood on one leg next to him and whispered respectfully in his ear, 'What you hate when done to you, don't do to anyone else.'

Ezra bit his lip in annoyance until he realised there was a case to answer.

'But, Jesus son of Joseph,' he said, defensively, 'Nebat deserved it and I only did it for his good.'

The boy thought about this for a moment before nodding sagely. 'So, Rabbi, that is what you meant by commentary.'

'Well,' Ezra hummed, 'well ... yes, partly.'

After another pause, Jesus added, 'Rabbi, are you sure we *need* commentary?'

Once the Rabbi had asked Jesus if he liked the Sabbath services. The boy had replied, hesitating, 'Most of them.' 'What don't you like?' The boy said, 'In the three Benedictions where you pray, "The Lord is blessed who hath not made me a Gentile, a slave or a woman."' 'So?' 'Well, Rabbi, I have not met a Gentile or a slave, praised be God, but my mother is a woman.' The Rabbi patted him on the shoulder. 'So was mine, my son.'

After that, Ezra omitted 'woman' from the Benedictions in spite of protests from some members of his assembly who were unhappy in marriage.

Ezra used to say in the best rabbinic tradition, 'I will have no pupil who cannot teach me.'

This morning, perched on his log, he scratched his head as he admitted that sometimes Jesus had taught him more than he cared to learn. The boy's questions were so direct, so guileless, that Solomon could not have answered them.

His mother's teaching must have had something to do with it. Ezra once remarked, 'Mary is so simple she is profound.' When he knew her better, he corrected himself. 'She is so profound she is simple.'

It rubbed off on the boy.

Ezra was expounding the glory of the Law. We have nothing else, he said. It is our teacher, our father, our fortress, our life, our joy, our patriotism. It is more precious to us than the land itself. Other nations have laws so they can live together, but really their laws are for them but a necessary nuisance. Our Law *is* our life together. Put a Jew in prison, leave him in the middle of a desert, he will still love and keep the Law.

By now, several children were playing games at his feet. Nebat was snoring aloud to draw everybody's attention to the grand scale of his boredom.

Only Jesus was attentive and Ezra realised it was for Jesus and only him that he was waxing eloquent.

Then Jesus asked, 'Does the Law make all Jews equal, Rabbi?'

'Of course, my son. We are all children of Israel.'

Inwardly, he was ready to make an exception for Nebat. 'Why, then, are there so many differences between us, Rabbi? Why do so few people own so much of God's land when others, like the widow Anna, have none?'

'It is wrong, my son.' The boy had been listening to that mother of his again. 'I cannot deny it.'

'Wrong?' Jesus opened his eyes wide like a baby owl. 'The Law has failed us?'

Ezra shook his head fast enough to fan a fire. 'We failed the Law,' he croaked.

'Ah, yes,' Jesus agreed. After a moment's thought, 'Does the Law say my mother cannot look in the mirror on the Sabbath in case she plucks out one of her grey hairs?'

'No-o.' He just about conceded it.

'Why do you teach it?'

'It makes *sure* we keep the Law.'

The boy shrugged his narrow shoulders. 'Wouldn't you make it more sure if we enjoyed the Sabbath?'

Ezra dismissed the class.

Jesus stayed behind to ask, 'Does the Law say we cannot lift a weight on the Sabbath or touch money or scrape mud off our sandals?'

The Rabbi shook his head, not attempting to speak.

'Rabbi,' the boy suggested, 'there is far too much commentary?'

Ezra, still not speaking, for a moment shook his head from side to side. Then honesty compelled him vigorously to nod his agreement.

Long before this, Ezra had lost his only son. That day, he decided that Jesus would eventually succeed him as Rabbi of Nazareth.

To have wisdom, he told the boy often, and not to teach it is as deadly a sin as to have a pupil and not learn from him.

'What do you learn from me?' Nebat asked, insolently.

Ezra retorted, 'To thank God you were born to someone else.'

Nebat so disrupted the lessons that Ezra finally had to exclude him from the class. Trying to get sense into him was impossible. Like putting a plum back on a tree or stabbing a stone.

Nebat's father, Shaphan, a burly ploughman, heard this astonishing news and came bounding in from the fields, his hands and feet heavy with mud. He was blind sober, as the villagers put it, hence dangerous.

'What's wrong with my boy,' he demanded, genuinely ignorant, 'that you toss him aside like chaff?'

'I cannot teach him,' the Rabbi said, cowering. 'I am sorry.'

'But you told us,' Shaphan insisted angrily, 'that no child is too young to learn Torah.'

While Ezra shifted from one leg to another, unable to answer, Jesus, quite fearless, tugged at Shaphan's sleeve.

'Sir,' he said, 'Nebat is not too young to learn the Law. He is too old.'

The Rabbi still chuckled to himself at the thought of a six-year-old saving him from physical violence.

Shortly after that, Jesus said to him, 'Rabbi, you have lines right across your forehead.' 'Old age, my son,' Ezra sighed. 'Why don't you write on them?' 'What, my son?' Jesus said instantly, 'You are a Rabbi. What else but, *Hear, O Israel, the Lord our God, the Lord is one.*'

Then there was that time when Ezra ran into Joseph, so good and so respected, walking with Jesus in the cool of evening. Jesus was fourteen years old, still small for his age and with a pimply face. Joseph could not see by this time, though Ezra felt that in the dry lands of the spirit, he knew exactly where he was headed, just as there are blind desert guides who direct caravans unerringly from one water-hole to another.

Chatting to Ezra, Joseph said, 'For me, my Jesus is the light of the world. Without him, my friend, I would have to walk in darkness.' The adolescent offered his father his arm and Joseph sighed, 'See, Ezra. My son is a green bough for a very weary bird to rest on.'

Perhaps that meeting stuck in Ezra's mind because, soon after, Joseph went to God and Ezra became more and more involved with the boy. He watched him shoot up like a castor-oil plant, fill out, develop muscles, move with the speed and grace of a gazelle.

The boy had never lost his innocence; he kept himself, as Ezra would have it, 'undamaged'. Every misfortune, every slight injustice done us closes a little crack or crevice, sometimes a big door in the heart. In Jesus, Ezra realised, *nothing had been closed*.

He was uncomplicated in a way not appreciated by complicated folk, but, for all his childlikeness, he had more secrets than a camel. Yes, Ezra thought in more solemn moments, that boy is born to trouble as sparks are born to fly.

No one knew better than Ezra the wood-cutter what flying sparks can do in a dry wood.

Mary had fed and watered the ass and put Jesus's lunch in the palm-leaf pannier. Today it was salted meat, bread, two small cucumbers and a flask of wine.

'May you be blessed, my son,' she called after him.

He waved back. So tall was he that, seated on the jogging donkey, his feet almost touched the ground.

On high ground, he looked down on the plain where turtle-doves were still searching for the last of the clover. Since they arrived in waves in spring they were to be seen and heard in every garden and grove and on every wooded hill from dawn to dusk.

On this day, Jesus too had his memories. How he loved this crusty old Rabbi with the pinched look of a man with permanent indigestion, who scratched himself a lot. 'Alas,' Ezra used to moan, 'fleas find me more of a companion than God does.'

He was grateful to Ezra for coaching him in Hebrew when Joseph died. At the study table in the synagogue they had read the sacred books of the Bible for hours. Jesus had never read anything else, nor wanted to.

Over the last few months, Ezra had complained that his eyes were good for nothing any more except for weeping. Added to that, he had lost most of his teeth, so that he had a tendency to swallow his words even more than the average Galilean.

The first time that Jesus, at Ezra's insistence, proclaimed God's saving word in public tears sprang to his eyes. More than ever he was a true son of Israel.

He not only read the text, he translated it into colloquial Aramaic. The assembly, apart from Nebat and his father, approved his strong, clear, vibrant voice. It made the services go quicker, which was a blessing.

Being the Rabbi's star pupil was not a sinecure, for Ezra was a man of luminous contradictions.

Once he invited Jesus to sit with him in his garden. A basket of oranges was by his side. Nebat, the ever mischievous Nebat, asked if he could have one. 'Of course, my boy,' Ezra said, and handed one over. Jesus noticed he hadn't said thank you. He kept silent but Ezra knew it worried him. 'Ah, my son,' Ezra said to him, 'when you do good, you must not expect gratitude.' Hearing this, Nebat poked his tongue out at Ezra. The Rabbi was on his feet in an instant and thwacked him on the head with his staff. 'Neither,' he said, turning to Jesus, 'should you expect ingratitude.'

And what about when Ezra pleaded with him, for friendship's sake, to extract a tooth that was bothering him. Jesus protested he was not qualified. 'Never you mind, my son,' Ezra said, understandingly, 'a man of God must school himself to endure discomfort without a murmur.' Jesus took out a pair of pincers, fixed them over the tooth and pulled. It came out with a crack, causing Ezra to scream with pain. Afterwards, he refused to speak to Jesus for three days.

He allowed himself a last reminiscence. It was a few weeks after Ezra had misaimed and chopped off the three middle fingers of his left hand. They were in the woods on a day like this and Ezra was raging against God for leaving him with only one effective hand. A storm blew up without warning, the sky turned as black as night. Then a fork of lightning zipped past Jesus's ear and struck Ezra on the heel, throwing him full-length to the ground. The Rabbi was bruised by the fall but otherwise unhurt. Without pausing for breath he bounced back and, raising his fist to heaven, cried, 'That is no *argument.*'

In spite of being close to disaster, Jesus had laughed aloud.

Chapter 4

Jesus dismounted from the donkey, bowed to Ezra and asked his blessing. Ezra gave it and embraced him.

How he loved the sheer beauty of the boy, now that he was mature, fully fermented, with that kind of extra dimension youth brings.

'Thank you for coming, my son.'

The wood to the west of Nazareth had remained green after the heavy spring showers, but it was not well planted. The rocky soil was more suited to olive-groves. Still, there were numbers of trees, oaks and the ilex, also terebinths, carobs, a few pines and one medium-sized sycamore to which Ezra pointed.

'We'll leave that to last.'

He was short-winded, his lungs in poor shape.

Jesus tethered the ass, stripped off his outer tunic and set to with a big axe.

While working, they spoke little, preferring to chant a psalm together or some other passages from scripture. When Jesus had the initiative, he might sing:

> *Praise the Lord,*
> *Praise him in the heavens and the heights,*
> *Praise him, all his hosts,*
> *Praise him, sun and moon,*
> *And all you shining stars.*

The Rabbi, as cross as Moses at times and revered in the village for his practical peasant wisdom, tended to reproduce the darker side of the writings. He thrived on Ecclesiastes, Proverbs, Job. 'Why not?' he joked. 'Bad luck has been loyal to me all my life.'

When Ezra got in first, he chose:

> *By the waters of Babylon, there sat we weeping*
> *When we remembered Zion*
> *And on the willows there*
> *Hung up our harps.*

At which point he spat and, without his saying so, Jesus knew that was for the Romans who strutted across their land.

Sometimes, in even more sombre mood, the Rabbi chanted in memory of his dead son:

> *Out of the depths I cry to thee, O Lord;*
> *Lord, hear my voice.*

Today the Rabbi was in a mellower frame of mind. He could not contribute much because he had a touch of dysentery. He kept having to retire into the wood to 'cover his feet', as he expressed it.

Returning, he watched with admiration the rippling muscles of his adopted son, the keen eye, the broad shoulders, the strong hands with skin as tough as the pelt of an animal.

Jesus worked hard, he enjoyed work. Above, a small rare hawk, the black-winged kite, hovered and, later, a

25

honey-buzzard; he did not look up. He only heard the wood-pigeons with their throaty voices calling in the depths of the wood.

Ezra used to say that Jesus was as industrious as an ant. High praise. For Ezra, sloth was not only a sin, it was the father and mother of sins. The Most High had ordained that a man should earn his bread by the sweat of his brow, *especially* rabbis and future rabbis.

'Has Shaphan paid you for the work you did last summer?'

Jesus, still wielding the axe, shook his head. Farmers often refused to pay up, even after a good harvest. Nebat's father was no exception.

'Get him to cough up, my son, it's good for his soul.'

'Money's not important,' Jesus puffed.

'Is it not?' Ezra said, pouting comically. 'Bread is for laughter, wine for joy, but money is wiser than Solomon.'

'How is that?'

'Because, my son, money has the answer to *everything*.'

Jesus put down his axe for a breather. A chance for him to do his imitation of Shaphan when asked for payment.

Jesus screwed up his eyes, looked slowly round him.

'Shaphan,' the Rabbi cried, delightedly.

Jesus yawned, smelled his armpits, scratched his belly, spat – not the prodigious shiny stream that Shaphan managed – and, in a passable mimicry, said, 'What's the hurry, boy?'

Ezra applauded a fine effort.

They chopped down a few more scraggy oaks and removed the bark and cut the logs into sections. Such wood was no use for the support beams of houses but it served to make stools, kneading-troughs, ploughs, doors, candlesticks, even yoke for oxen.

They worked for four hours till they were dripping with sweat and burned raw by the sun. The Rabbi called a halt. They retreated into the shadows where the ass was tethered.

There was a healthy smell of resin and sawdust in the air. Trees, Jesus thought – more than reconciled to his trade – trees are wonderful things.

Out of direct sunlight, the buzz and whir of hidden insects was less noticeable, though the flies remained as persistent as sin.

'When God made us,' Ezra complained, 'why didn't he give us a tail to keep the flies away?'

'Why ask me?' Jesus said.

The Rabbi settled himself down against a tree with the mechanical, jerky movements of a camel. He was old, he said, barely turned on his hinges.

After they had washed their hands and said the blessing, Jesus, seated cross-legged, unwrapped his food from a linen cloth. It looked appetising.

Ezra had nothing but a flask of rough, scarcely fermented wine – 'It would set my teeth on edge,' he said, 'if I had any' – a few honeycombs and a chunk of dry flat barley bread.

'Look,' he said, holding the bread up and comparing it unfavourably with the light, almost fluffy substance Jesus was digging into.

'You could use that without sin for Passover,' Jesus said, his mouth full.

The Rabbi examined his own bread critically, like an expert wood-cutter. 'I think you could make from this a posh table-top, my son.'

Jesus held out his own bread, but the Rabbi refused it. He started on the honeycombs.

'Better,' he explained, sucking noisily, 'when you have no grinders left.'

Soon his beard was awash with a golden, gluey substance.

Touching Ezra's beard in fun, Jesus said, 'Greetings, Aaron.'

That was enough to spark Ezra off. 'Ah,' he chanted in his best Sabbath voice:

> How good it is and joyous
>> For brothers who live as one.
> Like precious oil on the beard,
>> The oil that streams down Aaron's beard.

Jesus joined in with:

It is like the precious oil that runs
Down the collar of Aaron's robe.

The Rabbi smacked his lips and eyed the young man proudly. Jesus had said that with a mixture of fondness and devotion that moved him deeply. 'This boy,' he said often to his wife, 'may be plain and blunt in speech, but his heart is all green leaf. And let me tell you, he can find God anywhere, as a camel can sniff out water in the Negev.'

They ate for a while in a contented silence. Ezra broke it by saying, 'That mother of yours looks after you too well, my son.'

Jesus stiffened. Ezra was about to broach a topic Jesus did his best to avoid.

'She is a good mother, Rabbi. Says little, does much.'

It was undeniable. Mary was always employed: kneading, baking, pounding the washing with a stave on stones, spinning wool, weaving cloth on two spindles round a chain so as to make a seamless robe, tending the garden and talking to the vegetables, fetching water, cleaning every nook and cranny of the house with a bunch of chicken feathers and, in between, nattering with neighbours and sympathising with their complaints.

'I was wondering...' Ezra hesitated. 'Isn't it about time you, well, you took a wife?'

Jesus cleared his throat nervously.

The Rabbi wiped his mouth with his sleeve. 'Remember the scriptures, my son. Enjoy life with your beloved of the years.'

Jesus had difficulty keeping a straight face. Ezra and his wife – he insisted on calling her 'my Rib' – were renowned in the village for their arguments. They rowed loudly enough to make cocks crow at midnight. How often had Ezra complained on days like this that the breath from Sarah's mouth could pluck a chicken.

'Buzz, buzz, buzz, Rabbi.' Jesus was reminding him that only last week Ezra had likened his wife's nagging to being stung by six swarms of bees.

'Ah, yes,' Ezra said defensively, 'but doesn't she look

after me better than a horse?'

'If you dig a pit,' Jesus responded in kind from the Writings, 'you will fall into it. Disturb a snake and –' He thrust two fingers in the direction of the Rabbi. 'She will *bite* you.'

Ezra jerked his head back and banged his fist on the ground in irritation. 'Do you want to stand before God on Judgment Day without the sweet partner of your bed to plead for you?'

Jesus moved the handle of the axe towards Ezra. 'Split the log but mind your toes.'

'Always an answer, eh?'

'I had a good teacher.'

The Rabbi's nervous gestures became more florid but, with three fingers missing on one hand, hardly convincing. His thin, almost transparent nostrils were quivering.

'To stay unwed at your age, my son, is not natural. It's like a dance without a song.'

'Or a song without a dance.' Jesus's old cheekiness was reappearing.

'It's like a land without water. Like a tree that bears no fruit.'

Jesus knew that Ezra was too hurt to add what he would have wished. To die without a son is to die twice and for ever. It is to pass through the world and leave no trace.

'What is an unmarried man,' the Rabbi went on, steamily, 'but a blunt axe. Whet it with a woman and the job takes half as long.'

'Without a wife, I have all the time in the world.'

The Rabbi, sulking, made as if to get up and walk away, but rheumatism nailed him to the spot.

'I'm serious, my son. How will you ever be a rabbi without a wife? People will say, "How can he know what he is talking about? He has never suffered."'

Jesus finished off his wine. Then, 'Did you have, um, anyone in mind for me?'

Ezra lifted his bony hands with the seven black, cracked fingernails. He had rehearsed at home but failed in the performance. He examined his palm as if it were a

29

scroll of the Law.

Everyone in the village above the age of six knew he was hoping to get Jesus to marry his daughter. Jesus avoided Jedidah with as much courtesy as he could. She made him edgy.

'My Jedidah, now.' Ezra mentioned her name as if it had just sprung unbidden into his mind. 'No beauty, she. No dove's eyes. No hair like a flock of goats streaming down the slopes of Gilead.'

Jesus was unable to help him out there. Jedidah, in fact, did not possess any of the attributes of beauty as outlined in The Song of Songs. She was flat-chested, with thick greasy hair, rough complexion and a squint that was common among village girls. 'A frog with feathers on,' as one lad put it.

'But how she loves the scriptures,' Ezra said, glowing, as if this more than made up for ugliness.

Jesus merely sat there, his hands joined, going redder.

Ezra was dejected. Sometimes a thousand words said nothing, and one burst of silence said it all. But he so wanted Jesus as his son-in-law.

'A beautiful woman without sense, my son, is like a gold ring in a pig's snout. My Jedidah not only has sense –'

'She is like you,' Jesus broke in, 'a treasure.'

Ezra brightened up. Was there hope, after all?

'Better to sleep beside a plain wife than only dream of a pretty one. Warmer in winter, too.'

'Rabbi,' Jesus said gently, 'you are very kind. But for marrying' – he shrugged – 'I am not ready.'

How could he tell his old teacher that he was pledged already to his people? How explain that he had ended his night's vigil on the hills by saying to his people in his heart:

> Open the door, my sister, my beloved,
>   My dove, my dearest one.
> For my head is wet with dew and my locks
>   With the laughing tears of night.

They finished eating and Ezra went to sleep with his

fathers for an hour. Afterwards he helped Jesus until mid-afternoon.

They both noticed it about the same time. Something strange was in the air. The sky was unseasonally overcast, the humidity so stifling as to be unnatural. The ass was braying and lashing out with his hindlegs. The wood-pigeons had ceased to sing. And where were the flies?

They soothed the donkey and loaded it until it was almost invisible under the boughs. The Rabbi took on his shoulders all he could manage. Since Ezra wanted the trunk of the sycamore in one piece, Jesus hoisted it on his back. Bowed in two, he carried it downhill to the village. In that wet heat, it felt like the weight of the world.

On the way, one or two idlers busied themselves by passing remarks.

'Look at the Rabbi,' one said. 'A walking tree.'

Another said of Jesus, 'Look at *him*. You'd think he was on his way to crucifixion.'

Chapter 5

At Nazareth, they saw a sky dark grey to the horizon. The sense of menace they had experienced on the edge of the wood was even more pressing in the village. Dogs were howling, asses braying, even the cocks were crowing out of time and fretting over the hens.

Someone gave an unintelligible shout from a hilltop, more like a scream. Soon word filtered through that a yellow-brown cloud was coming their way.

A group of men ran to higher ground. From there they could see, to the south-east, blue sky seeming to chase the grey clouds which were passing in fury over the

31

landscape. Blue overhead again, but that other cloud was still coming, a mile long and fifty yards across.

One of the older men let out a cry which was taken up in a fearsome wail by all the watchers:

'*Locusts.*'

The Rabbi was sitting outside Mary's house, sucking a sweet lemon and mocking Jesus openly in front of his mother for not getting himself a wife.

'Locusts?' he croaked, incredulous. 'Are we Egyptians that God sends locusts to infect our land?'

Jesus was already racing to his workshop through the panic-filled streets. He handed out the rushes and flails he kept there to men who were clamouring for something, anything, with which to defend their property.

Women and children were running wild in all directions, shrieking. Older women like Anna and Sarah sat down in the dust, mourning as for the dead.

The able-bodied men scampered to the fields, waiting apprehensively under the olives, the fig-trees and the vines. Some risked life and limb by sliding down sheer rock slopes to the cornfields in the plain.

'Shut your doors.' Jesus shouted it out to every housewife as he passed the houses, making for high ground. 'Tight as you can.'

They didn't argue, closing windows, barring doors. Tiny children with rush brooms readied themselves to defend a pathetic vegetable patch while their mothers threw sacks, even clothing and bed linen over the berry-bearing bushes in the gardens.

Mary forgot her arthritis as she hurriedly picked every remotely ripe vegetable and piled them in spare pots and baskets. Next, she sealed all the cracks and fissures in the house with mud and sawdust.

From his vantage point on the hill Jesus could see the locusts advancing in their hordes, on glazed wings. It was like the approach of a deadly snowstorm.

He prayed that it would turn aside or pass them by, but he knew this was unlikely, since the locusts were following the path of the moist grey cloud.

The dry months had been preceded by a long damp

spring. The summer crops were abundant. The locusts knew it.

They came relentlessly with a noise like the roaring of a distant cataract. When nearer, they sounded like stampeding horses.

Their snowy whiteness against the blue turned to a moving yellow band. So deafening were they now they drowned out the screams of women and children.

Hundreds of people were banging pots and pans and hand-drums, smiting the trees with spades and broken boughs, and nothing of it could be heard for the roar of locusts flying on the wind.

The leading locusts were bound to head straight for the grain fields and spread out from them to orchards and vineyards. Jesus had just reached a field of ripe corn when he was enveloped in a wave of locusts eight to ten feet high. It was as easy to walk through a wall.

The creatures were huge, nearly an inch long with bright-coloured hind-wings, sharp mandibles and tiny cushions between the claws of their feet.

He lashed out at them with two heavy seven-pronged flails, bound together to make a more lethal weapon. With every stroke he heard the crunch of disintegrating bodies, but still they came on without a splinter's gap between them. His impression was of being trapped in a dense shoal of fish beneath the sea.

Dry, grasshopper-like, they spilled everywhere. They clung to every leaf and stalk and blade of grass. Millions of them gnawing away hungrily so that a crackling sound went up like fire in stubble.

In the cornfields they began chomping low down on the stalk, working upwards to pick out the growing kernel, often biting off the whole ear.

The cornfield Jesus was trying to defend just disappeared. Like the field of millet he had seen that morning, gone. Men were brandishing clubs, threshing-hooks, branches, spades, palm-leaves, as if they were fighting Satan himself – and making no impression.

Tiny rock-chats and other insect-eating birds swooped down, spiked a locust and retired to a place of refuge to consume it. Cats were up trees, pawing crazily and

33

having a prodigious feast. The chickens, especially the cocks, had never been so well fed.

And still the locusts came.

They denuded the fruit trees: pear, apricot, plum, orange, walnut, almond. All that was left were bare pits and stones on the cherry and peach trees. Only the fig-trees went unharmed.

One farmer, in desperation, set light to a batch of straw on the edge of his cornfield. He must have misjudged the direction of the wind. The whole field exploded in an orange flame that devoured everything in its path.

Jesus scrambled his way to where he could see a number of men fighting vainly on their own. With ferocious gestures he organised them and, in a straight line, they went threshing through a barley-field. They killed hundreds of locusts, which were replaced by thousands.

Many gave up and went home where their wives told them the locusts had entered the houses. The smaller and darker of them had managed to squeeze through cracks in the doors or the stone walls and devoured the stocks of fruit and grain, leaving only the salt. They had even chewed the woodwork. They were insatiable.

Hour after hour the thunder of the hordes filled the village and its fields, echoed round the hills.

One by one, the last of the fighting men withdrew from the fray, exhausted by their efforts, still more by the uselessness of them. With bowed heads and drooping shoulders they went home as though they had buried an only son.

Jesus battled on.

Ezra did not know where he was. Hobbled as he was by rheumatism, he searched for him a long time. He passed one of those streams that gush miraculously out of the limestone rocks in the height of summer, teeming with fish. He stood in amazement as the fish lifted themselves out of the water, snatched a locust and descended with it to the depths.

It convinced him that nature had gone mad and God had abandoned them.

At last, he found his favourite son, threshing away with his double flail, solitary, uncaring of its futility. The boy never knew when he was beaten. Something was forcing him on and Ezra looked at him, proud yet pitying. For it was, however heroic, in vain. Like trying to bridle the wind and the waves.

The sun had set. With the coolness of night the locusts became sluggish. They settled down in the stubble which was all that remained of once fertile fields.

Jesus went on flailing, possessed of superhuman energy.

On a mound above him, Ezra stood, arms extended like Moses, railing at God for stretching out his hand against his faithful people.

Finally, in utter contempt, Ezra sat down.

'Ichabod!' he cried again and again, as he sprinkled dirt over his bared head. 'The glory has gone from us. Ichabod! Ichabod!'

Even as Ezra watched, Jesus collapsed like a drunkard on a rock. There was nothing left in him. Before the locusts came, he had already done the work of two men. He slept as he had never slept before, with a few locusts still twitching in the folds of his garments.

Ezra descended the slope. He blessed Jesus and covered him with his cloak, muttering, 'You cannot fight God, my son,' and kept guard over him all that night as though he were honouring a soldier who had died bravely on the battlefield.

Chapter 6

Locusts were still flying overhead next morning in a broad yellow band. They did not alight on Nazareth. They had no reason to.

At first light, the villagers were able to take stock of the damage.

Fields and forests had been picked clean. The animal fodder had been consumed. Gardens were as desolate as in winter. Not a sign of the season was to be seen, except that a few fig-trees and two eucalyptuses were unscathed. Even the evergreen oleander and the ilex were stripped of foliage.

The grass, usually adequate, was cropped so close that the sheep were bleating their hunger. On the margins of the village, the rocks reflected the sun, smooth and white as camels' skulls in the desert.

The far-seeing gathered up dead locusts to feed themselves and their animals but soon a stench filled the air and sickened them.

After two more days, the locusts came no more. They had flown westward on a gale and the sea had swallowed them. It was too late for Nazareth.

It was hard to stir anyone into activity. The women sat on the ground, tearing their garments and moaning. The men stood against walls from morning till dusk, blank-eyed, saying not a word. The children had forgotten how to play.

Jesus prevailed on a few farmers to plough the land so that any locust eggs laid in the stubble would be destroyed. They ploughed and sank back into apathy.

Landowners wept openly at the desolation, knowing that this year they would be gleaners not farmers, would thresh less than they had sown. Women and children scoured the fields, scrabbling in the dust for food like famished crows.

That Sabbath, Ezra in his rabbi's gown read from Deuteronomy. His piping tones had gone, he had recovered the voice of his youth.

The synagogue was packed. A few women were there, even the local tax-collector. Nobody objected to his presence. Why should they when the entire village was cursed?

The box of a room was usually noisier than a stable. Menfolk chattered, complained to their cronies about their wives and children, concluded business deals, arranged marriages, picked up local gossip, swopped the latest jokes.

It was different now. Ezra did not have to call out, 'Quiet! God cannot hear himself think.'

'Take possession of the land, the Lord says, that you may live there, a land flowing with milk and honey.'

The yawns began. The Rabbi was inspired but they were listless, dispirited. Only Jesus watched him warily.

'Indeed,' Ezra went on, *'the Lord's eyes are upon this land, from the year's beginning to the year's end.'*

He paused, gazing down the throats of the yawners. They had come to bring each other comfort; there was none, they had decided, in God's word.

Ezra slammed the book shut.

'We have kept your commandments, God,' he cried in a voice that made the congregation sit up, 'and see how you have treated us. You have revoked your covenant, you have abandoned us.'

Coughing, an uneasy stirring of feet. They were bruised, yes, broken by recent events but this was heresy. The covenant with God was all they had.

'Our village,' the Rabbi went on, 'was yesterday a garden of Eden, today a desert. Our meadows yesterday had lush green grass and you have shaved them closer than the face of mourning.'

A few nodded their heads slightly.

'Was it for this you called us out of Egypt? Was it for this you made great promises to our father Abraham?'

Jesus had been standing opposite Ezra, his head bowed and his eyes closed in prayer. He stepped forward. In a ringing voice, he said:

'Return to the Lord your God, for he is full of grace and mercy.

The assembly buzzed with excitement, tapped each other on the shoulder, whispered in one another's ears.

As to Ezra, he glared malevolently at Jesus and called out in response:

'My God, my God, why hast thou forsaken us? Why art thou so far away, from the words of our crying, now when we need thee?'

Jesus rode the storm and came back with:

'The threshing floors will be full of grain, the vats overflowing

*with wine and oil. I will restore to you the years which swarms of
locusts have eaten, yea, the jumper, the destroyer, the cutter, my fierce
army that I sent among you.'*

The assembly sat up, watching wide-eyed, listening to
challenger and challenged. Maybe Jesus was staking his
claim to be their teacher from now on.

Ezra opened up a sack and dramatically emptied the
contents on to the cracked mud floor.

'This, God,' he snarled, 'is the offering I make you.'

Out of the sack tumbled hundreds of dead and
crawling locusts. The sour odour permeated the
building. Many pegged their noses, a woman vomited, a
few with weak stomachs rushed for the exit.

'Behold, God,' the Rabbi said, 'the odour of sweetness I
give thee.'

Some of the assembly tore their garments, others
raised their fist at Ezra or spat at him.

For his part, Jesus saw the gesture as in the tradition of
the prophets. It was, in one sense, appalling. In another,
proceeding as it did from Ezra's tremendous love and pity
for his people, it was superb. The Rabbi had *become* his
people in their misery and sense of distance from God.
He dared to express what was in everyone's heart and, by
voicing it, Ezra raised them from their apathy. Even their
noisy hatred of him had a positive effect. They were
coming alive again. There was hope for the village.

'*God has ceased to bless us,*' Ezra croaked.

'*What God hath blessed,*' was Jesus's instant rejoinder, '*is
for ever blessed.*'

'Amen,' cried Achbor, an elder, and many echoed him.

Ezra fixed his eye on Jesus again, but without hostility.
Jesus's tone made it clear that he was not in opposition to
the Rabbi, was merely complementing his message.
Wasn't the Bible the book of hope in despair, of hope *in
spite of despair*? Even when Ezra called out, '*Why hast thou
forsaken me?*' he addressed God as '*My God.*'

The Rabbi wanted to speak but his tongue stuck to the
roof of his mouth. He tried to wrench it free but could
not. His whole body shook like a leafy branch in the wind
a moment before he fell, unconscious, to the floor.

With tenderness, Jesus picked up this little bird with

broken wings and kissed the top of his head for all to see the respect in which this great man should be held.

'Our Rabbi,' he said, pointedly, 'is unwell, but he will recover.'

Ezra was not heavy but Jesus's arms ached so much that it was not easy carrying him. But carry him he did to his own home where Mary looked after him until evening, feeding him grilled fish and buttermilk.

Late that night, before Jesus went up into the hills to pray, his mother wanted to know, 'Is it now?' and, gripping her shoulder fondly, he said, for the first time with a hint of sadness, 'I am waiting.'

Chapter 7

Crushing days followed for the villagers. They had to purchase grain and foodstuffs for themselves and their animals from villages – some surprisingly near – which had escaped the locusts. Prices soared and some families had no savings. Promises bought no bread.

To Ezra's delight, they helped one another. Proud of their resilience and comradeship in adversity, he was loud in his praises of the Lord.

Jesus and Mary had no money stashed away and no supplies to barter with. Jesus was working for practically nothing; for once the farmers really did have an excuse for delaying payment. What he did take home his mother spread among the needy.

'There are always people much worse off than us,' she said, though it was hard to see how.

They rejoiced to go without, blessing God for the little that they had and for each other.

Though Mary could not read or write, she knew the Psalms by heart and much of the Writings. She was constantly asking God to be kind to the poor, not to send them away empty.

Because of the food shortage, there was much sickness in the village. The skin of many turned a deep orange-brown. An insect bite was likely to cause a swelling as big as a cabbage.

The doctors, who knew practically nothing, except how to collect their fees in advance, put it down to pollution of the land by locusts. Mostly, it was blamed on the release of demons into the air which the sick had swallowed or otherwise imbibed.

Children had rickety legs and swollen bellies and babes in arms had the wizened look of old people. Jesus could scarcely bear to look on their wrinkled faces, their big damp gloomy eyes. Mary wept openly for them.

Without milk, some children died and the number of the lame, especially among the young, increased.

Some cashed in on the calamity. A shepherd gave to dreams interpretations more bizarre than the dreams themselves. Shaphan the ploughman turned fortune-teller and sketched the future with marvellous imprecision for the price of a loaf.

Many families left Nazareth to search for a holy man, a faith-healer, a sorcerer – anyone who boasted he was able to heal their sick children. All of them charlatans.

The families returned, their numbers depleted, sometimes carrying their dead.

A few came back with incredible tales of how a healer, for a modest sum, had laid hands on hundreds and cured them of sickness, blindness, lameness. Or gave them the recipe for an infallible cure.

You had to bury the sick up to their necks in sand or mud; or make them eat the raw heart and liver of a fish or the turds of camels mixed in butter and milk; or douse yourself in vinegar and salt while reciting various incantations; or drink the juice of three oranges out of a dead man's skull.

Jesus loathed these quackeries. These so-called healers gave the sick nothing of themselves or God. But chiefly he pitied his people who saw no alternative but to put their trust in them.

40

He cautioned many villagers to stay home and wait for better days.

Except that better days were long in coming.

Winter's rain was sparse and gentle, but the villagers thought little of it at first.

October, when rains customarily last for days on end, gave only a few brief showers that barely wetted the lips of the land. There was no short, second spring that so often brought out bursts of pink and purple colchicums or meadow-saffron.

November passed, mild and dry. The farmers found it hard to plough in the seed they had scattered over the brick-hard fields, especially as the oxen were without sufficient fodder.

The rains of December to February fell but more modestly than anyone could remember and precious little snow whitened the flanks of Hermon.

On his journeys to surrounding hamlets, Jesus noticed that river-beds were almost dry, nor did wadis, dry in summer, sing sweetly with the usual winter's rain. It was quite common for parts of the plain of Esdraelon to be impassable at this season. But no meadows were turning into lakes, no quagmires forming to snare the feet of oxen. It was mild, clear, beautiful weather and what rain fell drained quickly away in this mostly porous, limestone land.

Jesus was growing anxious. Could it be that the desert, always terrifyingly close to fertile places, was over-stepping its bounds? Even the dews from Hermon were not as thick and juicy as in normal times.

By day, the sun was a furnace spewing out red coals. On the hills at night, when he scanned the horizon for clouds out of the west there was not even one as big as a man's hand. The land shuddered and the air smelled of rust. He returned home after a night out of doors with dry clothes and a burning throat.

No matter, everyone said, provided the latter rains are generous. They prayed for a wet spring.

In vain.

Still there was no fatal alarm until it was rumoured

that one of the fountain-heads of the Jordan had dried up completely. This was taken as an omen: worse was to come.

With a sharp shower, spirits soared and flowers showed. Anemones, verbena, cyclamen, marguerites – all of them blossomed. So did whole fields of narcissus and purple bougainvillea. They blossomed like hope itself and withered in the self-same night.

The impoverished villagers groaned under the burden, not knowing what to do. Nine out of ten of them worked the land and all depended on it.

Days passed, weeks, and no seasonal breezes blew from the north-west. Instead, a burning sirocco swept from the east, raising sand-clouds that obscured the sun. Mary was able, even in spring, to make pancakes for widows and orphans on the stones outside her house.

When finally they despaired of the future they despaired of God. That was when brotherhood wilted, perished.

This was not hardship but penury; not poverty but destitution; not hunger but starvation.

Communal misery was replaced by individual and family avarice. It was each for himself.

Ezra limped around the village, moaning, praying, plucking hairs from his beard as if they were strings of a musical instrument. Every woman was becoming a temptress out of the overwhelming need for bread. Nursing mothers offered themselves as whores to save a starving child. Bread was their only aim, their one god.

No one fed blind beggars any more. They wandered through the village, wailing from cockcrow to sunset. One of them sat in the gap between two houses and died. He was not missed for two days, until they smelled what was left of him and saw the sizzling mass of flies.

A widower, whose family had lived in Nazareth for generations, sold his house for a mouldy loaf of bread. He ate it slowly, with dignity, walked down the hill and was never seen again.

Feuds broke out, everybody lied on principle. Some were suspected of hoarding vast quantities of meat and grain while others starved. Thefts, once rare, became commonplace. Trust died. No housewife put washing on the bushes to dry in case it was stolen.

Children hid behind the women, the women behind the men, and men hid behind faces as cold and hard as a wall.

Nazareth, sweet kind Nazareth, became a village of staring eyes. Every householder made efforts to protect his property, efforts out of all proportion to what they were protecting. At night, in spite of the forge-like heat, every door and window was double-barred.

The bazaar, usually filled with ear-splitting noise, was deserted. An aged crone led out her prized goat, milked it into a small container and offered the contents to the highest bidder. At the street corner, a butcher stood ready to slice off a choice piece of an ass's head if the price was right.

It was the final humiliation when Cain appeared in the village. There had never been a murder before. A lonely man, elderly, had his head smashed in. He was found one morning in a pool of blood near his empty food-bin.

Ezra saw this and blamed God. What could they possibly have done to deserve this? Why, when they prayed so hard, did their teeth find no meat to bite on, only gristle and bone?

Nothing changed, except for the worse. The whole land quivered under the silent earthquake caused by the sun. The soil, dry and crackling like parchment, started turning to dust. Every step in it raised a puff like smoke. The very dust gave off dust, finer than the motes that danced in sunlight, finer than pollen, plugging nostrils, choking lungs. They walked on dust and had the weird feeling that no solid earth was underneath them any more. No one left his house for a minute without a kerchief over his nose. When a child sneezed a jet of incandescent dust shot out.

There was no wine or oil or gladness or dancing or music, no marrying and giving in marriage. Sons left the village to the sound of keening; many of them never returned.

The migrant birds departed in the wrong months. No

43

more sparrows hopped and chittered at the doors; no more crows stamped crossly over the fields. The turtle-doves, the swallows that normally even wintered there were not to be seen. Nor the swifts that had screamed overhead pursuing gnats since spring. No more skylarks rose and fell in song. The solitary song-thrush, the boast of Nazareth, sang no more.

A plague of mice enveloped the village, nibbled at every stick of wood, in some cases bringing down the support beams of the houses, and went away as suddenly as it had come.

Gnats, without the swifts to check them, increased astoundingly. Lice multiplied and flies found no other source of moisture than children's eyes.

There were no cats and the few remaining dogs no longer barked. The owners guarded them day and night lest they be stolen and slaughtered for food. Dogs, once common property belonging to no one and everyone, were the subject of heated disputes about ownership – and, once appropriated, promptly disappeared.

But there were troubles no one spoke of. Young girls ceased to menstruate so that their mothers sighed, 'We have no future,' and their fathers groaned in the night, 'How can the Messiah come now?'

There were miscarriages and the milk of many nursing mothers dried up. Behind every door children whimpered and moaned and quietly expired. Then were buried within the hour, to protect those who were left.

Chapter 8

It was for Jesus a wrench and a relief to quit his village. In any case, it was a necessity. He had no prospects there. Even when he found work, afterwards people gave him their hand, with nothing in it. Farmers had been forced to eat their seed-corn and, with it, their livelihood. People can sustain all calamities but one: the dearth of water.

Jesus said goodbye to his mother and to Ezra and walked down the hill. It was strange to see the olive-trees, usually so laden, without fruit or foliage. A metallic sky had produced metal trees with metal branches from which buds and soft leaves could not grow. It made a mockery of Micah's promise: *Every man under his own vine and under his own fig-tree.*

He took to travelling to villages where the locusts had not struck and the fountains still gave water.

Having chosen his spot he worked from morning till night for a pittance. What he earned he sent back to Nazareth for his mother to distribute to the neediest. He was mostly paid in kind: barley, wheat, olive-oil, dried meat, salted fish. He kept for himself only what he needed to conserve his strength. Hunger was his bond with home.

He moved around a lot but never slept in the local hostelry. He preferred to build a booth in the fields as on the Feast of Tabernacles, or he made his home, like a fox, in a bat-infested cave. He was scared at first, but he got used to it. More than once, though, he woke in the night to find a pair of green eyes gazing at him.

A migrant worker without roots, he was friendless and, especially in the beginning, as lonely as a pioneer. With no one to invite him in or to talk to, his spirit was in chains. It was not good for a man, any man, to be alone. Homesickness was the most terrible illness: his whole self was out of joint.

If only one of the children from his own village were there, say, little Shimon, his favourite, he would give him a fig or a peach and feel better for it. If only he could share his bread with someone, a dog that recognised him would do. Even the dogs here knew he did not belong. He felt that the rocks and trees, the very sky, knew it, too.

In his workshop at home he used to play a game with the children. He had carved a human figure out of olive wood, then cut it up into smaller, interlocking pieces. He had written a child's name on each piece, jumbled them up and left the children to put them together again. On occasions, he kept a piece hidden in his hand.

The children set to with zest. Until they realised they could not complete the figure. They searched high and low for the missing piece. They turned out every drawer, shifted every tool, up-ended every container. Jesus finally took pity on them and opened his hand. There was the piece and on the back of it not a name but a word: 'Us.' In this way he taught them that we are all parts of a bigger whole, we belong to each other. If one part is missing, all of us are incomplete. Together we make up mankind.

Jesus had always felt that he interlocked with everything – persons, places, things. With parents and children and the unmarried, with the wind and the stars, with the stones of the streets and the rocks on the hills.

Why, then, in this village, in so many ways like his own, was he not allowed to interlock with anyone? He was excluded from their sorrows and joys, from the deaths of their old people and the excitement of their new births. He was not permitted to laugh or cry with them. They were *complete already*.

One night he had a dream. It began with him trying to pull a tooth out of Ezra's mouth. But Ezra's mouth changed into his mouth, he was pulling out his own tooth. Except he, Jesus, was the tooth more than he was the rest of himself, and finally he was *only* tooth. Identified with the tooth, he screamed that he, the tooth, was being pulled out of what was once himself. All his feelings, his memories, his hopes, *were* the tooth. There was a fearsome crack and he, the tooth, came out and was tossed away. There it was on the dust, blood-spattered, the roots showing but attached to nothing, lying upwards like the legs of a dead insect. *He* was in the dust, a discard, alone for ever, rotting in the sun. And this tooth which was himself looked up at his old self, gigantic, foreign, far away, like a mountain towering over him, over the poor little tooth, so insignificant, so useless, so uncared for.

He sat up sharply to wake himself. He bit his lip until it

bled, felt all his teeth with his fingers, squeezed his arms, legs, belly, thanking God this was he. He was whole and entire again. His relief was enormous.

Then he remembered who and where he was. A migrant worker, a refugee from home. In his waking life also he was an uprooted bloody tooth. A nothing and a nobody who was forced to smile at strangers in the hope of disarming them, had to pat snarling dogs, had to bow down before an employer who might, just might, want to use him or abuse him for payment.

Whereas before, he had been buoyed up with thoughts of home, the sights, even the smells of the bread and laundry of home, now he pushed them out of his mind. With everything else, the pain was too much for him to handle. But the pain was there all the time, an unthought pain. Like a growth you ignore but which will not ignore you.

Hard work made his lot easier to bear and the memory that the Ark of the Lord, containing the tablets of the Law, itself had no home for many generations.

The longer he stayed in a place the less he was paid. Employers sensed his desperation. He, the outsider, was chosen for the toughest, dirtiest, most menial tasks so that work, until now a joy, became his chief humiliation.

When he put himself forward as a carpenter he often ran into hostility. The local carpenter accused him of undercutting him, of taking the bread out of the mouth of his babes. Jesus sympathised with them, stayed only as long as he dared.

As summer wore on, he no longer declared himself a carpenter. He was an odd-job man, a fixer. No task was beneath him. No hour was too early or too late for him to be of service.

The pain surfaced most on the Sabbath. At home, it was his favourite day, the Good Sabbath, a day of joy and magic, shared with Mary and Joseph, then with Mary alone. The Sabbath created its own sacred space inside their little house. They were together, growing in the Law of God. Mary had watched for sunset so she could light the seven lamps and Joseph, whom he adored, kissed and blessed him and wished him 'A happy

Sabbath, my son.' Ah, yes, on the Sabbath his soul had grown big within him.

Now it dwindled with the pain and he had to fight hard against a crippling self-pity.

During the week, his employers sometimes pointed out spurious defects in his work and paid him less than the agreed wage. Jesus went white with anger. For the sake of his people back home, he swallowed it like a cup of vinegar, said nothing.

In the market-place before sun-up, he was first in line. He drew himself up to his full height, put his shoulders back, flexed his muscles, to show that anyone who took him on would get their money's-worth and more.

He worked at whatever came up, claiming like all migrant workers he was 'expert' at everything. Ploughing, shepherding, shearing, he could do it all. He was not ashamed to draw water with the women if that was part of the deal.

Some jobs he preferred to others.

Tending sheep like his forefather David, for instance. And working in the vineyard. He learned to dig it and clear the stones away and plant a hedge to protect it and prune and hoe it and rid it of thorns and briers. He was impressed as never before by Isaiah's words:

The vineyard of the Lord of Hosts is the House of Israel.
The men of Judah are his pleasant planting.

At harvest time, working in the vineyard had another advantage: he had something to eat. He rested at noon in the long cool tunnel beneath the vines, the ends of which were supported on fig-trees. There he sat in comfort, nibbling a bunch of grapes. That year, even grapes were warm and clammy, though straight off the stalk. But how good they tasted. He chewed them slowly, savouring each one. Once he was fired without pay because the steward said he was eating too many on the job, which was a lie.

The Law said every man should be paid the price of his labour the same day, before sunset, *because he is poor and with his labour he sustains his life*. A workman might know nothing else of scripture but he certainly knew that line by heart.

Yet often, hours after sundown, Jesus was still labouring like a beast. The stars came out and he was, afraid to complain in case he would not be taken on again. He was the marginal man, he was dispensable. They could bully him and he had no come-back. They did not have to employ him, but he had to work.

Sometimes he hid so much fury inside him that it hurt. His brain was a full bladder that wouldn't empty.

But they were not the worst days. The worst days were when he stood in the market-place, eager, raising his hand whenever an employer approached – and was passed over. His long hours of enforced idleness under a stinging, bone-aching sun, breathing thin air, were punctuated by sudden bursts of hope: Maybe this man will hire me. And at the end of a day of total inactivity, he was physically and mentally exhausted. His arms were strong, his heart yearning to work, and it was all wasted. A day, a precious God-given day was wasted. A part of himself was wasted.

On days like this he would willingly have placed the ox's yoke over his head, on to his shoulders, and with a yell dragged the plough through the stony soil. Anything was better than being *a worm and not a man*. Anything was better than *waiting* for nothing to happen.

They did something to him, those wasted do-nothing days when he stood in the market-place like a stone a child has thrown away. The rejection – it was cruel, however unintended – toughened his soul.

He remembered, with a grim smile, words his mother was fond of, 'It is good to be poor, my son. You learn so many beautiful things the rich know nothing of.'

Chapter 9

During that long hot summer, Rabbi Ezra did not let God off lightly. Each of his sermons became the topic of the next week's gossip in the village.

'Lord,' he prayed, one Sabbath, 'we are not worthy of all this suffering you send us. Give it to more deserving cases.'

'Amen,' came from old Reuben who was practically deaf.

'Where is *Meschiah*, Lord? Not in Nazareth, certainly. We have searched in every house and wood for him. But no, anywhere but in poor little Nazareth. Your Messiah has passed us by. Poor us to be so far off the beaten track, so easily forgotten.'

'*Meschiah*.' Reuben echoed the only word he could make out.

'Yes, Lord,' Ezra went on. 'Where *is* the Messiah, purger of hunger and guilt, bringer of glory and bread?'

'Where, *where*?' came from a dozen hungry throats.

'Take no notice of our hunger, Lord,' Ezra said, encouraged, 'we are only your chosen people. People you have chosen to forget. So we can glorify your name.'

He looked with pity round the tattered, starving assembly before adding, 'If this is to be chosen, Lord, you are lucky we did not choose *you*.'

As the weeks of famine passed without relief, attendance at the synagogue increased. Ezra was their only form of entertainment.

He had never been over-religious nor, under Jesus's 'tuition', one for observing the minutiae of the Law. He advised pilgrims to the Holy City not to pay the Temple tax; it only went, he said, to enrich 'the fat priests of the

Capital' and their numerous Levite hangers-on who lived in idle luxury down in Jericho. Those Sadducees, he bellowed, would tax the tongue we pray with if they could, and the smoke from our fires.

But this was irreverence of a different sort. With the bare head and shaved beard of a mourner, his present onslaughts were directed not against the clergy but against the Most High God.

Behold the days are coming, says the Lord, when the ploughman shall overtake the reaper, the treader of grapes the one who sows the seed.

Ezra had put an iron chain over his shoulders. He chanted this piece from the prophet Amos with ferocious irony – not to the packed assembly with their thin worried faces.

'Our sheep, Lord, have flat noses from searching for grass among rocks. Are there no windows in heaven that you alone cannot see?'

'When, Lord, *when?*' someone cried.

They watched the Rabbi tearing his garments, until he stood before them in nothing but rags and this great iron chain. There was no coughing, no feet-stamping, it wasn't a Jewish assembly at all. They let him have his way as he spoke in their hearing with God, as Abraham and Moses spoke with him.

He banged the empty drum of his belly and called:

'Behold I stand all day at your door knocking and you do not answer me. Give us bread, Lord, and we will return to you. Can I expect loyalty from my dog or labour from my ox if I do not feed them?

'Yes, Lord, you are angry with us. But we are angrier with you. Our tears are the only rain there is.

'Strike the rock, strike *me* if you so wish, but give us water. Turn *my* body into bread, only feed my people. Tell us what to do and we will do it. Speak, Lord. Speak to your people.'

A few grumbled aloud, 'Stop it, Rabbi. Haven't we enough troubles without you turning God more against us.'

The rest agreed it was profanity; it was also irrefutable. They wanted more of it.

'What else do we have a rabbi for?' they said. 'If Ezra doesn't tell God what's what, who will?'

Achbor, a dry and formal elder, with a lean face and silver beard as scaly as a fish, was scandalised. Really, Ezra was so wicked, Achbor was enjoying himself enormously.

'The Rabbi,' he said to the packed synagogue, 'is wanting to put a hook through God's nose and a bit in his mouth.'

'Amen,' said Reuben.

Achbor, who only laughed at what disgusted him, said gleefully, 'Is the Most High God an ass, Rabbi, that you coax him and curse him and take a stick to him like this?'

But Ezra, without Jesus to curb his holy insolence, had started a fashion.

'Don't worry, Rabbi,' someone called out. 'God never listens to you praying, why should he listen to you cursing?'

Grumble followed grumble in the same vein.

'God has eyes but he sees not; he has ears but he hears not.'

'Take the stone from your breast, Lord, and put a heart of flesh there, instead.'

'Forget your Messiah, Lord. We'll settle for rain from heaven.'

One man suggested, 'Try him in Greek or Latin, Rabbi,' and another called for volunteers, 'Who's for Egypt? Who will come with me to Egypt?'

Most agreed that between praying and cursing there was little difference. Anyway, a man had to do one or the other to relieve his mind.

One day, Ezra borrowed Mary's ass and went to fell trees. The copse was so dry it had caught fire. Ezra stood in the path of the flames, defiant, daring God either to strike him down or end the village's famine.

'Choose!'

By this time, his face was scorched and the trees were exploding a few feet away from him. Without warning, a branch whistled past his head like a spear. A few more inches and Goodbye, Rabbi Ezra.

Ezra acknowledged that God had made his point. He bowed to the ground and hastily withdrew.

Not that it stopped him from complaining in the synagogue.

The butcher said to Ezra's wife, 'Your husband is mad.' Sarah nodded. 'Ah, at last someone else has found him out.'

Then came the memorable Sabbath of the Rabbi's blasphemy. That week, two babies had been still-born and another, one month old, had choked to death.

'Lord,' he cried, 'have we bowed and scraped to Baal or kissed his lips that we have deserved this?'

He unrolled the scroll as if it were the tongue of God and put his ear to it.

'Do you hear me?'

No answer. God's tongue was still.

'You kissed us, Lord, only to destroy us?'

Shaphan was old now and racked with rheumatism, but he had never forgiven Ezra for the crime of throwing Nebat out of Bible class. Shaphan called out:

'God will turn our synagogue into a latrine if this goes on much longer.'

Nebat, a man-flower grown unmistakably from the boy-seed, took his own revenge. 'The Rabbi is yearning for the fat onions and flesh-pots of Egypt.'

Ezra paid them no heed. He addressed the assembly as if he were Elijah mocking the false prophets of Baal.

'Come along, my friends, cry aloud to your God. Is he not the only God? Maybe he is dreaming or he has lost his way.'

'Wipe him clean like a plate, Lord,' Achbor said, rubbing his bony hands. 'Show us your kindness and cover him with boils.'

'Maybe,' Ezra went on, in a frozen voice, 'your God has left home? Or he is asleep? Then we must wake him.'

'Stone him,' Achbor demanded, squirming with pleasure, as Ezra took up cymbals and clashed them noisily.

When the reverberation had died down, Ezra said, 'God? No answer?'

'Stone him. Stone the Rabbi,' Achbor repeated, happy as an ox with his face in grass. 'Sabbath or not, stone the Rabbi.'

Ezra took up the ram's horn. With his puny breath, he barely squelched out a sound.

'Not enough to bring down the walls of Jericho,' he said, puffed, 'but surely God, the only God will hear it if he is not asleep.'

'Amen,' said Reuben, who had just woken up.

'Not even a little thunderbolt for Rabbi Ezra, your devoted servant in Nazareth?'

'Fetch me stones,' Achbor shrieked. 'A big pile of stones.'

The assembly sighed contentedly. The Rabbi had acquitted himself far beyond their expectations.

Chapter 10

Summer was waning, the harvest was in. Jesus was finding jobs harder to come by and local hostility was growing.

Two or three times he was forced out of a village. Under cover of night, a few men crept to his booth, kicked it to bits with him inside it and melted into the shadows.

He shifted to a coastal village not far from Carmel. The locusts had overflown it, the weather had been kind to it. Mulberry-trees, figs, oranges, lemons, cactuses – all blossoming.

After three days' drudgery in the fields he was given as payment a basket of unripe dates.

He took them to his employer's house and, opening the door, threw them in, in his wrath. Then he shook the dust off his sandals. At that moment, he felt as ferocious as Elijah when, on Mount Carmel, he defeated the prophets of Baal and slaughtered them to a man by the Kishon brook.

It was a whole hour before he could bring himself to pray for the man who had stolen his labour.

This he took as a sign he should go home for a few days' rest. He was washed out. Even his great strength had waned, he needed a break. He had this searing pain for his mother, for Ezra, for the quiet village where dogs did not snarl at him, where people accepted him.

He needed to be re-created. He would hurry home before the Sabbath began.

He was much thinner than when he had left. His big rough hands were scarred, calloused, with hard shiny whorls on them. Several of his fingers were raw from over-work; the skin had peeled from them like the bark of a eucalyptus-tree. His feet were swollen. Tired and undernourished, he had developed a painful stye in his left eye. There was the first, premature streak of grey in his beard and a small bald patch on the crown of his head.

With his small store of corn, olive-oil, salted meat and animal feed, he headed for the most sacred spot in the world: home.

How he longed for rest, the Sabbath rest. It was always like drawing a curtain round his soul. It was the day to which every Jew was entitled. How else could he prove to himself, in spite of all appearances, that he was a free member of a free race?

Excited to be going home, his unease grew the nearer he came to Nazareth. From a couple of miles off, he could see the air shimmering over the village in the relentless heat. He stood for a moment, resting, and it seemed to him that the place was 'out of shape'. It was like a black-draped widow on a hill. Words from Jeremiah's Lamentations sprang to his lips: *The Lord has trodden as in a wine-press the Virgin daughter of Judah.*

There were signs of fresh graves on the edge of the village. Death had done a brisk trade, so his anxiety grew.

The rocks were bare, no touches of verdure anywhere,

and over all this unearthly silence. Until, at a bend in the road, he ran into a crowd of mourners.

Why had he not heard them before? Because at this double funeral, the wailers were silent. There were none of the usual sounds of keening like night-owls or wounded doves. The mourners had not the strength for it.

In the centre of the group he was relieved to see the black-shawled figure of his mother. She was alive, thank God.

Mary was hired for most funerals. She was excellent, everyone agreed, at lamenting. Not that she accepted payment, as she was entitled, like other women. She did it out of respect for the dead and hoped that one day neighbours would do the same for her. Today, there was a bundle in her arms.

Jesus tried to voice his own sadness, at these deaths, at everyone's death, but his throat was dry and clogged with dust from the long march. It was left to a boy drummer lightly tapping to express the quiet grief of the village and of all mankind.

The bundle in his mother's arms was the child whose parents they had just buried.

Deborah, four years old, looked and weighed less than a child of two. For days, Mary had carried her everywhere. The girl, mewing like a kitten, had the pained look of someone continually disturbed in sleep.

Jesus was glad to be home. He propped himself up inside the door, his eyes closed, breathing in until the pain ceased – *Go away, pain* – feeling how good it was to be in his own place, among his own, belonging. He would never leave again. Never.

He spoke and chains fell from his heart. She even noticed his voice had changed to a lower register.

Only those who love you *listen* to you, he thought. Others – business acquaintances, employers – at best listen to the words you say, but not to *you* saying them. Here at home his words fell not on rocks as they did in a strange village but like seeds on good soil.

He always knew these things, of course. But now he *felt* he knew them.

His mother was serene as ever, rejoicing in the greatness and kindness of God. No calamity would ever break her, no disaster undermine her faith.

And now her boy was home again. The big creaky hollow in the house was filled. All would be well.

She was feeding goat's milk to the child, all the little one could keep down. Mary kept the milk in a skin container in the recess of the house. The door and window were permanently closed against the sun's searching fingers. She had even surrounded the house with branches to give it extra shade. She lived mostly indoors in the dark, lighting the lamps only occasionally at night and on the Sabbath.

Jesus had brought milk with him but it had curdled, it was only good for cheese.

Mary could not hide her disappointment. She had but a small supply of milk left. When that was gone, Deborah would go to sleep with her mother and father.

Jesus washed, anointed his head with oil his mother had kept for him and put on his best robe for the Sabbath. It was a comfort to see that his mother had put out a candlestick and a vase with flowers – wrinkled like ferns before they unfold, but a token of her devotion – and a cup for the wine. Things had not changed too much.

He was proud of her. She was a rare woman, one who could handle joy as well as grief. To handle joy can require the more courage. She was one of the few women who are not perturbed by, or suspicious of, happiness. She could accept it without flinching, carry whole armfuls of it like a pile of washing. She used to say, 'You don't have to say sorry for being happy.'

When he was changed, Mary looked up at him, with a smile. 'You look very handsome, my son.'

She had not been expecting him. While she took care of the meal, he held Deborah, cooling her forehead with a damp cloth.

The little food in the house did not surprise him. His

57

mother was not one to hoard anything while others were starving. She brought out bread, honey, olives and a few chopped vegetables.

Once she paused, looked up shyly and said, 'You have waited a long time.'

It was less a question than a reproach. She had never used that tone before.

He nodded.

Deborah was a dove's feather in his arms and precious. He was in awe of her. He had never held anything so precious before. He never could understand what people saw in silver and gold but a child, any child, a child deformed, *especially* a child deformed, edged him to a precipice of wonder. Such frail containers of his Father's love and glory.

Only, this starving child made him ashamed, too. It should not be like this, not for a single child in the whole world.

Deborah's breathing came in gasps as though her lungs were bellows with a hole in. Her throat was red and spotted, she had a prickly heat rash. He dipped his finger in honey and almost leaped for joy when she sucked it and was consoled.

Tears ran down his cheeks from pity, from wonder, from anger; and his broad shoulders shook.

Mary stopped her preparations, causing him to brush his tears aside in a hurry.

'Don't be afraid of your tears, my son. There is a time to weep as there is a time to laugh.'

'There is a time to work,' he responded, harshly. 'Tears are for women.'

She took his shoulder gently. 'Abraham wept for Sarah, didn't he? Joseph, too, seeing his brother Benjamin after the years. Didn't Moses, even Moses, weep? And good King Hezekiah? David for Absalom, his naughty boy? Jeremiah for King Josiah? Pious Ezra after our return to our land?' Her voice took on a momentary edge. 'Were these *women*?'

He shook his head.

'Blessed are you for weeping, my son, for you will be comforted.'

Jesus rocked the child and as he did he chanted softly
from the Lamentations like a cantor in the synagogue:

> *My eyes are weeping and in turmoil is my soul,*
> *For babes and infants to their mothers cry:*
>   *Oh, where is our food?*
> *They fall down in the streets*
>   *Like men wounded in war*
> *As their life is poured out*
>   *On their mother's breast.*

Tears coursed down his cheeks but he was no longer
ashamed of them. Today, his mother said in her heart,
my boy has become a man.

Chapter 11

He spoke sparingly of his recent experiences. He put
them behind him, among things best forgotten.

But she knew.

Knew how anger and resignation had fought a bitter
unresolved battle within him. Knew the pain that had
gripped him while he was away. This she knew because
she had been holding the other end of the thread. How
could she *not* feel each tug on it, each twitch?

She spoke of people who had left the village, those who
had not come through the trials and gone under, those
who had survived. She mentioned babies dying whom he
had not known were born. She listed too acts of heroism
– her own not included – and stressed normal, womanly
things: sharing with neighbours, being present at births,
little jokes at the well.

But he knew.

Knew she had been putting lots of patches on her

'todays'. Knew that since he went away there had been a succession of torn, ragged, muddied days which she had washed and mended and folded away, as good as new. Or almost.

He knew that for such as her the world goes on. It has done and it will. All bad things end. If it is God's will that bad things come, it is also his will that people try to turn them into good. So they do, God willing...

Strange how he worried about her when she was so protected. Her soul was like a lamb with always plenty of grass to feed on. But worries came whatever you told yourself.

They spoke of Joseph and felt refreshed. Joseph, in death, was a deep private well to them. Whenever they were tired or low they met around him, drank cool water from him, laughed at the old tales, centring on him, told already a thousand times before.

They sat down to eat. Jesus noticed his mother was not sharing the fresh food he had brought. He was given leavened bread, she was making do with bread fried in a pan. It was flat, heavy, hard. Bread for a desert wanderer, for someone without a homeland. His whole being protested against it. Were they not God's people? Had they crossed the Jordan into the land of promise for this?

He leaned over and sipped the wine in her cup. That, too, was without yeast, more like grape-juice.

Mary gestured as if to say, What does it matter?

She tried to divert him by recalling her first meeting with Joseph and what she thought of him. Usually he liked to hear it – it was like gazing under the soil at the roots of things – but not today.

It *did* matter to him. Where was that bread and wine of a free people they had been promised, in their own country, under their own sky? Was it for this God had brought them out of Egypt? For this unending Passover? Was the only freedom left them, the right to bury their dead?

His mother read his anguish. It showed in the veins of his forehead, under his eyes, at the corners of his mouth. She smiled to reassure him that all was well with her.

'I am getting old, my son, well used to hardship.'

He suddenly realised Ezra had not been at the funeral. He had been so relieved to see his mother there he had forgotten about Ezra.

He asked after him and received an evasive reply.

'He is not ill?'

Mary admitted that he was being investigated by an official from Jerusalem.

Jesus was astonished. 'Why?'

Rumours had reached the Sanhedrin that the Rabbi Ezra was not loyal to the *Torah*. Achbor the Elder was rumoured to be behind this, but she did not mention his name.

Jesus pushed his food aside and stood up. He felt as he had felt when he was six years old: the Rabbi had a big bark but no bite. He needed defending.

'Eat first, my son,' Mary pleaded. 'You are tired and hungry.'

He shook his head. 'The Sabbath will soon be upon us.'

His mother shrugged and made him bow for her blessing.

Ezra was not at home. Sarah, his wife, a woman with a face flat and featureless as weathered stone, said he and the investigator went to the synagogue two hours ago.

'They have caught up with him at last,' she said.

When Jesus opened the door, there were Ezra and the middle-aged official facing each other across the study table. Between them was the scroll of the Law. It was a cheap copy, ragged and dog-eared, all they could afford. Like Ezra, it contained the unvarnished Word of God.

The Rabbi was somehow smaller than when Jesus last saw him, more battered; and gasping for breath like a fish in the Salt Sea. He was trying to explain himself to this tall gentleman from the metropolis with his sculptured beard and white translucent eyes like cucumber seeds.

Jesus waited. The strain was telling on Ezra. An old man with swollen legs, had he really been kept standing there for two hours?

To Jesus it was obscene that this polished priest should

be investigating Ezra, 'the Rumbling Rabbi' as he had become known. It was clear that the official had decided, probably at first glance, that he was wasting his time. Ezra was senile, not accountable for his words and actions.

'Does not Torah tell you,' the official said in a high, silky voice, 'when in trial and distress to return to the Lord and obey his voice?'

'Amen,' the Rabbi said, beating his bird-like breast.

'You believe this?' The official sounded sceptical.

'With all my sinful heart, Reverence.'

'There is *no* truth in the stories that you expressed anger towards the ways of God the Most High?'

Jesus had had enough. Why should Ezra, who presided free of charge over a village of dead lamps and silent millstones, be tormented by this plump, gentlemanly scholar?

Before Ezra could plead guilty or not guilty to a charge of blasphemy, Jesus slammed the door to, making the synagogue ring.

The official turned to face him, but slowly. He was not impressed by the bad manners of provincials. He had once written a treatise on usury, of which fifty scribal copies had been made, proving conclusively by a thousand fallacious arguments what no Jew had ever doubted. Authorship had endowed him with an unassailable sense of his own importance.

Jesus felt the official's gaze creeping over him like a spider. Yes, a wild youngster, as he thought.

'Of course the Rabbi is angry with God,' Jesus said, in a hostile voice. 'Has not a man who trusts the covenant and is left to starve like a slave the right to be angry?'

'You mean well, young man, I am sure,' the official said, in the same smooth manner. 'But, take it from me, to be angry with God is to hate him who made us.'

'Did Job hate God? Did all the prophets? No, the Rabbi's anger is proof of his love and zeal and fidelity.'

'If you say so.'

'It is not I who say so but the Book. When long ago Jerusalem suffered drought as Nazareth does now, what did Jeremiah say?'

The official had him now. 'You tell me, my boy.'
Jesus spoke as though he were the prophet and this was his prayer.

> Lord, thou hope of Israel, its saviour in times past,
>> Why dost thou wander
>>> Like a foreigner in our land,
>>> Like a journeyman who stays but a night
>>>> Then travels on?
>> Why deal with us like a drunk with a muddled mind,
>>> Like a man with colossal strength
>>>> Who will not use it?

The investigator was impressed at the youth's ability to quote scripture by heart and in flawless Hebrew. He had promise. One day he might even write a book.

As God's representative, he was pledged to be patient with beginners.

'Come, come, young man,' he beamed. 'Surely the Rabbi does not put himself on a level with Jeremiah. For ordinary mortals, to question God is to disbelieve in his ordinances.'

'To question God,' came the instant rejoinder, 'is to show him our hearts as our Rabbi has done, how bruised they are and in need of God's healing hand.'

'You think so.' A ghost of a smile lingered on the official's face. He had the equanimity of a man who cares for no one but himself.

'The Rabbi expects something from God and getting God's attention is not always easy. You, sir, expect nothing, except to be left in peace.'

The official was distracted from the speech by the curious provincial dialect.

'Obviously,' he neighed, 'you have a somewhat different view of God from me.'

'It is true,' Jesus said, with sadness, 'your God is not my God.'

At this, a fresh fire burned in Ezra's eyes.

Jesus added, 'My God is not afraid to take the blame.'

'You look tired, young man.' The official shaped his

plump cheeks into a paternalistic smile. 'I will forget you said that.'

Jesus asked abruptly, 'Have you brought us food from Jerusalem?'

The official shook his head, making a face.

'A promise of food?'

'My dear boy,' the official said, indulgently, 'the poor are a perennial problem. I am here not to discuss bread and wine but the Rabbi's orthodoxy.'

Jesus said, almost to himself, 'If only I could become bread and wine so my people could feed on me.'

The official looked disgusted at the unappetising suggestion, but Ezra was thinking, Yes, my Jesus will be Rabbi here when I am gone.

'You,' Jesus said to the official, 'are one of those who herd their flock from behind.'

The man from the big city said, with a smirk, 'Are there such in Galilee?'

'Yes,' Jesus said. 'We call them butchers.'

The official wanted to reply but his tongue was a plate in his mouth. Better, anyway, to retain one's dignity.

'Rabbi,' Jesus said, as if the investigator had just disappeared, 'I am off to the plain to look for work.'

Ezra touched his arm fondly. 'You are forgetting, my son. Soon we will be lighting the Sabbath candles.'

'I have not forgotten, Rabbi.'

Ezra looked at him with a dismay that slowly turned to understanding and, finally, to pride.

'The Sabbath is for the free,' Jesus said. 'Starving men are not free.'

The official scowled at him. 'You would honour God by breaking the Sabbath?'

'Man came before the Sabbath and takes precedence over it.'

'But, young man' – after all, the boy had promise – 'next, you will be saying that you can honour God by breaking his commandments.'

'I tell you,' Jesus said, 'a man like you may keep all God's commandments and not love him at all. Whereas a man who loves God like Ezra can do *whatever he likes* and he will never give offence.'

The official's good temper was at last exhausted. The young man was nothing but a smelly, inedible fig.

'Blasphemer,' he spat out, tearing at his robe.

'And you,' Jesus countered, in his same even tone, 'are a hypocrite.' It pleased him to see his adversary flinch. He went on:

'I have left a house in which a child is starving to death and you, though you *know* our condition, bring us "enlightenment" but no milk. That, *sir*, is blasphemy.'

'So be it.'

The investigator kept his temper this time. No point in building this into something bigger than it was.

'Who sent you, by the way?' Jesus asked.

The official wished he had mentioned the name of his illustrious patron earlier. It might have smoothed his path.

'I am of the household of Caiaphas.'

Jesus had not heard of him. He said, 'Tell Caiaphas that Jesus of Nazareth is leaving his ass behind to keep the Sabbath in his stead.'

'I will pray for you,' the official said, with a polished scorn.

Jesus could not be fond of the man but he said, with genuine concern, 'And I for you.'

Tenderly, he kissed the Rabbi on the cheek and asked his blessing.

The Rabbi raised his hand over him.

'The Lord bless you, my son, and keep you. The Lord make his face shine on you and grace you. The Lord lift up his countenance upon you and give you peace.'

It was more than a benediction, it was a massive gesture of defiance that was not lost on the investigator from Jerusalem. For it was the prayer spoken over a child of Israel who has dutifully kept the Sabbath.

Chapter 12

Jesus did not bother to go home. Ezra would tell his mother where he was. He went by the southern path in the direction of Esdraelon.

The journey gave him no pleasure and, in spite of Ezra's blessing, no peace.

He was fatigued and the pain inside him had begun again. Only an hour ago he had promised himself he would never leave home again, *never*.

It was hot and humid and he was going unprepared. Incensed by the treatment of Ezra he had not brought an extra coat for the evening and had forgotten to eat. That was a bad mistake, but it was too late to turn back now. There were more important matters on his mind, like obtaining milk for a four-year-old child with the body of a two-year-old.

While still far from his final destination, he just knew he was in luck. Several strings of camels, some fifty or so strong, were journeying from the north on the trade route across the great plain.

When he was within hailing distance of one promising-looking caravan, he saw that the bull camels were laden with timber – cedar and pine – while the cows had a lesser load, probably of gum, balm and myrrh.

The sun was sinking rapidly, so was his stomach. Soon it would be the Sabbath.

The camel-train he was following halted at a small water-hole, indicated by a clump of trees and chattering birds. Time to do the hard thing: ask for work. Always hard but never more than now.

He was weary, he knew nothing about camels. Dusk was coming on and with it the Sabbath when he should be resting from the work of a slave. He felt guilty about this, as a father feels guilty when he has injured his own child through no fault of his own. Guilt, like anxiety, came and went when it wanted to. At least his conscience was clear.

His mind went back to the days when he was a boy. His father had taught him how to carve camels, donkeys, pairs of oxen in olive wood. He had taken them, with some rabbit skins, down to Esdraelon and sold them to travellers in passing caravans like this. They paid well and he had been proud to contribute to the family purse.

During those youthful business deals, he had picked up a smattering of Greek. If only it would come back to him now. When he spoke, he was bound to sound as idiotic as any man wrestling with a foreign language. That was another hardship he would have to suffer.

Forming in his mind the phrases he intended to use, he approached the caravan, his hands open, his arms extended to show he harboured no weapons. Coming down the hill, he resembled a big white butterfly.

He went up to the caravan master, a turbaned man in flowing, brightly coloured robes with a face resting on an imperious black beard. He did obeisance and pleaded in scratchy, scarcely intelligible Greek to be allowed to serve him that night, to ease his lord's painful journey through the pleasant land of Galilee.

The master tugged on one of his gold earrings and looked him over as he would a camel or an ox. This Galilean had, to his trained eye, a strong, lithe body. He seemed willing to work.

Without addressing Jesus directly, the master ordered his steward to put him to work. He had lost a camel-driver that morning. The unfortunate man had struck a bull-camel and not taken the precaution of getting out of range before the beast bit his hand clean off. The injured man knew he had no value like a camel; no one would take care of him. When the others last saw him, he had tied a rope tightly around his forearm and was marching futilely back in the direction they had come, his blood spouting on to the desert sands.

The steward put Jesus in the charge of an overseer.

There was a strict hierarchy in that small caravan – it extended to the camels themselves – and Jesus, the newcomer, was at the bottom of the pile.

'You are sure you know how to handle a camel?' demanded the overseer, a one-eyed ogre of a man.

'Camels,' Jesus replied, bowing the better to conceal the truth, 'are my life, sir.'

He was given a date frond, the end of it sharpened to a point, and told to unload ten camels.

After a long trek, they smelled indescribably and their bellies made a noise like a retreating army.

The camels were roped head to tail. He untied his ten and led them apart.

The youngest of them, a frisky, untrained two-year-old, took an instant dislike to Jesus. It kept side-stepping him and knocking him over with its flank, much to the delight of the other two cameleers. The noisier and nastier of the pair looked a real ruffian as he peered from under his *keffiyeh*.

In this swiftest of apprenticeships, Jesus found the camel to be the haughtiest of beasts, as indifferent to human-kind as the deserts for which it was made. A dog can love you; a camel never. It is perpetually on the lookout for any sign of weakness in its driver so as to nudge him or snap at him.

The fiercest of the bulls – it was the one which that morning had broken its fast on its driver's hand – refused to have its halter removed. Following the lead of the two professionals, Jesus tied its jaws tightly together with rope, removed the halter and then, at the risk of being trampled to death, tied one of its forelegs into a jack-knife shape.

The animals had caught a whiff of water. Snarling and grunting, they turned huge, yellowy-black teeth towards the water-hole, digging into the dry soil with their enormous hooves. Already nearly blind in his left eye because of the stye, Jesus was practically suffocated by dust. It was ages before he had hobbled and tethered his camels and made them settle down.

He listened attentively to the other drivers, trying without success to imitate their sounds of command.

After unloading the beasts, he had to water them. The nastier of his companions, the one with a huge twisted nose, ideal for avoiding the direct odour of camels, gave him a bucket and Jesus made repeated journeys to fill it. The camels, not having drunk for six days, were insatiable. He no sooner filled the trough than it was empty. In between drinking, they crunched away at coarse grass and thistles.

Jesus worked harder than he had ever worked in his life. Even so, the two cameleers were finished an hour before him.

The night was advanced. His white Sabbath robe was stained yellow with sweat and camel dung. Smells of cooking from the camp-fire reminded him that he had not eaten for hours.

In the darkness, someone grabbed his arm. Instinctively, he wrenched it away, fearing an attack. It was the cameleer with the twisted nose.

'Come,' the man said. 'Eat.'

Jesus followed him eagerly until he saw, to his horror, that the overseer was cooking camel meat.

His companion handed him a plate and lifted a dipper full of camel stew from the pot.

Jesus shook his head violently.

'Not hungry?' his companion enquired.

Jesus had no words to explain that, for Jews, such meat is held to be unclean. He was breaking the Sabbath for the sake of a sick child, not for himself. He was famished but strong, he would survive.

He asked for a chunk of bread and a small onion. Having purified his hands by running sand through them, he ate his scanty meal, drank some of the brackish water, mixed with sand, flies and hairs, which the camels had left over, and went apart to rest.

This was the most wretched and humiliating night of his life. On his recent travels to outlying villages, he was among his own people, able to observe Jewish laws. Here, now, he was an outcast.

His sense of isolation grew when one of the men by the fire put a flute to his lips and played a high-pitched, wailing, foreign-sounding tune. His peace of mind was still more disturbed when he found near him, in the print of a camel's hoof, a little horned viper.

Jesus lay on his back, hungry and weary, looking up at the night sky. The crescent moon and the stars were Sabbath candles, God's blessing of light, the proof that he, Jesus of Nazareth, was still beloved. Then, in his tortured imagination, the stars faded and the crescent moon turned into an evil yellow mouth, leering at him and all his misfortunes.

He was too tired to sleep and too hungry, and his eye was very sore. The flute player ceased. The cameleers rose from the fire to lay themselves down beside their charges.

Jesus presumed it was for warmth and protection, and he wondered how they could stand the stench of the beasts, equally nauseous at the front and the rear.

Really, they were guarding their camels. If one of them was stolen, they might have to pay for it with a hand or a foot. Jesus did not know this was part of the deal or he might not have slept at all.

He wrapped his mantle round his head and eventually drifted into a fitful sleep in which he was dimly aware of being bitten all over by ants. It was a chill night and he was not dressed for it. Twisting and turning, he dreamed he had a twin, except he was himself the twin as well. And this twin loved and served God perfectly and was commended for it. But he himself was dragged before Moses and Elijah, gigantic figures with great green beards, who angrily demanded to know why he had deserted his people and desecrated the Sabbath.

During the hours of sleep – *when* he could not judge – someone approached where he lay. Jesus tried to wake up but hadn't the strength. If this was to be the end of him, so be it.

It was the evil-looking cameleer, taking pity on him by covering him with a black goat-skin blanket.

In the morning, before sun-up, he awoke to the stirrings of the caravan. Without taking food, he had to load the camels. He saw them reclining there at first light, immense, forbidding, statuesque.

To stop their snorting and gurgling, he muzzled them as before and began loading them.

He was balancing a pile of timber on a camel when the overseer approached and yelled at him in a language he could not follow. The others took no notice. No help from that quarter.

Jesus tried to say in Greek that he didn't understand but the overseer continued berating him and digging the point of his stick in Jesus's back. Again and again, he felt the point piercing his skin causing blood to dribble down his back.

'Do it properly this time,' the overseer said at length, in broken Greek.

Jesus, throbbing from head to toe with an anger which the overseer took for fear, nodded, not knowing what he had done wrong.

The cameleer with the twisted nose sidled over to him.

'I am Asuph,' he said in recognisable Aramaic, baring his teeth in a smile.

He had made the journey through Galilee a hundred times and picked up a bit of the local dialect. He offered his name 'Asuph' as though it were a gift of a loaf or a flower.

'I am Jesus of Nazareth.'

Asuph explained that Jesus was putting heavy timber on a cow instead of on a bull. Also, he should load the camels in the right order, since they were used to a rigid routine. 'They no work for you otherwise, man from Nazareth.'

Jesus thanked him and loaded the camels as directed. It was not as easy as loading an ass.

Once loaded, the camels had to be persuaded to get to their feet. Having had their fill of water the night before, they were not inclined to move.

Jesus did his best to drag them up, snorting and gurgling grossly, by the halter. As soon lift a boulder with his bare hands.

Once more Asuph came to his rescue. 'We are friends, no, Jesus of Nazareth?'

71

Jesus nodded. He and Asuph were friends for life. Such was the nomads' way. It was friend or foe at once and for ever.

'If you are well,' Jesus said, 'I am well.'

Asuph showed him how to get the camels to their feet with the palm frond. He tapped the leading bull camel on the knees, while making a clicking noise with his lips. Reluctantly, the beast lurched forward, back, forward again and, after this succession of diagonal movements, it was on its feet.

'Remember, friend Jesus of Nazareth,' Asuph said, 'the camel never go backward. Waste of time to try.' He banged a camel on the nose. It snarled with pain but looked at Asuph with respect. 'His only weak bit. Punch his nose and he follow you for ever like a woman.'

Jesus thanked Asuph and, to test the method, tentatively tapped a bull on the nose. The beast immediately coughed, regurgitated a filthy yellow foaming cud and spat it at him.

His task was completed just as the sun rose. The men prepared a hot drink before the caravan departed.

Asuph took Jesus aside and said, 'The overseer, he hit you when you were south-east of the water-hole. Why you not smash him?'

Jesus shrugged. 'Not a good idea.'

'You very wise, my friend,' Asuph said behind his hand. 'He would not have paid you.'

Jesus smiled. 'That is not why I did not hit him.'

Asuph was interested. 'Then, why?'

'Because,' Jesus said, 'we are brothers.'

'You and –' He made an obscene gesture towards the back of the overseer. He spat and the spittle plopped on to the ground like an egg.

'Yes, Asuph.'

'But,' Asuph said, in wonder, 'brothers do not hate each other.'

'Correct. I do not hate him, I love him.'

'He pokes you worse than camel and you love him?' Under his keffiyeh, Asuph's eyes were twinkling in fun. But he frowned as he added, 'Even his own mother has to hate that pig.'

'That makes me even sorrier for him,' Jesus said.

'What he needs is –' Asuph made a slicing motion across his throat. 'And one night when no moon I do it.'

Jesus shook his head.

'No?' Asuph asked. 'Then you hold him, I push his filthy head in the fire.'

Jesus moved his hand negatively in front of Asuph's chest.

'Why you come here, my friend?' Asuph said, his lips tightening.

'To get milk for a child who is ill.'

Asuph made a sound like 'Ai, ai, ai. Your boy sick, now I grasp.'

'It's not a boy, it's a girl.'

Asuph touched the wrong side of his nose as if he were trying to straighten it.

'Why you worry about your girl?'

'It's not *my* girl.'

'Your brother's?'

'No.'

Asuph was really amazed. The whites of his eyes showed it. 'You slave for another man's little girl?' He put his hand to his head to indicate this man from Nazareth was not quite right in the head.

Having recovered, he took Jesus to the man in charge of stores and begged him, as a brother, to give him camel's milk.

'Richer it is,' he explained to Jesus, 'than milk of goats.'

Jesus's last job was to gather up the camel dung in a bucket to fuel the fires of the caravan that night. Then he was paid in kind: oil, bread, vegetables and flour.

Before the caravan left, Jesus took Asuph of the fierce eyes and broken nose into his arms and held him tight.

'Brother, thank you,' he said.

'One day,' Asuph whispered in his ear, 'you help me cut out overseer's tongue, agreed? And we eat it together before him, then kill him pleasantly.'

Jesus squeezed him for the last time. 'I will give my own life for you, my friend.'

'Ah,' Asuph sighed, happily, 'may your ass and my ass be brothers for ever.'

Jesus waved him goodbye and started up the track to his village.

On the outskirts, at a twist in the road, he was confronted by a hideous female figure. She emerged from a cave, decrepit, dressed in widow's weeds.

'Alms, kind sir, for the love of the Most High.'

He would have recognised that whining voice anywhere. It was his mother's friend. Anna perhaps did not know him because his mantle was up and the left side of his face was badly swollen.

'Give to the poor and lend to the Lord,' she cried.

What was Anna doing here? Had she already been driven from her house for not paying the rent?

She was plainly starving. Her neck was like a bare stalk. The skin under her eyes lay open and tattered like husks of corn. Food given to her would be wasted. She looked close to death.

He put down his parcel of provisions, divided them into three and handed Anna one portion.

'God sent you,' she said, in that familiar wail. 'You are Joshua to me, my saviour.'

She clutched the food in her withered arms and retreated to the cave in the hillside.

Jesus chuckled to himself. If only it was that easy to be a saviour.

He quickened his pace over the last stretch of his journey. It was midday. The village was in the bosom of the Sabbath; not a cat's whisker was to be seen.

He opened the front door of his house, holding up his precious flask of camel's milk like a trophy, to find Mary in the darkness softly singing and rocking in her arms a dead child.

Chapter 13

The drought ended. The Lord ordered his angel to sheathe his fiery sword at last.

That year the winter rains were long and heavy. More important, the spring rains did not fail. Great marble clouds came out of the west and deposited their load over the bare heights of Nazareth.

Ezra had remained as Rabbi. The official who had reported back to Jerusalem had aroused much mirth by his account of what he had seen and heard. The priestly aristocracy, convinced that Ezra was weak in the head but no political threat, left him to minister in a place where there were no other takers – apart from an informer called Achbor who seemed even more unsuitable.

Ezra stepped out into the market-place during a downpour and honked his hymn of thanksgiving. The villagers sloshed through the mud to surround him. The raindrops were as big as grapes, they sipped them like vintage wine and slapped him on the back. 'God's gift, Rabbi. Prayers of yours did it,' they said. 'Now grow your beard again.'

Only Achbor, with nothing to laugh at any more, relapsed into prayerful misery.

In the spring, the bare bones of the trees were fleshed green again; swifts, swallows and turtle-doves returned; the grass grew as they watched. Someone swore he had heard a frog croaking, and everybody cheered. It was back to normal.

Hence Ezra's wrath. The people had come through hell and now they would not repent. They stopped attending the synagogue, they even broke the Sabbath on the plea that work had piled up.

'We need a break, Rabbi,' they said. 'We have had two years of nothing but Sabbaths.'

Ezra muttered darkly to himself. Jews were not Jews without suffering. Suffering was the real circumcision. Suffering created spaces in the soul for God to breathe in. Fat, laughing, contented Jews were invariably blasphemous. He wished he had a forehead of flint so he could butt them into submission.

'Maybe the Lord was right, after all,' he confessed to Jesus, 'in sending us locusts and drought.'

'Ask him to send us persecutions,' Jesus said, joking, 'so we love him all the more.'

Ezra lifted his eyebrows in mock irritation. 'You still are making fun of me, eh?'

'No,' Jesus insisted. 'You are confusing God. First you tell him: No more troubles, *please*. Next you say: Troubles are what we need.'

The Rabbi stroked his chin, bare as a plucked chicken, and raised his eyes, including the half-closed one, to heaven.

'No more troubles, God,' he pleaded. 'We're happy to be miserable sinners for a while.'

Sorrows seemed to have been forgotten. Children played in the streets again. A few cats and dogs drifted back. Soon they overran the place as before and most dogs belonged to no one and everyone. Old Anna, skeletal, with only a tuft or two of hair left on her head, had survived and was continually in Mary's house, begging and borrowing.

'Your sweet, darling first-born will do great things, Mary. Such a pious boy.'

Children crowded Jesus's workshop again, reminding him of what his father used to say, 'If God had made a bunch of children on the first day of creation, he still wouldn't have finished making the world.'

They asked questions, implored him with rolling eyes to teach them how to saw and carve and use the chisel. They could be cruel to each other and cheeky, but they were eager to learn, ready to begin at the beginning. They did not 'know it all'. They had no airs and graces.

76

God's Kingdom belonged to such as these.

Once, when the rest had gone, seven-year-old Shimon stayed behind, wiggling his toes, rubbing his left calf with the ball of his right foot.

'Sp-sp-sp,' he whispered. 'Jesus.'

'Yes?'

'My sister Rebecca,' he said, opening wide his big black eyes, 'she told me to say she likes you.'

Rebecca was sixteen and the prettiest girl in the village. If Jesus had been thinking of marrying he would have looked Rebecca over more than once.

'Thank you, Shimon,' he said, getting on with shaping a yoke.

'She gave me two peaches to say that.'

Jesus patted the boy on his curly head. 'Glad to be of help.'

'You, have you a message for my sister?'

Jesus did not hesitate. 'No, no message.'

Shimon rolled his eyes in a mortal agony. 'But you must have some message for her.'

'Must I? Why?'

'Then she'll give me two more peaches.'

Jesus reached into a basket. 'Here.' He handed the boy two peaches he was keeping for his lunch.

They vanished in an instant, inside the boy's tunic. 'Now the message, Jesus,' he said, 'then I'll have four peaches.'

Seeing the Carpenter's mouth was firmly closed, Shimon pleaded, 'Shall I tell her you love her?'

'No.'

'*Please*, Jesus.'

'Not even to please you, Shimon.'

The boy turned mischievous. 'Then I'll say you don't love her.'

Jesus grabbed him before he could disappear. 'Not that, either.'

Shimon looked genuinely puzzled. Probably a pose. 'Either you love her or you don't.'

Jesus released the boy. 'Neither,' he said.

'Then you love some of her? Or some days you love

her and some days not? I don't understand.'

'There are some things children are not supposed to understand.'

'Ah,' Shimon said, as if enlightenment had dawned. 'You love someone else!'

'I don't.'

'Good,' Shimon said, running away fast, 'my sister will be very happy when I tell her you don't love *anyone else.*'

Jesus was left wryly wondering if children were altogether suited to God's Kingdom after all.

Then it was Ezra's turn to get at him. He whispered in Jesus's ear, 'My Jedidah, even in the harshest times, she did not...'

'Not?'

'She did not cease to be the way women... should be.'

Was Ezra expecting congratulations?

'Ah,' Jesus said.

'Of good stock, like her mother, you understand.'

Jesus nodded approvingly.

'That girl will produce fifty sons,' Ezra affirmed, 'every one as strong as Samson. A whole flock of children for the lucky father.'

Jesus said he would pray for her. That was when Ezra knew his cause was hopeless. He used that strategem himself.

In spite of appearances, Nazareth was not back to normal and never would be. Too much had happened to it. It had been torn limb from limb.

More stomachs than food. That was the root of their problem. In the final stages of the drought, they had put pinches of food in their mouth when they wanted spadesful.

Fathers and mothers remembered their children with black tongues, hard little heads they couldn't keep still, accusing eyes, bare bones showing all the way up as if they had swallowed a young tree.

Remembered how they had less to eat than once they threw away, how they trained boys and girls to be spies, thieves, scavengers.

Remembered the 'economy of the crumb'. They had

saved every crumb and whatever looked like a crumb.

Remembered how, with the final fear, conventions slipped, masks dropped from their faces which, till then, they never knew they wore.

Remembered – for many still clung to the practice – how they barred their doors and windows at night; remembered the cold faces and the stares.

How could they go on as if these things had never been?

A neighbour once roundly cursed, in some ways is never a neighbour again. No wonder there were now so many eyes that did not like being looked at. Trying to catch eyes in Nazareth was like catching flies. They were off as soon as you got anywhere near them.

For maybe you had accused them in anger of starving your child by hoarding food. You said, 'You are killing my sons and daughters with your greed as surely as if you stuck them with a knife.' True or false, it was of no consequence. They were now your neighbours only in name.

It came to the people of Nazareth that you can rely on others up to a point. Others can rely on you up to a point. But when there is trespass beyond that point by so much as an inch, each man is on his own, as closed up in himself as if his head were under water.

You could not forget his cruel savage eyes glaring at you. Oh yes, his eyes are gentle enough at present. But what about those *other* eyes behind his eyes? You know they are there. You have seen them with your own second set of eyes.

His voice is sweet enough at present. But on other days it shrieked hatred at you and you remember – ah, it pierces you still – how you shrieked back.

And you know and he knows that if it had come to a choice between his children dying and yours, you would have *killed him and his children* so yours could survive.

The villagers had discovered, that is, that there is no difference in brutality between the very rich and the very poor, between those who have everything and those who have nothing.

They would never be 'normal' again because they

remembered all this.

With the rain, conventions were hooked back on, masks were replaced, but no one was fooled. Not any more.

The cruellest shock of all was to discover that their religion was not, had never been sincere. That too was a mask, a convention.

When they prayed after the rains, they *saw through their own prayers.* They had never relied on prayers, only on rain. Their prayers were as empty as bubbles. The only time they had meant a prayer, really meant it with their whole soul, was when they said Amen to Ezra in his blaspheming.

This was why they hated Ezra more than before. He reminded them of when Nazareth had become sin. He reminded them that the locusts had stripped more than fields and trees; they had stripped *them.* For ever afterwards, in spite of the appearance of normality, the men and women of Nazareth were wintry people.

Jesus saw all this and did not despise them for it. He had shared their agony, had become the sin with them. And so he ached for them. He loved and pitied them all the more, felt how much they needed him.

He longed to show them in his own life that God cared for them, show them more than he had so far shown them.

But his Father had given him a work to do. The first stage of that work was perhaps the hardest: waiting.

Chapter 14

As soon as Jedidah was born, Ezra felt sorry for himself. The midwife called him in and he saw this big bundle with a red raw face in his wife's arms.

80

Most babies are ugly but this one, he knew somehow, would never recover.

More than ever convinced of ill-luck's loyalty towards him he announced, 'She is not beautiful.'

Sarah lifted the baby up to his face. 'This is only a mirror, husband. What do you expect? She must have caught something from your side of the family.'

Ezra loved his daughter dearly, but he had long groaned over the problem of marrying her off. All those years, it was like carrying a big bucket of sand around.

For some time, he feared Jedidah was rusting into the place. She was moping, so that, for all his fatherly devotion, he had to admit she was increasingly good fun not to be with.

When Jesus declined his final offer – he would have paid Jesus well, too – Ezra went by night to David the matchmaker, a small man with a mousy beard who sold bad-quality candles for a living.

He told Ezra his fee. Ezra nearly collapsed.

'Rabbi,' David said soothingly, 'Rabbi. After all, to work miracles, *costs*.'

Ezra was a modest man. 'I wouldn't know,' he said.

David persisted, 'You want a miracle on the cheap? What do you take God for, and you a rabbi?'

Ezra agreed the sum. What choice? If he didn't pay up David would spread the word not only that the Rabbi came to him but was too mean to pay the fee.

What Ezra did not know was that only the week before Shaphan the ploughman had been to David, asked a similar miracle. His Nebat had not only killed his wife when he was being born, he had been a burden ever since. The cost of his miracle was even higher than Ezra's.

A week later, after pretending he had not slept in the interval, the matchmaker whispered to Ezra that Nebat was free and his father willing.

Ezra was reluctant to say yes. Like Shaphan.

'What?' Shaphan had shrieked, as though trying to stop a team of oxen out of control. 'I don't mind the girl having a face like my elbow. But the father! A rabbi with no teeth, three fingers missing and only one and a half eyes! A rabbi who can't even pray right! If I couldn't plough straighter than he can pray I'd give up.'

'You refuse, then.'

'No, I accept.'

By that token, Shaphan proved that his main concern was not gaining a daughter-in-law but getting rid of a son.

Now it was Ezra's turn to squirm and wriggle and, in the end, acquiesce.

The matchmaker called a meeting between the fathers. It was less like arranging a wedding than a cease-fire, with one of the parties holding all the weapons. Shaphan demanded and received unconditional surrender.

Ezra had nothing to bargain with. As well argue that a massive debt is a prime asset or try to sell an egg laid last year.

He went home, doleful, to tell his Rib 'the good news'. Sarah showed that she too was capable of the prophetic gesture. She spoke not a word, simply kicked him. As he rubbed his shin, he had to admit justice had been done. If she hadn't done it he would have kicked himself.

'You are getting married, Jedidah, my pet.'

Jedidah was so overcome that for two hours she forgot to ask to whom. When she was told, she broke down and cried.

'My pet,' Ezra pleaded, 'I know Nebat is not first on the list.'

That was true. He wasn't on any list, that was why Jedidah was getting him.

He added, 'But you could do worse,' and was relieved she did not ask him to prove it.

For practically the first time in their married life, Sarah backed him up. 'Of course you could do worse,' she said. 'I did.'

To their surprise, after the early tears, Jedidah seemed reconciled to her fate. To be no longer the oldest virgin at the well was worth any sacrifice, even marriage. Also, she followed her mother in religion. She was not too concerned about resurrection after death, provided her body gave rise to other bodies before death. Wasn't *that*

82

resurrection, she argued, the most important to any woman? If there was another resurrection on top of that, it was a bonus.

That is how Nebat and Jedidah became yoked together. It was settled by two old men, fierce antagonists but partners in despair. They wanted a grandson before their eyes were shut for good; did not want the longest road of all to end in them but to rise on through their children to a thousand generations.

When Jesus heard the news he said he could not have been more pleased. He promised to sing cantor at the wedding.

Ezra bore him no grudges. Jesus was bound to do better for himself. Besides, his daughter was now an old woman of eighteen Passovers.

Months later, on his greatest day, Nebat did not smile. But, to everyone's surprise, neither did he smell. He had been prevailed on to take a bath, the first since he was born. Unless he fell in a river, he would not take another until he died.

At the wedding-feast, the whole of nature seemed to be overturned.

Sarah: a stone crying. Nebat, the groom: a wolf looking sheepish. The bride, Jedidah: a sheep pretending she was a lamb.

There was Shaphan, preening himself, as if he had done the world a favour. There, too, was Ezra, a mild donkey next to a wild bull, his face the face of one trying to look happy while his last tooth is being pulled.

It was no lavish affair. Shaphan contributed nothing to the reception. His attitude suggested he had already given too much away by letting his son go.

Ezra's attitude was the opposite. To provide food and a dowry after pledging his daughter to a ploughman's son was more than any Jew should be asked to bear.

The few guests came, bearing presents and muttering, 'It's only a little something,' and invariably it was. Times had been hard, as everyone knew.

'It's not the gift,' Ezra sighed, 'it's the thought behind it that counts.'

But it didn't count much because there wasn't any.

Achbor, the informer, was too hateful not to be invited. He was certain to spread a bad report of events but it would have been twice as bad if he hadn't been there.

Naturally, the widow Anna was a guest for the entire three days, eating and drinking heartily and reminding everyone of how good her dear man had been to her in the days of his virility.

Mary helped with the catering, smuggling in some of her own food to supplement the little Ezra and Sarah were able to provide.

Jesus sang at the Rabbi's house – 'beautifully', Anna said, nudging Mary. He was relieved that he would be badgered no more into becoming Ezra's son-in-law.

Bride and groom wore crowns of myrtle as the Rabbi wished his daughter fertility and long life. To the groom, he said:

'May your fountain be blessed. May you be happy in the wife of your youth. Let her be to you a lovely hind, a graceful doe. Let her affection always fill you with sharpest delight. And may her tender love infatuate you for ever.'

Jesus said the loudest amen.

Chapter 15

Long after the rains, the tradesmen and farmers who attended the synagogue kept complaining to God and to each other about the hard times and devoutly cursing their debtors. They knew no other way of being happy.

Mary made and sold linen garments to boost the family income. Jesus was never idle, making tools and implements for farmers who put off payment as if they were the only ones in the world who had to eat.

One day news came of a disaster on the Lake of Galilee. A storm, ferocious even for the Lake, had smashed dozens of boats and drowned some of the crews.

They would need carpenters. Jesus decided to try his luck.

This time he was glad to get away. After its sorrows, Nazareth, always conservative, brooded, stuporous, enclosed within itself.

Mary prepared food for his journey and told him to take care. The Lake was a rough place, she had heard. Unspeakable things went on there.

'Keep away from Tiberias,' she warned, 'and don't talk to pagans.'

'As if I would,' he said, in the tone of a man who pretends, for his mother's sake, that he is still a boy.

Suddenly she said, 'What are you doing, going away again?'

'Practising,' he said.

She put three silver denarii in his purse. No question about it, she had saved them for just such a need as this.

'I worked hard for them' – her chin was beginning to wobble – 'so don't give them away all at once.'

She knew this son of hers.

He glanced from her worn fingers to her tired eyes. 'You work too hard.'

It was his constant refrain. If it were possible, he often said, she would wash the early morning sun like a doorstep and dust the moon and stars.

He held her tightly and, after, she fingered his face like a woman who is blind.

'The Lord watch between you and me,' she said, 'when we are absent from each other.'

He brushed her tears aside with the back of his hand. 'For those who love,' he said, 'there is no absence from each other.'

It was true. Separation, she knew, had always brought them closer together, even as Joseph's death had planted him like an ever-spreading oak within her. Hearts shape their own eternity. There is hurt, too, naturally; but somehow the hurt and the love are one.

He left the donkey in case she needed it. He took only food, the basic tools of his trade in a basket swung from his shoulder and a staff.

He waved to his mother but she did not wave back. She had had enough of goodbyes. She kept her hands by her side, pretending.

He set off in high spirits, in the last mists of a spring morning. The mists were clearing with the sunrise just as he reached the top of the rise. It was like being present at the Creation. He cried aloud for sheer joy: *Sing to the Lord a new song; sing to the Lord all the earth.*

Nazareth was circled by tulips, and lamb's wool clouds dotted an immense sky in which, almost lost, was a thin white eyelid of a moon.

He went north on a downward path that brought him into a rich green dewy valley with a stream running through it. Women were singing as they washed clothes. Children were playing outside cottages, their voices and the barking of dogs gently splitting the silence of the morning.

Never had Jesus felt so alive. He was like someone who, having recovered from a long illness, is beginning to remember what it is like to feel well.

In the months of the drought he had been tried to his limits. In his mind was the image of felling a tree. You chip and chip and at first the tree seems impervious to you. Then it sighs a little, and it shudders and it creaks and it groans, it even cracks. But not yet the decisive crack, the fatal crack that tells you it is all over. *That* crack is quite different from any other sound, though it is not necessarily the noisiest. It can be very soft, like a heart breaking. But when you hear it, you know you don't have to touch it any more. It will fall because it has already gone. Its own weight will topple it now ... In all his recent trials he had never reached that point. Not quite. He was chipped at, he sighed, he shuddered, he creaked and groaned a lot, even cracked, but not decisively. He was never *toppled*. His Father, in whom he trusted, had seen to that.

No wonder he felt so vital now. He breathed deeply and moved on. Lambs were gambolling in the fields; the gossamered grasses, feather-tipped or with heads on like corn, were combed by a wind, and all the flowers were out. Crocuses of three colours, the deep blue iris and the royal purple of the grape hyacinth. There were whole stretches of ruby-coloured anemones and cyclamen with their red eyes and marble-coloured leaves and the occasional prickly pear with yellow flowers.

His heart soared in gratitude to God and he felt overwhelmed by his presence. He wanted to hold up every flower and blade of grass and offer it up in thanksgiving to his Father.

In awe of his surroundings, he whispered a psalm.

> *Bless the Lord, my soul, bless the Lord.*
> *Thou art great, very great, O my God.*
> *Thy tunic is majesty and honour,*
> *Thou art wearing a garment of light.*
> *Like a tent thou hast pitched are the heavens,*
> *The walls of thy room rest on seas.*
> *The swift-moving clouds, these thy chariot,*
> *Thou dost ride on the wings of the wind.*
> *Thy voice we can hear when the wind blows,*
> *See thy face in the flame and the fire.*

He soon found himself opposite Sepphoris, the capital of the territory. It was ruled by Herod Antipas, son of the monster, King Herod. Remembering his promise to his mother, he gave Sepphoris no more than a glance.

The countryside became more varied. Bare hills, the haunt of jackals; wheat-fields and a wide green plain with rabbits that scuttled away at the sound of his steps.

From a distant meadow he heard a clear liquid call, 'Whit-we-whit', repeated over and over. Then in low flight, on whirring wings, a plump, sandy-coloured bird with dark stripes took off: a quail.

Farther on, he came across a big poisonous viper in the process of swallowing a full-grown hare. Next to it in the dust was a turtle-dove. A mere scratch on one of its wings, but dead all the same. How sly the snake must be to be able to capture fleet creatures like these. He thought, If only a man combined the shrewdness of a snake and the innocence of a dove.

A couple of hours' steady walking had brought him to a hill at the foot of which was Cana. A mere hamlet set in a thicket of trees: dark oaks, terebinths and carobs. Fruit-trees, too. There were olives, apples, apricots, pome-granates and a solitary almond with pink blossom.

His mother had been born at Cana and her sister, Mary Cleophas, still lived there in a house surrounded by broom bushes, white, yellow and wasp-coloured.

His aunt was delighted to see him. He gave her a present from his mother and in return received the kindest hospitality. They brought out the best wine.

Jesus met again his cousin Ruth, a girl of fourteen who was engaged to be married, and James and Jude, her brothers. Also invited to the meal were friends of theirs, Philip and Nathanael.

They ate under the fig-trees, talking and laughing into the afternoon. It was with difficulty that they allowed Jesus to continue his journey to the Lake.

The path went upward for a while, past a twin-horned mountain. Rock-grey on the heights, it was brown on the lower slopes with a base-fringe bright blue with lupins.

Then all of a sudden, through a gorge, he saw the Lake. The shining waters took his breath away. Of all the things he had seen on this blessed day this was the most stupendous.

Still a thousand feet below him, it was wrapped in a soft, transparent mist. For all that, it was so blue it looked like a part of the sky, with a whiteness in the northern reaches which he realised was a reflection of Mount Hermon.

He wanted to call out to his mother, to Ezra, to anyone, to *everyone*, Come and see.

An elderly man with big tuber-like growths on his face was digging a ditch.

Jesus said, 'How wonderful it is.'

'What?' the man said, leaning on his spade.

'The Lake, it's wonderful.'

'Thanks for telling me, son.'

The man went on working.

'I believe it is,' Jesus said. 'Wonderful.'

'Been there a long time,' the digger said, puffing. He put down his spade again and eyed the stranger. He said, 'A poet or rabbi are you, or you got some other reason for wasting your time?'

Jesus appreciated the twinkle in his eye. He pointed to his bag of tools. 'A carpenter.'

'So you *do* work for your living.'

'When I can.'

'You're in the wrong line of business.' The man was becoming quite talkative. 'Me, now, I dig ditches. Graves, too. Good living in graves and, more to the point, regular.'

'I'm sure.'

'Mind you, it's not so easy dying round here. It takes an effort, but people seem to manage it.'

The man spat on his hands and resumed his digging.

Jesus had to force himself to carry on.

'Goodbye, sir.'

The man paused. 'Eh? Say something?'

'Only goodbye.'

''Bye. Don't forget what I told you. Dig ditches.'

In spite of the load on his back, Jesus walked with a brisk step. God was all around him. Even before he was out of ear-shot of the man he was chanting:

> *Where, Lord, can I go from thy Spirit,*
> *Where flee from thy face?*
> *If I climb up to heaven thou art there*
> *Or in hell make my bed thou art there.*
> *If I ride on the wings of morning*
> *And dwell in the depths of the sea,*
> *Even there thy hand shall hold me,*
> *Thy strong hand hold me fast.*

The digger wiped the sweat off his brow. 'Crazy kid,' he said.

The path went steeply down from this point, past lemon-trees and flowering oleanders. Blue birds, light as bees, settled on blades of grass without bending them. River tortoises peeped out of running streams to peer at him with inquisitive eyes. He saw a crested lark.

The temperature rose sharply with every mile covered, the air became hotter, stickier. For a fleeting moment he missed the breezes of his native village.

He kept to a northerly route, taking care to avoid Tiberias. Herod Antipas passed the summer there, he had been told, in a palace on a hill overlooking the Lake.

Above Tiberias was a Roman road. It ran straight across the broad plain of Genesareth. Fields of mustard, already shoulder high, dazzled the eyes and enchanted the heart with the songs of hidden warblers.

He pressed on, ever northwards along the road skirting the Lake. Looking down, he was impressed by the denseness of the lakeside towns and the number of people moving in and around them.

On the Lake were many boats but the sails were furled, for it was a windless day.

From the heights above Magdala, he had his best view so far of the pear-shaped Lake, seven miles across, and the pinks, browns and mauves of the Gergesene hills beyond. At the foot of those hills were the tiny Greek cities of the Decapolis. On the other side of the hills stretched the desert.

The road finally threaded through a narrow, rocky defile between the plain and the slopes. From there he saw where the Jordan fed the Lake. The water was fast-flowing, milky-green in hue. Cormorants were lunging at fish. Promontories were adorned with rose laurels and thorny caper bushes, and around the entire Lake was a broad band of lilies of the valley, the red anemones.

He had never been in this part of the world before. Yet it was so in tune with his soul it was as if he had lived here in a previous existence. As if he had opened the door of a strange house, only to find that he knew exactly where everything was: table, chairs, beds, lamps, ornaments. He felt less expectation than something close to nostalgia.

One day, he was certain, when his waiting was over, down there by the blue waters of the Lake of Galilee, he would work out his destiny.

Chapter 16

On the last stage of his journey the road was a crowded highway. It was exciting to be in such varied company. There were merchants from Phoenicia, Egypt and Damascus; Jews from places as far away as Antioch and Alexandria, many of whom could not speak and barely understood Aramaic; Roman legionaries. So many people in such strange attire and speaking foreign languages, Greek mostly and Latin.

Though he had spent ten hours on the road he could not afford to waste time. He had to look for a job at once.

From several towns around the Lake he chose Capernaum. He liked the look of the hills above it, shining with lemon and orange groves. In the approaches to it he came across masses of geraniums and hibiscus with multicoloured butterflies fluttering in and out of the enormous flowers.

Capernaum had to be prosperous. The streets were crowded. There was a number of imposing government buildings and, judging from the soldiers on view, a heavily-manned Roman garrison.

He had just whipped past a fish-seller's when the owner threw a bucket of fish-heads, bones and scales into the narrow street. Jesus watched with fascination as the whole putrefying mess began its long winding descent into the Lake where it would doubtless nourish the next generation of fish.

In search of coolness, he walked down to the water's edge. Shrubs were heavy and resonant with bees.

Sparrows in their hundreds were making an incredible din. Pied kingfishers, on branches overhanging the Lake or hovering on invisible wings, were watching intently before they swooped. Sometimes they speared a fish and flew off with it to feed their young in mud banks along the shore. The swifts, too, veered and screamed in their never-ending flight up from the water to the streets of the town and back again.

Jesus walked along the beach in a mist of happiness, crunching underfoot the small white and yellow pebbles. He took in huge draughts of air; it smelled good in spite of the humidity. He looked up and saw fish spread out to dry on the flat roofs of basalt houses. Boys with palm fronds were screeching and flailing away, warding off the birds and the flies.

He jogged himself again. He would not earn his daily bread by idling.

He ventured along a narrow jetty by the sides of which fishermen were repairing their boats. The surface of the jetty was strewn with fish scales as thick as sand and the sour smell of fish nearly made him vomit.

The boats were definitely in bad shape. Hulls, rudders, sails, had received a tremendous battering. Wreckage was everywhere and more was being washed in all the time.

Now for the bit he never liked.

'Pardon me, I wonder if I can be of help.'

He took his bag from his back, showed his tools, spread them out in front of him, muttered something to the effect that he knew about wood and fixing things.

The fishermen with black wind-scoured faces did not bother to reply. Not a turn of a head.

Embarrassed, Jesus gathered up his things, said sorry and withdrew. He prayed for them. They must have troubles he knew nothing of.

This experience was repeated all along the shore. One or two older men told him kindly to come back tomorrow. 'Tomorrow, who knows?'

Jesus knew. It was hopeless. Extensive repairs were under way but there was, if anything, a surplus of workmen.

His hunch had been mistaken, then. He would not be staying by the Lake, after all. As he wiped his brow, he consoled himself with the thought of returning home next day to his village among the hills with its cool breezes and its big sky.

Jesus sat by the shore, ate the remains of his food and washed it down with cool clear water.

A boat was coming in. Two men were at the oars and progress was slow.

As it drew near, he saw the boat was holed near the water-line. After every few strokes, the rowers had to bail out.

The boat landed and out of it leaped a man massive as a rock. A turban on his head, fastened under a jutting chin, fell down on to his broad shoulders. Well over six feet, he was about Jesus's age, maybe a year or two younger. He wore a fisherman's tunic, the sort that can be thrown off quickly in an emergency.

Jesus heard him whisper to his slighter companion, 'Quick, Andrew, hide that barrel, will you?'

Too late. A small, sharp-eyed customs official had materialised out of nowhere.

'Like a blasted kingfisher, he is,' the bigger of the men snapped.

'How many baskets, Simon son of Jonah? The truth this time.'

'Listen, Levi,' Simon said, picking at his curly beard, 'we've had a stinking day, that *is* the truth. Any wind out there and we'd have been done for.'

'How many?' Levi said, as if Simon had not spoken.

'Three.'

Simon's subterfuges were so utterly transparent Jesus had to smile.

Levi was peering over the edge of the boat. 'That's funny,' he said. 'I can see four. Maybe you took one basketful with you, just to confuse me.'

'It's four,' Jesus said.

Simon glared at him but only for a second because Levi had jumped on board the boat for a closer look. There might be a fifth basket hidden somewhere.

In an instant, Simon had leaned over and lifted Levi by the top of his tunic as if he were a babe in arms. Still holding him aloft, he roared, 'Who gave you permission to get in there, eh?'

'I'm sorry,' Levi managed to splutter. 'Really. But –'

'All right, traitor,' Simon said, dropping him on the sands. If I wasn't a Jew I'd break you in half with my bare hands and scatter the sawdust to the winds. It's four. But listen carefully. Never, *never* put your filthy trotters in my boat again.' He rubbed his hands together as if ridding them of clinging dirt. 'Now I'll have to get the Rabbi to pray over it a second time.'

Levi had retreated in the short sharp steps of a frightened chicken. 'Come to the office tomorrow,' he said, from a safe distance, 'and pay your dues.'

'May you have nothing but skinny daughters,' Simon yelled after him, thumbing his big red nose.

He beached his boat securely and brought the baskets ashore. Andrew had disappeared on an errand of his own.

Simon was swearing to himself about the sinful taxes decent people had to pay and customs officials who were worse than pigs.

Catching sight of Jesus sitting there, chewing his last crust, he said harshly, 'Who are you laughing at?'

'I wasn't laughing.'

'Don't contradict me. I said you were. Don't grin at me, I don't like it.'

'I can believe it,' Jesus said, trying to keep a straight face.

It was clear to him that, for all his bluster, this fisherman had a big funny bone. Touch him anywhere and he would laugh. He only hoped he was right!

'What're you doing working with that scum?' Simon said, nodding after Levi. 'You his new assistant or something?'

'I've never seen him before.'

'Never?' That made Simon madder than ever. 'Then why the blazes did you split on us?'

'Because, well, I'd like to be your friend.'

94

'Friend!' Simon spat it out. 'You certainly acted like one.'

'*I* think so,' Jesus said, quietly. 'I knew you didn't mean to lie.'

'They steal from us every day, they grind us in the dust. How can I lie to *them?*'

'Lie to God, I meant.'

With that, Jesus got up to retrieve one of the heavy oars that had slipped from its lock.

Simon reached out and grabbed the other end. 'Will you *leave* it, you hear me, *stranger.*'

His emphasis made it plain he wanted no meddling of any sort.

To vent his frustration, Simon gave a big tug on the oar. To his amazement, the man did not let go, didn't even budge. For someone so slender, he was tough all right.

They stood there, each gripping his end of the oar, looking one another over, feeling each other's body – bone and muscle, spirit, too – through the wood. For a moment they seemed to be part of a single living organism.

Simon wondered if it was the hunger, but he felt stronger and not diminished by this contact. The man had fine olive skin, now he came to look at him, and eyes made for distant horizons and beyond.

He sensed it was wiser to let this man give back the oar rather than try to snatch it from him.

When he was ready and not before, Jesus took his hands away.

'That's more like it,' Simon said in a grumbly voice.

He took no more notice of Jesus. He stored the oar away and picked up two big baskets of fish, one in each arm, as if they were a couple of water-melons, and strode off in the direction of the main street.

Jesus picked up the other two baskets and shadowed him.

Simon had pushed some way into the evening crowd before he realised he was being followed. He turned round sharply.

95

'What the blazes do you think you're doing?'

'Lending a hand.'

'I've got nothing for you,' Simon said, curtly.

'Not even a kind word.'

'Yes,' Simon said, 'they're free. How many do you want?'

Jesus shrugged. 'One will do, if you can spare it.'

'Thanks,' Simon said, through clenched teeth. 'Now put 'em down, blast you, and leave me be.'

Jesus put the baskets down, smiled in a friendly way and headed back towards the Lake.

Simon stooped to pick up the other two baskets and found he couldn't manage them.

'Hey, *you*,' he roared.

Jesus was expecting it. He turned back and stabbed himself with his finger. 'Me?'

'You can't leave my fish here,' Simon called out over the heads of passers-by. 'Someone'll pinch them.'

Jesus walked back, slowly. 'Sorry. I thought you told me to put them down.'

'Pick 'em up.' He was used to being obeyed.

Jesus did so.

'Now,' Simon said, 'follow me.'

He marched off but there were no footsteps behind him. When he turned about, Jesus was in the same spot.

'What's the matter now?'

Jesus said, 'How can I follow you? I don't know your name.' To smooth the way, he said, 'I'm Jesus.'

'And I'm Simon,' came the reluctant reply. 'Now, for heaven's sake, follow.'

'Willingly,' Jesus said, and followed him.

At the fish merchant's, Simon grabbed a big fish and tried to thrust it on Jesus.

'Better a fish today,' he said, 'than a promise of a flock of sheep tomorrow.'

'That's not necessary,' Jesus said, refusing it.

'Not enough, you mean,' Simon said gruffly, annoyed that he couldn't figure the man at all.

'Too much. I don't want anything.'

'Don't you ever do as you're told,' Simon said. He tried again. 'For you.'

'I'm satisfied with a thank-you.'

Simon waited, his hands twitching. Eventually, 'Thanks.'

When he offered it this time, Jesus took it.

'Cook it for your supper,' Simon said. 'Now, good*bye*.'

An hour later, when Simon returned to check the damage to his boat, the man was still there. Simon was belching prodigiously and muttering something about his wife's cooking. Still, the meal had done something for him.

'Enjoy your fish, Jesus?' he said, cheerfully.

'I wasn't hungry. I gave it away.'

'You got a good price for it, I hope,' Simon said, chuckling into his beard.

'Yes. A very nice thank-you.'

Simon went right up to Jesus's face. 'People don't just *give* fish away,' he shouted.

'*You* did.' Jesus did not raise his voice.

Simon chuckled again, less genuinely this time. 'You must be well off is all I can say.'

He was fingering the jagged hole in the side of the boat, probing to find the extent of the damage. He said, offhandedly, 'If your belly's full now it won't be come tomorrow.'

Jesus smiled. 'God gave me a fish today, will he not give me another tomorrow?'

Simon momentarily lifted his head to see if Jesus was mocking him again. 'Take it from me,' he said, 'some days God gives fish, some days he doesn't.'

Simon had really mixed feelings about this stranger. He liked him and he didn't like him. In any case, he wasn't prepared to argue with him. He had too much on.

He had brought wood with him, a hammer and nails. He set to, trying to patch up the boat.

Jesus watched for a few minutes before saying, 'That won't last, you know.'

Simon didn't look up. 'A sailor, are you?'

'A carpenter.'

Simon missed a nail and hit the boat instead, causing more splintering of wood.

'Any good?' Even as he said it he cursed himself. He, the fish, was swimming into the net.

'People say so.'

Simon appreciated that. He himself wasn't capable of understatement. The man did not boast, maybe he didn't need to. He was good enough for humility to come easy.

'What do *you* say, Jesus?'

'Nothing. My work speaks for me.'

Simon stood up and straightened his back. 'How long' – he belched again – 'would you take to fix this?'

Jesus eyed it expertly. 'I could patch it up in a day or so. To do a proper job on it, four days, maybe five.'

Simon had had his bellyful of narrow escapes in a leaky boat. 'What'll you charge?'

'Whatever is fair.'

Simon raised his head and let out a roaring torrent of a laugh. 'That's good, that is. Fair is whatever you can get.'

'No,' Jesus said. 'If my work is no good I wouldn't want a good wage.'

'Then you must be the only carpenter in Galilee who thinks so.'

Jesus shrugged. 'If so, so be it. But I can't believe that.'

'Look,' Simon said, rawly, 'if I said to the merchant who buys my fish, "I leave it to you, kind sir. Pay me whatever's fair," he'd give me nothing. He swindles me enough as it is.'

'Maybe,' Jesus put it to him, 'that's because he thinks you are trying to swindle him.'

'Which,' Simon said, with another ear-shattering roar, 'I would never do.'

'Of course not,' Jesus said, embarrassed.

Without warning, Simon grabbed Jesus by the shoulder. 'All right, Carpenter,' he said, 'you're hired. I'll pay you *whatever is fair*.'

Jesus, wincing a little, said, 'I know. Why do you think I asked to work for you?'

Chapter 17

Simon offered him hospitality for the night until he was settled in, but Jesus did not want to put him out. Instead, after watching the last purple weal in the west turn black, he wandered around town.

He liked the place, savoured the sights, smells and sounds of it. What he admired most was the water. It spread through aqueducts to every part of town. It was comforting to know you had water without having to travel to the well for every drop.

He tried the local hostelry. It was crammed and noisy. When he opened the door he had to step aside as a yellow sulphurous cloud floated past his head. The smell was overpowering, as if all the inmates had been dead for a week. Why pay to suffocate? He would make do out of doors. It was warm enough.

He returned to the water's edge, next to Simon's boat. The sky was a big bucketful of stars and a full moon was silvering the water. Some fishermen were taking out their boats. Maybe they thought fish, like men, are more foolish at night, or they hoped to avoid being seen by Levi, or simply because they were so poor they had to.

Fires had been lit along the shore where the men who had finished for the day were cooking fish on wooden spits.

Still no wind, and the smell of food hovered in the air. The sparrows had stopped their chattering. The water slapped the sands, making itself heard for the first time that day.

He had hoped it would be cooler by now, but great blobs of perspiration formed all over him and poured down his body.

As always on his first night away from home, sleep came grudgingly. He sat up, gazing at the stars and their reflections, like fireflies, on the sea. The moon was a precious pearl in the oyster of night that any merchant would give his all for.

He was relaxed. It was marvellous having a job, something to do. When they said, 'Nothing doing,' it was like being told there was to be no tomorrow. It gave you a *bad feeling*, as though you were an apple sliced across the middle. That was it. Like the bottom half of your body coming clean away from the top half and going its own way.

That was how he felt when he walked along the shore earlier, when he put down his tools and had to pick them up again in silence.

Then Simon said, 'You're hired,' and he knew tomorrow was going to come for him. That is what those words do to you. You know tomorrow is coming and you are going to eat your way right into it. And when it comes it won't hurt too much because you are protected: you worked today, your belly has something in it, you are a human being. You have a future. For one more day, at least. God willing...

It occurred to him that for too long he had been coddled. It had been an easy life until the locusts came and stripped the village. From then on, it was 'No work'. Two small words that taught him more than Rabbi Ezra had taught him over many years. 'No work' was a Bible in itself. It gave you thorough instruction in yourself, in humiliation, fear, dread, trust, despair, love and hate.

'No work' had also given him new ties. He was now kin to those in want. He belonged to the brotherhood of want. He, Jesus of Nazareth, was one of the have-nots, the dispossessed. That was why he *knew*.

He knew what happens to you when you hear 'No work'. You grit your teeth so tight you're afraid you won't get them open again. Words you want to say drop backwards down your throat like a pebble down a bottomless well; words that won't come up again, ever. You give a little, hollow laugh, the best – the only – substitute for tears.

He wanted to address himself to these, his people, his brothers and sisters. They knew what it was to be hollowed out; they had experienced this massive emptiness. They, like he, would at any rate be prepared to be beggars before God.

He was kin to these fishermen, too, pushing out their creaky boats, cooking and singing by firelight. What was it Simon said? 'Some days fish, sometimes none.' These fishermen knew what it was like to labour day and night – for nothing. They had had their livelihood snatched from them by a storm as capricious as locusts and drought. They also were ready for God.

In his mind, he could see Simon. He spoke to you right between the eyes but he was gentle, really. Like many big and powerful men, he was extra careful not to hurt anyone. Even when he had lifted Levi above his head, Jesus never feared he would harm him. He pounced on you like a lion, only to lick you like a kitten.

Simon had the innocence of a child. He reminded Jesus of little Shimon, the most mischievous child in Nazareth. He even schemed and lied like Shimon, made faces and defiant, mocking gestures like Shimon – and he, like Shimon, only succeeded in making you laugh.

In his imagination, Simon was reduced to Shimon's size, though he was permitted to keep his bushy black beard.

'Did you steal two peaches, Simon?'

'Oh no, sir,' Simon said, offended. While all the time the fuzz and flesh of peaches is spattered all over his lips and beard, and two peach-stones lie on the flats of his open hands.

Simon had lied to Levi because he felt it was his duty. It was a matter of principle and patriotism, of devotion even. Levi represented the foreigners who taxed and bled Simon's people. But he never expected his lies to be believed. He would have been upset if Levi had been taken in. It would have meant Levi had missed the insult.

There was something immensely lovable, touching, about the big fisherman. What if Simon, like the Lake itself, was to have a part in Jesus's destiny?

101

Someone was trying to attract his attention. He was startled. Why should anyone be calling him?

He made out the figure of a woman. She was dressed in a long robe and hooded.

'I'm sorry,' he said, politely, not sure of what she wanted. 'Did you mistake me for someone else?'

'No, you, dearie,' the woman said softly. 'Would you like to have a nice time?'

He was about to tell her he was enjoying himself already when he realised what was happening. So this was how such women operated. It was quite different from what Rabbi Ezra, in his preaching, had given him to expect. Ezra spoke lyrically about the honeyed tones of enticement, the harlot's soft bed, perfumed with aloes, cinnamon and myrrh and draped with the finest linen of Egypt.

What Jesus saw in the moonlight was a poor, bony, scarcely articulate young woman in a ragged robe.

Ezra had got his knowledge from a book, and was out of his depth.

For all that, Jesus found the situation interesting. He had never before spoken to a strange woman alone.

As she lifted the hem of her skirt, he reached up and touched her arm gently, to tell her she should cease.

'Thank you,' he said, 'but no.'

She laughed a hollow laugh and moved away, disappointed. It was exactly the gesture he himself instinctively made when he heard the words 'No work'. Before the drought he would have missed it. But now he recognised this woman was his kin. She too had been emptied out.

He called after her, 'Please, can I help you in any way?'

It was the 'please' that made her halt in her tracks.

As she turned towards him, the hood fell from her face. She was only a girl, about the same age as his cousin Ruth. She was very dark-skinned, long-haired, pretty, as far as he could judge in moonlight, with a mature woman's shape. She looked thin-lipped, though, and bitter.

'No one can help *me*.' The words had come up, just,

102

from the bottom of the well and squeezed through her gritted teeth.

'Sit down beside me, anyway.' He smoothed a spot for her beside him.

She lowered herself with a sigh. She was fatigued.

He got rid of the tension by saying, 'It's very warm tonight.'

'The usual.'

'You live here?' he said.

'Along the coast.'

'Bethsaida?'

'Magdala.'

'I've heard of it.'

'Probably smelled it, too.' Her voice had an acid quality, unattractive in one so young.

Magdala was well known as a place where dyes were made. A pall of evil-smelling smoke hung permanently over the place, and when the wind blew from the south-west it polluted the northern reaches of the Lake.

The girl herself smelled of cheap perfume, as much a tool of her trade as wood was of his.

'Mind you,' she said, her voice softening for one moment, 'lots of hollyhocks grow there. I love...'

She could not finish.

He jumped in with, 'I'm from Nazareth.'

'I think I've heard of that,' she said. There was a pause and she said, 'Where is it?'

'A day's march west of here. We're not famed for anything.'

She was relaxed, almost dropping off to sleep. He said, 'Have you left home?'

'Yes.'

He did not probe, simply sat watching the stars. When he looked at her again her nostrils were twitching at the smell of cooking.

'Please,' he said, 'have you eaten?'

'Not today.' The query touched something off in her, reminded her she had a living to make. She stood up. 'I'd better go look for some food.'

He hesitated before asking, 'Do you have any money?'

103

She too hesitated, hiding her eyes. 'Not yet,' she said. Reverently taking her hand, he sat her down again.

'Wait here, please. I will get you something to eat.'

She wished he wouldn't keep saying 'please'. Insults she could bear.

He went up the hill and, in a few minutes, returned with bread, olives, grilled fish wrapped in a palm-leaf and a flask of wine.

The girl was resisting the advances of a burly young man. He was taunting her.

'What's come over you, Mary? Don't you love me tonight?'

Jesus was shocked to discover the girl had the same name as his mother, shocked into an even deeper compassion.

Seeing Jesus hovering nearby, the man muttered an oath and went away. He must have thought he had arrived late on the scene. Mary of Magdala wasn't worth scrapping over. Besides, his turn would come.

The girl made no reference to what had happened. This, like the humid weather, was normal.

She ate ravenously and washed it down with sweet wine.

Afterwards, she talked. Not much. It was no great story.

Her mother, whom she adored, had died. She was the last child at home. Her father was crazy, always had been. Drink and religion did it. His drink brought the religion on. He beat her every night until she could take no more, couldn't see why she should. She was fending for herself, how needed no further comment.

'I'm sorry.'

She scrutinised him but there was no condescension in him.

'It's horrible,' she said, spitefully. 'Dangerous beasts, men are.' She turned her head aside. 'Most men are.'

A long silence followed.

She was not embarrassed by it. Usually, she had to keep up endless small-talk with the men she dealt with. Words hid the nothingness between herself and them. Here, silence was a bond, a way of listening, of sharing something important without words.

Jesus was relishing the silence too. He was thinking that this girl had nothing. Only the small capital of her youth and beauty. When that was gone, and it would go fast, so fast, she would have nothing. Nothing even to sin with. And he was thinking, She, too, is my kin.

In his spirit, God was luminous. God's Spirit shone in the eternity of his spirit. Undeniable, too, was the impulse towards his destiny. But the shape his destiny would take was still shrouded in darkness. When it did shape up, as he felt it was now beginning to, those hollowed-out people like Mary of Magdala would have a share in it. So, too, would Simon and other fishermen around the Lake.

At length, more confident by reason of shared silence, she said, 'You are different.'

He looked at her as if to say, I am?

She nodded. 'You don't want me or judge me. Most men do one or the other. Some do both.' Her head dropped on her breast. 'That's not fair, is it?'

He lifted her head with his hand.

'Mary,' he said softly.

It was the first time he had called her by her name. To this girl who despised herself it was like a bath or a benediction.

'I do not judge you because there is no need. You judge yourself.'

As if to confirm it, she said, in a grating voice, 'I am full of demons.'

He was not shocked. On the contrary, he smiled broadly. 'No, demons are not so fortunate.'

She could not fathom that. 'Why?'

'Because they would also be full of you.'

She jumped to her feet. 'I must let you sleep. I have work to do.'

Before he could stop her, she had slipped away into the night.

Chapter 18

He was woken by a cock crowing. It was unlike any he had ever heard.

He opened his eyes. Simon the fisherman was towering over him, his mouth agape, making this ridiculous noise.

'Wake up, Carpenter,' he bellowed. 'Time you started work if I'm to get value for money.'

He had brought materials: timber, nails, pitch, a small brazier.

He pointed. 'Food for you in the basket. Help yourself. I've got plenty to do somewhere else.'

Seeing Jesus still hadn't stirred, 'Get to it, man, you hear?'

He gave Jesus a final friendly dig with his toe before leaving.

Jesus stretched himself and saw the eyelids of the morning opening. The sun was not yet up, but already there was a broad, delicate orange glow over the trans-Jordanian mountains. A mist was breasting the Lake and he glimpsed a flock of roseate pelicans, a few herons and any number of white-headed ducks diving for food.

The water rustled silkily at his feet. When he looked to the rocks on the shoreline he made out delicate stock flowers with pink stars, while higher still he saw the colourful plain of Ghôr with mist lifting from it like the steam off a big pudding.

He worked hard under a broiling sun, would have enjoyed himself but for the mosquitoes. As soon as he began to sweat they came at him, big, fat and hungry, pitiless as frisky camels. Zoom, zoom, zoom. If this is spring, he wondered, as he squashed one on his forehead, what must summer be like?

He took a break at midday. He sat in the only few inches of shade. To his right, down the west coast, past the prosperous towns and hamlets, Tiberias rose from the lakeside to the hills above.

Its marble palace in a grove of eucalyptus-trees was an affront. Antipas hosted riotous parties there. There were rumours of sacrilege and debauchery.

The town itself was built over a cemetery. Practising Jews never put foot in it; those who did were reckoned defiled.

Jesus, like every young Jew, had been brought up on stories of the Herods. Antipas's father, Herod the Great, an Idumean, had received from Rome the title 'King of the Jews'. Another reason for Jews to hate Romans. Herod thought nothing of slaughtering his wife, his sons, his rivals, even babies of peasants if he considered his throne was threatened.

Jesus felt quite put off his dinner.

After a brief nap, he worked through the afternoon. Salt diluted in water and spread over his hands and face helped keep the mosquitoes at bay.

Towards evening, he went to the hamper again when two youngsters surprised him. They grabbed a hand-net and threw it over him. He was afraid to struggle in case he tore it.

The lads, both with short hair, were laughing and jumping around him. One said, 'Caught you.'

'What have I done?' Jesus asked.

'You were pinching our friend's food,' the younger, aged about fifteen, replied. 'Isn't that right, James?'

'Right, John,' confirmed the other, his senior by a couple of years. 'A big fish, eh?'

Jesus stood still, enjoying the joke. Through the net he caught John's eye.

The boy returned the glance and froze. He did not know who was the catcher, who the caught. He felt *outnumbered*.

In a kind of hoarse whisper, John demanded, 'Do I know you?'

'You've always known me.'

John was gripped by the mysteriousness of this reply. Felt it was true but did not see how it could be.

Jesus sat down, causing James to say, 'He's only a tiddler, after all. What do you say we throw him back into the sea?'

John did not answer.

Simon appeared at that moment with Andrew.

'He's no thief, you rascals,' Simon thundered. 'He works for me. Let him get on with it.'

To James, he said softly, 'You've caught a real man, let me tell you.' Louder, for all, 'Next time you lads want to play tricks, use your own nets. *And*,' he growled, 'let your hair grow.'

James only laughed. 'Is this the thanks we get for asking our father to lend you a boat?'

Simon was still muttering oaths as he started to extricate Jesus. John was assisting him.

'I bet you fooled that tax-collector today, Simon,' James was saying. 'He wasn't there when you landed on our jetty, was he?'

'We told him,' Andrew volunteered, 'we caught four baskets.'

'How many *was* it?' James asked.

With a glance in Jesus's direction, Simon said in a gruff voice, as if he had been caught out in a sin, 'You heard. It was four.'

The sun was down, Jesus had finished work for the day, when Mary of Magdala called his name. She had brought him a meal of bread, nuts, dates and wine.

'I cleaned fish all day to buy this,' she said in explanation.

He didn't question it. The smell of fish drowned even the smell of her perfume.

He thanked her from his heart.

It was not dark yet, a few people were whispering as

they passed. Mary said, 'I'm sorry. I'll leave you.'

'But you have only just come.'

She said, humbly, 'I'm not doing your reputation any good.'

'Reputation?' He took her hand and urged her to sit beside him. 'Am I a person of such distinction?' he asked, laughing.

He made her share the food she had brought. They ate, saying very little.

She appreciated his quiet generosity. Most of the men she knew had hearts as big as a noonday shadow.

Once again, the girl had this experience of not needing words. They were friends; there were no awkward gaps to fill. Silence was refreshment. Like sitting beside running water.

From time to time she glanced at him and he smiled. She had the feeling that he was *ready*, always *there* for her. If you wanted to talk, he didn't keep you waiting; he didn't have to wrench himself away from himself and his preoccupations. His availability was immediate and total. She found an image in her mind, ready formed: she was standing at a door, a very important door, and, afraid, was about to knock when from within he opened the door to her.

It was no fault of his that she could not yet trust him completely.

'I'll leave you in peace,' she said, rising abruptly.

Tonight he was ready for her. He was on his feet in an instant, taking her hand.

'Stay, *please* stay.'

'I can't,' she said, resisting. She was ashamed and, for the first time since she had left home, she felt it was *wrong* to be ashamed. In his presence, shame was out of place. With him, she was not a street-walker but herself, Mary of Magdala, her mother's child, a child of God.

'I will pay you.'

For an instant, horror showed in her eyes. 'Pay me? What for?'

His tone was apologetic. 'Not to work tonight. Here,'

he took a coin out of his purse, 'a denarius.'

She tried to hide her shame, the deepest she had ever felt. She had doubted him.

'A denarius?' she said, close to tears. 'For nothing?'

'I am sorry,' Jesus said. 'I am so clumsy. I mean well. If you could help me...'

'Of course.'

'I thought if you just went to sleep here'–he pointed to the sand in the shadow of the boat – 'I could watch. No one will disturb you, I promise.'

Mary took a few moments to work it through before lying down at his feet. She could not explain this great thing even to herself, but she felt peace inside her, the peace she had not known since her mother died.

Almost as soon as her head touched the ground she was asleep. The hard set of her mouth relaxed. She lost for a time her animal shrewdness and distrust of the world. She was a child again.

She awoke of herself in the morning to find herself refreshed, purified, after a night without dreams or bitter memories.

He was sitting exactly where he was the night before. Nothing had changed, except he was holding a bunch of hollyhocks.

He smiled a greeting at her and she smiled back. Without a word, she took the flowers from him and pressed them to her.

He offered her the remains of the previous night's food and she accepted gratefully.

'Tonight,' he said, 'will you come back tonight?'

She shook her head. 'No. Not again.'

It sounded final.

'You don't like me, Mary?' He said it half in sorrow, half in jest.

'Like you?' Instinctively, her hand reached out but was withdrawn before touching his. 'Oh, yes.'

'Then you don't trust me.'

'I *do*,' she said. 'So much it frightens me.'

He smiled. 'That is a strange thing to say.'

110

'It is strange what I feel.'

A sound sleep, conversation with someone she trusted, a meal, had put colour into her pinched cheeks.

She stood up.

'You said, Jesus, that your village was not famed for anything.'

He shrugged. 'It is a pity.'

'As far as I'm concerned, I will always cherish it. Because of you.'

She wanted to leave on those words, had planned it so. But he managed to slip in, 'And I will remember my first trip to the Lake because of you, Mary of Magdala.'

Her back straightened but she did not swing round in case he saw her tears. She saw Simon coming and hurried away, clutching her precious bunch of flowers.

'Who was that?' Simon asked, though he knew.

'A friend.'

'She spent the night here?'

'Yes. I was looking after her.'

Simon put down the hamper with the food. 'A man is judged by his friends.'

'Thank you, friend,' Jesus said, putting an end to that topic with a laugh.

It impressed him that Simon, for all his gruffness, was not scandalised. He was simply concerned lest Jesus compromise himself without knowing it.

Jesus said, 'I expected you earlier.'

'What's the hurry?'

'Aren't you going fishing?'

Simon snorted irritably. 'Not today.'

To Jesus's unprofessional eye, it was a good day for fishing. A clear sky, a gentle swell, a moderate breeze.

Simon pointed in the direction of the palace at Tiberias. A banner was flying from the battlement.

'Antipas?' Jesus said. 'Is he in residence?'

'The heathen's been there for a week. His Lordship has decided to take to the water.'

'So?'

'The rest of us poor blighters have to keep off it, don't we? So we don't "get in the way" of his precious guests.'

Jesus was dumbfounded.

111

Simon said, unnecessarily he knew, 'Hurry up with those repairs.'

Turning on his heels, he stomped off home.

Chapter 19

Sullen groups of fishermen had gathered along the strand, Simon and Andrew, James and John among them. Jesus heard plenty of unspiritual comment, especially in the late morning when the barge was floated. Antipas himself was on board and several doubtless distinguished guests.

Eight massive men with gleaming ebony bodies, clad in white loin-cloths, rowed the boat from shore. In deep water, at the first breeze, the sails were set.

Jesus stood for a few minutes, appalled by the fishermen's stolid indifference. When he could take no more he thrust himself into the middle of the group he knew.

'Why do you put up with this?' he demanded.

Simon brushed the question aside. 'Do you have a better idea?'

'But fishing is your livelihood.'

Andrew, a quiet genial soul who reminded Jesus of his own father, said, 'Better to lose a day's work than our lives, that's what we reckon.'

Only Simon noticed that Jesus was trembling, fighting to control his rage, as he watched the barge drift farther out to sea. The Carpenter reminded him of the Lake itself: for the most part completely tranquil; then, in an instant, without the least warning, a storm blows over him and he begins to boil.

What happened next was uncanny. Even as Simon was thinking this and Jesus was staring seawards, a

112

transformation came over the Lake.

First, a breeze scuffed the surface, then with a howl the wind came at gale force out of the north, driving through the gap from the mountains of Lebanon. In seconds, the waves which were previously a few inches high reared up like wild horses, ten to twelve feet tall.

The barge was immediately in difficulty. The mast snapped, the main sail was torn to shreds and the rigging dropped like a dead bird.

Swollen black clouds scudded low across the sky, bringing great sheets of rain that flapped around the watchers' heads, hissing on the water, the sands, the rocks, blinding them.

When the rain abated, they saw that the rowers had taken to the oars, but the boat was shipping water fast and still they were a long way from land.

On every rock and promontory, all along the northern and western fringes of the shore, men were on their feet, dancing and cheering, their robes and beards raked by the wind and flecked with foam.

In a demonic frenzy they were urging the storm to blow harder yet. They revelled in its ferocity, laughing and slapping each other on the back as if this was the most entertaining thing they had ever seen.

Jesus did not know what to do, what to make of it. Out at sea, people were dying.

James and John were shouting out scripture to each other.

> *Make them like whirling dust, O Lord.*
> *Like chaff before the wind.*
> *Pursue them with thy tempest.*
> *And terrify them with thy hurricane.*

Could they not see people were dying?

Simon, who prided himself on being a man of the world and not easily surprised, was staggered by what happened next. Jesus turned on the little group of rejoicing fishermen and redirected his wrath at them.

John, sensitive to this change, shouted to Jesus, 'Why aren't *you* enjoying yourself?'

'Never wish for someone else,' Jesus managed to convey, 'what you do not wish for yourself.'

James shouted back, 'Ridiculous. These are our enemies,' and another fisherman supported him. 'They're worse than Samaritans.'

Jesus shouted back but all John could make out was, 'God's children.' The wind stole the rest.

John could see tears of compassion in Jesus's eyes. He wanted to comfort him, took his arm.

Jesus shrugged him off, crying, 'What sort of God do you serve?'

John, angry at being rebuked, returned, 'The God of Israel.'

Jesus cupped John's ear. 'The God of Israel,' he cried, 'does not only love Israel. Or else he is not worthy of Israel's love.'

John only got the drift of the words. 'What?'

'We were only chosen to witness to a God who loves all men.'

His words were in tatters, broken into pieces by the wind, but Simon grasped well enough what he was saying. And hearing it, he was struck by an awesome, terrifying fact: Jesus's God was different from his. His mind began racing.

If you're right, Carpenter, the rest of us are wrong. The whole of Israel is wrong. You are wanting us to love our enemies, is that it? Impossible. We can hope and pray that one day our enemies will convert and be our friends. But to pray for our enemies and love them while they're still our enemies... Common sense is against it, the Bible is against it. Who ARE you?

The wind and waves were rising higher, making all communication impossible. But the fishermen still managed to show their jubilation. They clenched their fists and raised them to heaven, thankfully.

If you're right, Carpenter, and we're wrong, everything but everything has to change. Do you realise that? We would have to love and pray for the heathen who are in peril out at sea. Even Antipas? That's a big idea, Carpenter. Too big for any mind. The mind can't stretch enough to take it in. What right have you, Carpenter, to throw out such a big idea? Keep quiet or else you'll end up going crazy. Stick

114

to wood and fixing things, stop busting my head with a big idea.

'Look at that... The back's broken, surely... They're going down... Reckon they're sinking... Come on, wind. Blow, blow...'

The world is simple, Carpenter, don't mess it up. Friends and enemies. You love friends, you hate enemies. It's as sharp and lovely as the distinction between land and sea, fertile places and deserts. Once you start shifting boundaries, dissolving them, we get confused, see? All mixed up inside ourselves. We need boundaries, fences, so we can think straight, make plans, know who we are. Right at this moment, we're a family. All the bonds between us are established, they're plain, unquestionable. What if everyone else starts wanting to move into our place, into our house and clan, claiming they belong to our family? What then? Before we know where we are, we won't be a family any more. Just a rabble. Enlarge the family, get rid of its boundaries, and there is no family, you've destroyed it. We can't risk that.

'Come on, wind, blow, blow harder.'

You can love your family. Your enemies you HAVE to hate. If you don't hate, you go crazy as surely as if you don't love. It's natural. The mind would collapse. The walls of allegiance wouldn't be there to stop it collapsing. Enemies and hate are needed to keep alive the very idea of love and the family.

'Blow, blow, blow.'

I'm only a fisherman, a practical fellow, no education to speak of. So answer me this: If I'm to love my enemies, does that include the man who rapes my wife and kills my children? Answer. To me – and I'm just a plain, blunt man – to me, hating such people is not self-indulgence. My responsibility, my God-given duty is to destroy such people if I can. Otherwise, I'm not even a man. What sort of big idea is it that stops you being a man? Loving those who hate you does no good. It will make them despise you more and embitter you. Only a holy hatred can purify. Doesn't the Bible say that?

'They're shipping more water... It won't be long now and, glug-glug, exit Antipas.'

And, by the way, Carpenter, since I can't help relying on common sense, what about pigs like Antipas? What about the Romans who have raped our land and murdered our children? Are you asking us to stop hating THEM? If we do, we won't be Jews any more but Romans, part of their Empire. Think. Is that what you really want?

115

Do you want to put an end to Israel? Can't you see it's hatred not love of the Romans that enables us, obliges us, to keep our covenant with God?

Jesus cut across Simon's thought by moving directly in front of him and, with blazing eyes, addressing the group. 'Peace. Peace.' They could not hear him but they read his lips.

John stopped cheering and waving and tugged on James's arm so he stopped, too. The whole group stopped. Then, one by one, beginning with the nearest, soon all along the shoreline the men ceased chanting and leaping and dancing. Like Jesus, they gazed out to sea, subdued and silent.

Simon saw that Jesus was in pain.

I do believe, Carpenter, you suffer when anyone is suffering. You would prefer to suffer yourself rather than see someone else suffer, wouldn't you?

Jesus's whole body was rigid with the agony he was going through. He was praying and willing that boat back to shore.

It was only three hundred yards from safety but it took half an hour to reach it. Half an hour in which the men stood motionless on the strand, thinking their own thoughts.

The wind dropped, the storm ceased as suddenly as it had begun.

'That was no lark,' James conceded. 'It might have been us.'

John said, 'A few days ago, it *was* us.'

As the barge made it to land, Jesus sank to his knees, exhausted.

The fishermen, muttering to each other, 'A close thing... By God, it was,' drifted away.

Soon, only Jesus and Simon were left on the shore. Simon helped him up and said, 'You're a strange fellow, you know that, Carpenter? First, you get livid with those people for depriving us of our livelihood. Next, you are wanting them to be saved.'

'Is it so strange,' Jesus said, beginning to recover, 'to hate evil and to be concerned for the evil-doer?'

'Some would say so.'

116

But Simon was saying to himself:

Damn it. I had it all worked out, Carpenter. Now you have sown another doubt, thrown out another big idea. You are saying, love and hatred do remain, they are both necessary. Only, we have to love ALL men and hate ALL wrongdoing. So there are still boundaries, allegiances remain crystal-clear. But they are not allegiances to race or family or clan. They are to right and wrong, regardless of which race or family or clan do one or the other. Is this enough, Carpenter? Can there be a family, a kingdom of nothing but right and goodness? Blood is still the ultimate allegiance, surely. We Jews are a family in blood. Isn't that what the Bible tells us? Or is the Bible pointing us in the direction you are wanting us to go...?

Jesus said, 'Simon, what do *you* think?'

Simon whispered, 'I'm still thinking.' Then he came to with a roar. 'What the blazes! Jump to it, man, and fix that boat.'

Chapter 20

On the Sabbath, Jesus attended the synagogue. It was constructed not of black basalt like the houses but of gleaming limestone.

For a provincial like himself, it was an experience. After ascending the imposing stone steps, he found himself inside a vast, Greek-style building with decorated columns – carvings of grapes, dates, a pot of manna.

The basin of purification was a work of art. The seats were of marble. The Ark containing the scrolls of the Law had on it exquisite mosaics: stars, vines, grapes, eggs, a soldier's arrow. There was a Roman double-eagle on one of the paving-stones and on others the shields of David and Solomon, the one a star with six points, the other with five.

He contrasted the opulence of the place with the

synagogue at Nazareth, so poky and dirty, with its few battered wooden benches and its mud floor.

He had arrived early and took his seat. How many officials there were in their splendid Sabbath attire, and what a lot they had to do!

The *hassan*, the general factotum, was greeting well-dressed visitors, fussing over the President of the synagogue, an elderly, benign man with the face and manners of a scholar.

James and John came in and sat opposite Jesus. John was signalling him and he returned the greeting. Why was John continuing to shake his head and wave his arms?

Jesus soon knew.

The sacristan approached him, coughed and whispered in his ear.

Jesus could not make out what the man was saying. The *shammash* was good enough to repeat it, louder: 'You are in the wrong seat, young man.'

Jesus stood up as if he had been stung. 'Sorry.'

'This place,' the *shammash* said, 'is for'—another cough—'someone important, you understand.'

Embarrassed, Jesus crossed to where his fishermen friends were seated. In Ezra's synagogue, everyone was equally important – except for Ezra who considered himself less so. The poor, Jesus concluded, would inherit the earth, but they would have to keep out of certain seats.

The assembly was more subdued than at home. Not as much coughing, talking, foot-stamping. No business deals or rumour-mongering. It was very suspicious.

After the readings and Benedictions, the President called on whom he wished to read and expound the text from Leviticus. The lucky person stood on a stone dais to speak. Then another and another.

Jesus offered to contribute, as was his right, but the President studiously ignored his hand in favour of more distinguished worshippers.

The service dragged on. All chaff and no grain, was Jesus's verdict. The advantage of being in that delightfully cool and spacious place was lost. The dry formulas, the lengthy interpretations took their toll.

It was the President's turn. He was bowed by the *shammash* to the Ark and prayed before it. Prayed and prayed and prayed. It was prayer everlasting. He prayed as if he feared that when he stopped he would drop down dead.

When finally his prayer turned into preaching, he gave his interpretation of the sacred text and every tradition based on it. Distinction followed distinction, each finer than the one before, so that soon they were all transparent.

'There are twelve ways of looking at this,' he said at one point, and proceeded to elaborate each one. It was fascinating in a grisly way, like watching a dog picking out fleas.

Jesus was tempted to think the building was responsible for this. It encouraged insincerity. The President and his assistants, doubtless good men where religion was not concerned, were being forced to put on a show *because of the building*. They had to come up to its grandiose designs. It was not God and his will but the building that dictated to them how they were to pray and conduct themselves. On a hillside, under the open sky, the President could not possibly have used those polished, empty phrases. Why *did* he use them, except the building expected it of him?

Jesus, bored, smitten by the heat, saw the President turn before his eyes into a cock – a red, purple and black-sheened cock – crowing on a dunghill.

The topic under discussion was purification. How to clean cups and plates, the ritual of words and actions, the symbolic meaning behind the words and actions, the different interpretations of such according to the schools of Hillel and Shammai and, wonder of wonders, how the President could reconcile these differences.

Jesus was thinking, If a father of a family made all the rules God is supposed to have made, everyone would leave home, including the dog. Better to go hungry, live on the street, in a cave, in the hills, than tolerate this spiritual bondage.

The preaching was coming to Jesus like the distant hum of bees. He did his best to stay awake but he had had a hard week and the air had acquired the consistency of cooking oil. Much to Simon's amusement, he kept nodding off. Each time he straightened up, blushing wildly, only to find the President still at it, a blind man leading a long line of other blind men in a labyrinth.

In spirit, he was back in his own house, small yet cool, listening to his mother pray in simple, direct words to God. He was in his own synagogue, listening to his beloved Ezra with his endearing impudence, his holy irreverence. If only Ezra were here now, a man of the people who told God what he really thought and who prayed aloud the way the people prayed when they knew their neighbours were not listening.

He tried everything to keep awake. He counted the number of uses of olive wood, bit his thumb, the inside of his cheek, his tongue. He clenched his fist, pressed the nails deeply into his palms, wiggled his toes. No good. Everything went rosy, grey, black, blank as he finally succumbed, snoring softly for ten minutes at a stretch.

Simon was delighted. The Carpenter was human, after all. So much for a man who propounded a new vision of humanity!

John nudged Jesus awake just as the *hassan* was returning the scroll to the Ark.

The scroll was covered with a superbly-embroidered mantle on which precious gems had been sewn. Above it was a canopy with silver bells arranged in a sort of diadem. The bells were tinkling as the *hassan* proudly bore the sacred scroll, scattering benedictions in his path.

Until the unthinkable happened. A mouse scratched its way down the mantle and jumped. It hit the flagstone with a bump, scampered under a stone seat and disappeared down a hole.

There was a dense silence before the whole place erupted. The consternation would have been no more had a lion leaped through the window. Decorum, the monumental show of correctness built up over two hours dissolved into chaos – because of a little grey mouse. The gilded roof echoed with a babel of conflicting opinions.

'A rat ... No, a mouse, you could tell by its tail ... Let

the Rabbi decide ... Was it in the sacred scroll? Possibly
... Certainly ... It's unclean, the scroll is unclean ...
How can the pure word of Torah be unclean? Not Torah,
the parchment it is written on ... This is God's judgment
upon us ... What have we done to deserve this? We have
not prayed long or hard enough ...'

The *hassan* was in a state of shock. He was publicly
disgraced. There was no way he would be able to hold on
to his office after this.

The President, his dignity tested, called for silence.

'Unroll it,' he commanded. 'Unroll the sacred scroll.'

The *hassan* obeyed.

'Has that creature, *Hassan*, nibbled at the word of God?'

With trembling fingers, the *hassan* spread out the scroll
and examined it. 'There is no sign of nibbling, Rabbi,' he
reported.

The President, renowned for his tidy mind, enquired,
'No ... droppings?'

The *hassan* spotted one and tried to brush it aside with
his sleeve but he was noticed. That, too, would tell
against him.

'There is a dropping,' someone called out, and another
said, 'I saw it, too.'

The assembly boiled over again.

'Do we have to get another scroll? That one was so
expensive ... And the mantle? Surely we can keep the
gems ... And the bells?'

The mouse, unwittingly, had created an entirely new
field of casuistry.

'How many ... droppings?' the President demanded.

Scrupulously this time, the *hassan* laid them out on his
handkerchief and gave his final tally: 'Seven, Rabbi.'

'Seven,' was echoed by all. Some said, 'It is a sacred
number, no harm will come to us.' Others were more
pessimistic. 'It is blasphemy ... A mockery of our sacred
number.'

'What did Rabbi Hillel and Rabbi Shammai say?'
someone enquired.

The President, for all his learning, was not sure they
had ever debated this issue. To mask his ignorance,
firmness was required of him, and *wisdom*. After all, it

crossed his mind that what he decided was bound to become standard practice henceforward.

'The sacred scroll is no longer sacred,' he said, in an authoritative tone. 'It behoves us to have it destroyed.'

'Destroyed,' came from three hundred throats.

It took a while for the seriousness of this decision to sink in.

Someone said, 'Tie a stone to it and throw it in the Lake.'

The President overruled him. His name and only his was to be associated with this case.

'By fire. Fire is sacred.'

'Of course.' Everyone could see it now.

'But not today,' the President went on. 'We must not desecrate the Sabbath.'

'No, no, not on the Sabbath.'

'The *hassan* will leave it,' the President said, pleased to have resolved the issue so smoothly, 'outside the synagogue. At the rear.'

This was banishment, indeed.

Out of pure mischief, the sort that had endeared him to Ezra when he was a boy, Jesus stood up and enquired, in a solemn voice, 'Have you considered, Rabbi, there might be a desecration of the Ark itself?'

'The Ark?' The President was white and terribly shaken.

'Might there not be ... droppings' – Jesus matched exactly the President's interval before the offending word – 'in the Ark itself?'

The President regretted not having called on this young man to contribute to the proceedings earlier. He could have sworn he dropped off to sleep. Instead, he was evidently a man of God.

'*Hassan*,' he thundered.

The luckless *hassan*, more wretched than any mouse, was already at the door of the Ark. He put his head in and scrutinised every inch.

'None,' he reported.

'Two witnesses,' the President said with relief, for he had been wondering if the Ark itself was destined for combustion. 'I want two witnesses to testify there are no mouse ... droppings in the Ark of God.'

There was a mad scramble to perform this sacred function. Afterwards, four important personages insisted on their names being registered as witnesses of the Ark's integrity.

Jesus was so happy that his Sabbath had not been entirely wasted.

The congregation trooped out of the synagogue, led by the most prestigious members, discussing the unspeakable scandal of the mouse.

Andrew touched Jesus on the elbow and whispered, 'You had the right idea, Jesus. God himself would have slept through that sermon.'

Chapter 21

Outside the synagogue, Simon was less sensitive in his approach than his brother.

'I saw you catnapping, Carpenter. Prayers too long for you, eh?'

Jesus was tempted to say he hadn't heard any prayers. Not the sort God would think it worth while listening to.

'Long prayers, long life,' Simon said, quoting a rabbinical saying.

'Who wants to live that long?' Jesus asked, before admitting that endless talk about purification did not appeal to him.

'Too hard for you, Carpenter?'

'No, too easy.'

Simon chuckled, taking it as a joke.

'Really, Simon. It keeps a man away from religion.'

Simon, still tickled by the events in the synagogue, said, 'What's your idea of religion, then?'

Meaning it to be his parting shot, Jesus said, 'Loving God and doing his will.'

Before he could escape, Simon grabbed him and made him sit alongside him in the shade of a fig-tree.

'What we just did was our Jewish way of loving and obeying God.' He looked hard at Jesus, just as the *hassan* appeared and deposited the once holy scroll behind the synagogue. 'Agreed, Carpenter?'

Jesus shook his head. 'That was just an exercise in making people feel safe and secure.'

Simon had a premonition that Jesus was about to develop another of his big ideas. How did he manage to carry so many big ideas inside his head?

He said, gruffly. 'What's *wrong* with feeling safe and secure?'

'Our God is not a God of security,' Jesus said. 'Did Abraham feel secure when God called him from his own country and his own family? Did Moses when God told him to go into the desert?'

Simon gulped. 'Anyone would think God is dangerous.'

'Like a fire,' Jesus returned, with a distant look in his eyes. 'He is calling us all the time to foreign tasks in foreign places where often there is no foothold.'

Simon chuckled again, less comfortably. 'Sounds wild to me.'

'Yes, God is completely wild and unpredictable and lovely. Like a rose in the desert.'

'No wonder,' Simon said, disparagingly, 'you get bored with talk of dirty cups and plates.'

'Dirty cups and plates do not matter. A man's heart does. Only what comes out of a man's heart can dirty him.'

Simon went on the defensive. 'The Rabbi meant that, surely.'

'It's odd, then, that in two hours he never got round to mentioning the one thing necessary. The truth is simple, it should be simply put.'

Simon took Jesus by the hand and hauled him to his feet.

'I've come to the conclusion, Carpenter, that under that quiet exterior you are a bit of a rebel.'

'No, no. I merely state the obvious.'

'That's what I mean,' Simon said.

124

That Sabbath was anything but a day of rest for Simon. He blamed the Carpenter. First, it was his big idea about loving enemies and, now, his equally big idea about religion offering no easy security.

At the end of an exhausting day, he resolved never to talk to him about religion again.

Next morning, he brought it up as soon as he handed Jesus the food-basket.

'I reckon you ought to show more respect for rabbis.'

Jesus took no notice, but went on working on the boat.

'Did you hear me, Carpenter?'

'I'm fixing your boat.'

'Fix *me*,' Simon said. 'Don't I count?'

Jesus looked him over. 'Are you leaking?'

'All over.'

The rain was beginning to fall. Tentatively, at first.

'What can I do for you, Simon?'

'You could start by keeping quiet.' Realising the contradiction, Simon added snappily, 'What did you object to in yesterday's service?'

Jesus, still hammering, said, 'It seems to me some rabbis want to build fences round God's word. Fence after fence. After, they are pleased to show you a hole here and a hole there for you to squeeze through. Provided you follow their directions to the letter. I prefer to be without holes and without fences. Pass the nails.'

Simon obliged. The rain was coming down heavier. Fat rain, big as leaves. Simon said over the patter, 'What about religion? I don't just mean cups and plates. But the Temple, sacrifices. Is nothing sacred to you?'

'To me,' Jesus said, hammering in a nail, 'everything is sacred.'

The rain splashed in Simon's eye, annoying him even more. 'That's not good enough, Carpenter. Some things are specially sacred.'

'I agree,' Jesus said. 'The poor, the gentle, the lowly of heart.'

Simon clicked his teeth with disapproval. 'I mean, *religious* things.'

'What is more religious than someone who is filled with God's Spirit?'

125

'Think like that,' Simon said, 'and that's the end of God's laws.'

'That's right,' Jesus said.

Simon gasped. He had not been expecting anything like this. 'That's *right*?'

'Of course. If you act with love towards God, what's the point of laws? You don't break them or keep them. They just don't figure. More nails, please.'

'*And* religion, is it the end of that, too?'

'A heartless religion,' Jesus said, evenly. 'A religion as neat as Levi's ledgers: credit, so much; debit, so much.'

'I wonder why you bother to go to the synagogue, Carpenter. Maybe to sleep.'

Jesus acknowledged the dig with a smile. 'No, like you, I go because I have hope in my heart. I go to be one with my people, to celebrate with them in joy the love of God.'

'Damn and blast this rain,' Simon roared. 'All right, Carpenter, you've done away with laws and religion, what can you do with our traditions?'

The rain was lashing down, so it was hard to see. Jesus ignored it.

'Our only true and unchanging tradition,' he said, 'is that God is calling us out of our past into a future no one can see.'

'Not even you?' Simon said caustically. 'A word of warning for you. Don't let the rabbis hear you say that or you'll be thrown out of the House of Israel.'

For the first time, Jesus stopped working. 'Why?' he asked, innocently. 'Because I put the Law-giver before the Law?' He touched Simon's beard, causing water to stream down his neck. 'Still leaking?'

'Sinking,' Simon said, with a grin. 'I don't know, Carpenter. You sound sure of yourself.'

'No.' Jesus bowed his head humbly. 'I am very sure of God.'

When Simon went home to dry out, Jesus was still hammering away.

Levi the tax-collector was another one to come under Jesus's spell. He was impressed by the fact that he had

126

made an honest man of that insufferable rogue, Simon son of Jonah.

True, Simon had tried arguing with Jesus.

'No one round here pays the full amount. Even Levi doesn't expect that. Stretching things a bit is all part of the game. Besides, any fisherman who revealed his full catch wouldn't be able to compete. He'd go out of business. Only a fool would do that.'

Jesus had said, 'If so, he is God's fool.'

Now, in the evenings, Levi did not even lie in wait for Simon. It was part of the routine for Jesus to come to the customs house. Levi said, 'How many?' and he accepted whatever Jesus said.

Why? He did not know. What was even more difficult to fathom was why Simon employed a man who wouldn't tell lies for him. Maybe Jesus had some hold over him.

Realising that Simon wasn't getting away with anything, Levi felt sorry for him. One evening, when Jesus reported the day's catch as five baskets, Levi winked and said, 'We'll make it four, shall we?'

'It's five,' Jesus insisted.

Levi giggled at the obtuseness of the man. He couldn't recognise a favour when he saw one. He said, 'Can't you see, man, I am allowing you to write four?'

'Thank you kindly,' Jesus said. 'But even tax-collectors haven't the power to turn five baskets of fish into four.'

'God has come to earth,' Levi whispered to himself when Jesus left. 'At last I've found a man who doesn't fiddle his taxes.'

Though Simon no longer tried to deceive Levi, he loathed him, all the same.

Jesus, with that half-smile he often had, suggested, 'Why not pray for him?'

Simon pulled a face. 'I've given it a try. I wasn't made for it. Like a fish up a tree.'

'Try harder, Simon. Make yourself a nuisance with God, make yourself unbearable until he says yes.'

'You know I can't stand the man.'

'I noticed. But God makes his sun shine and his rain fall as much on Levi as on you.'

'God can't make exceptions for things like that,' Simon said, 'but I can't wait for Judgment Day.'

'He may be your enemy,' Jesus said. 'There's no need for you to be his.'

Next evening, Jesus reported the day's catch to Levi and was invited in for a cup of wine. Jesus was in the inner room, out of sight, when Simon appeared at Levi's table at the customs house. He looked very agitated.

Levi went out warily, afraid that Simon was reverting to his old, rough ways.

'Yes?' Levi said.

From behind his back, Simon drew out an enormous flounder with a big head and a rocky spine.

'For you,' he said, thrusting it in Levi's hand.

'But ... But ...' Levi stammered. 'Why give it to me?'

'Because,' Simon began. 'Oh, damn,' he snapped, all confused. 'It's because you're my enemy.'

Chapter 22

Repairs to the boat took three days longer than planned. As Jesus said, 'We all make mistakes.'

Simon was delighted to have the boat back. He took it out at once with Jesus as his mate to test its seaworthiness.

Jesus was in the stern, trailing his hand in the water. It was a day of unbearable humidity.

In a sudden burst of high-spiritedness, Simon swooped on Jesus from behind and lifted him up.

'You want to cool off, Carpenter? Let me oblige.'

With a heave, he threw Jesus overboard.

The water was icy cold, it took Jesus's breath away.

Simon failed to understand why he was struggling and spluttering so much. Until Jesus managed to lift his head above the water and cry. 'I can't –' Then he went under again.

At first, Simon thought it a huge joke. Realising it wasn't, he cast his tunic aside and jumped in with a splash. In moments, he was holding Jesus up.

'Come on, Carpenter,' he shouted. 'It's about time you learned to swim. You're all theory, you know that?'

Jesus had swallowed too much water to argue.

'That's right,' Simon said, delighted that for once he had the upper hand. 'Stretch yourself. Go flat, you hear? Trust me, that's the secret.'

Jesus threshed around wildly, like most beginners.

'Don't *panic*,' Simon yelled. 'Don't lift your backside up like a duck. Stay *on* the water, man.'

Jesus made a few tentative strokes and Simon, satisfied, ended the first lesson. He helped Jesus clamber aboard and threw a blanket over him.

'So, Carpenter,' he said, in his cheeriest manner, 'you've learned *something* from your stay with us.'

'One day,' Jesus replied, through chattering teeth, 'one day, I will teach you to walk on water.'

Simon looked at him cagily, wondering if this was another of Jesus's big ideas.

'I look forward to it,' he said.

Ashore, Simon wanted to hammer in a new landing-pole. Jesus held it while Simon swung a heavy wooden mallet.

On the third blow, the mallet missed and glided down the side of the pole, crashing down on the knuckles of Jesus's left hand.

Jesus let go of the pole and sank down on his haunches. His face turned a deathly white, he was breathing heavily but the only sound he made was a barely audible moan.

Simon was disgusted with himself. He flung the mallet as far as he could into the Lake. He waited, grieving, until Jesus was able to hold out his hand for him to look at it.

No bones seemed to have been broken but there would be a bad bruise and swelling for quite a while.

As Simon took hold of Jesus's hand, blood began to trickle through a perforation in the skin.

'Did you mistake me for Levi?' Jesus managed to say, as he shivered from pain and cold.

Simon raised Jesus's grubby, calloused hand to his lips and kissed it. It was more than an act of sympathy, more like an act of homage. Afterwards, he had the tang of blood, like salt, in his mouth.

What went through Simon like a sword was, *I foolishly shed this blood. I can taste it. His life is in my mouth.*

In spite of his remorse, he felt in an indefinable way that the accident was a bond, a communion between them and the promise of better things to come. He would be careful not to hurt the Carpenter again.

He looked down on Jesus and what he saw almost broke him up. Though strong, Jesus was as a child, helpless, undefended, with a goodness that went down to the marrow of his bones.

In a moment of insight, Simon knew you could do what you liked with him – taunt him, tease him, throw him into the sea, bruise him, draw his blood – and he would not hold it against you. He did not blame you, harboured no resentment. He hadn't even the *instinct* to retaliate, which meant – and Simon was to reflect a great deal on this in the years ahead – he hadn't the rough, ordinary man's talent for survival.

Even his anger, Simon saw this now, was innocent. It was a pure, untarnished anger, without self-pity, without self-indulgence, because it was *wholly* directed against wrong-doing and swept harmlessly past the wrong-doer himself. He was a man who hated injustice, not because it threatened him or touched him at any point, though it might, but simply because such things ought not to happen in God's world.

Ultimately, then, it was not what Jesus had said about loving enemies that won Simon over but the proof that Jesus had no enemies. The accident enabled Simon to see that Jesus was as big as his ideas. Bigger. Because in him they were not just ideas.

Simon was sufficiently self-aware to know that if someone had smashed *his* hand, he would have roared

and hopped about and rounded on the person responsible
and borne him a grudge for many a day. The pain would
have done the cursing for him.

But Jesus did not shriek. His pain did no cursing.
Nothing nasty was hidden inside him, not even the kind
of nastiness that pain invariably brings to the surface.

Simon felt you could hammer away at Jesus all day and
he wouldn't hate you for it or think of you as his enemy.
Even if you banged nails into him he'd say, 'Never mind,
it's not your fault.'

So, Simon concluded, *in Jesus there is no gap between saying
and doing. He is a man of his word, he is one with his word. And his
word is good; God's. God's word has become flesh, so to speak, in this
carpenter from Nazareth.*

'Don't *worry,'* Jesus said, looking up. 'In my job, you
have to put up with this sort of thing.'

Chapter 23

'Behold,' Simon said, introducing his plump wife, Timna,
'the place where I lay my head.'

Simon insisted that Jesus stay with him until his hand
was better. For the next few days, Jesus saw a lot of
Simon, Timna and Timna's mother who lived with them.

He liked Simon more and more. Liked his generosity,
his impulsiveness so like a child's, his enthusiasm for
everything. When Simon gave a kiss to Timna, who was
carrying their first child, it sounded like a giant's foot
being drawn out of thick mud. When he chewed his food
you could almost see the sparks fly.

Andew lived near by. Three years older than Simon,
he was content to take orders. The family joke was that
as soon as Simon was born, he said, 'Andrew, will you
listen to *me?'*

Andrew was not married. Simon told Jesus confidentially, 'He's asked three girls to marry him.'

'And they said no?' Jesus whispered back.

Simon slapped Jesus on the shoulder and bellowed, 'Not at all. They didn't even hear him.'

Once again, Andrew reminded Jesus of his father.

Jesus entered fully into the life of the fishermen. By day, the brothers took him out with them in the boat. At night, he joined them and other fishermen on the strand. Someone lit a fire, and they cut lines into the fish, rubbed them with salt and toasted them on a stick. They drank wine and sang boisterous sea-shanties and, less often, chants from the synagogue. Jesus sang as loudly as anyone, but he did not speak much.

One evening they were discussing in hushed tones the misery of being ruled by a heathen like Antipas and the burden of the Roman military presence. Israel was the Lord's, they believed, they should rule themselves as in the glorious days of David and Solomon.

Their chief sorrow was that the voice of prophecy was silent. For more than a hundred years, since Zechariah and Malachi, God had not spoken directly to his people.

One of the men chanted the words of the Psalm:

> *Signs we do not see;*
> *There is no longer a prophet among us.*
> *Yet not one of us dares ask,*
> *How long will these things last?*

The cantor finished and there was a long, sad silence around the fire.

James spoke up. 'What was it Malachi said? *Behold, I will send my messenger to prepare the way before me.*'

'Where is he, then?' someone said, and Andrew mumbled into his beard, 'We're a long time waiting, brother.'

Simon called across the fire, 'What do *you* think, Carpenter?'

Jesus seemed reluctant to join in, but he eventually said, 'I think we should ... wait.'

'How long for?' several said.

'Until God needs us.'

All of them seated around the fire became instantly aware that the Carpenter had altered their perspective. It was the sort of experience they had when their boat overturned. Sea and sky changed places. What mattered was not what they wanted but what God wanted.

'After all,' Jesus went on, 'we did not choose God, he chose us.'

'But what are we doing for him now?' James asked.

'Witnessing to him, as always.'

'What sort of witness is it,' James said, 'when we're not even masters in our own land?'

'Nor have any hope of it,' John added, fiercely.

'God is with us, he knows *that*,' Jesus said. 'If we are exiled in our own land, so is he. He can be found anywhere, so if it is his will that we witness to him in suffering and want, so be it.'

John was far from satisfied. 'If he is our God he should take better care of us.'

'John,' Jesus said gently, so that it did not seem a reproach, 'he is not *our* God.'

This was greeted by mutterings from the group.

'Of course he is ... We don't worship Baal ... Or Zeus or the Emperor ... *We* kept God's name alive, no one else did ...'

'True,' Jesus said, when there was quiet, 'without us God would be without a name in the world. But he is not our God. Not in the sense that he belongs to us.'

A cheeky youngster called out, 'Then we must be the only people in the world to worship a God who doesn't belong to us.'

Jesus waited until the laughter had died down before saying he took this not as a joke but as the expression of the profoundest truth.

'We alone worship a God who says, "You are mine but I am not yours. You have no rights over me. I am the God of everyone."'

Someone grunted, 'If God *was* a Jew he'd know how terrible we feel.'

The group settled into a more thoughtful mood. For a time all that could be heard was the lapping of water and

133

the crackling of thorns in the fire.

Then John spoke up in his thin, young voice, 'Are you saying, Jesus, that our God is the God of all men equally?'

Jesus did not hesitate. *'Equally.'*

Simon was staggered by this development, outraged. This was obviously another of the carpenter's big ideas.

'After all our trials,' Simon spluttered, 'after all the Jewish blood that's been shed, are we only *equal* with the rest of men?'

'Only equal with the Romans?' someone called out to hoots of laughter, and a wag added, 'I'd like to circumcise Pontius Pilate, I can tell you.'

Two or three of the group got up and walked away. They were deeply upset at Jesus's irreverence in equating Jews and grasshoppers. They refused to share food or fire with him again.

'Israel's glory,' Jesus went on, in the same untroubled tone, 'is that we kept alive faith in the God who made all men and who is, therefore, the Father of all men, equally. He is only *our* God, the *true* God, if he is the God of all.'

James was very puzzled. 'But aren't we sons of Abraham? Doesn't that give us the rights of the first-born?'

'And were not all nations blessed in Abraham?' Jesus replied. 'God's will is all that matters, not our flesh. God could take the stars up there and this' – he held up a handful of sand and let it fall through his fingers – 'and make as many sons of Abraham as he wishes.'

Simon was still in turmoil. He could not get out of his head that Jews had gone through hell since Abraham, had suffered under the Philistines, Babylonians, Greeks and now the Romans. Why? What was it all for?

Deeply perturbed, he said, 'Is there nothing special about being chosen by the blessed God?'

Jesus nodded. 'Our feet, our tired bloodstained feet first trod the path to God all men must tread. Do we expect to be rewarded further for this? Is it not enough that we did it?'

Simon half nodded assent to that.

Jesus went on, 'We have been chosen, yes. Chosen to

134

suffer more than others for the truth. But what do you think, Simon?'

Simon's head jerked back. Jesus was always asking him, only him, what *he* thought, as if he attached special importance to it. But what could he say?

What Jesus is saying, he thought, *is not possible. IS it possible?*

This isn't, after all, just one of Jesus's big ideas. It's the biggest, the one in which all the others are rooted. Because if God IS the Father of all men equally it would explain why we must love our enemies. They, too, are God's children, members of the family.

And didn't Isaiah speak often of Israel as being a light to the Gentiles, so that God's salvation can reach to the ends of the earth? 'For I am God and there is no other.'

But does that mean all men must become Jews? Would people like Antipas and Pontius Pilate and the Emperor himself have to submit to the Law and worship in the Temple?

Simon was confused and his fugitive moment of insight passed.

He became aware that Jesus was still waiting for his answer.

Simon shrugged. 'I don't know,' he said. 'Maybe.'

Inwardly: *Why is the Carpenter picking on me? What would I know? And where in the name of heaven did he get all his knowledge and wisdom?*

Another night the fishermen were grouped around the fire. John was singing to them in his sweet clear childlike voice a sad song from Israel's greatest poet Isaiah, and accompanying himself on a small harp.

> *Take comfort, my people, take comfort from me,*
> *Remember my love is so strong.*
> *'Speak to Jerusalem tenderly,*
> *Tell them I have pardoned their wrong.*

The men were listening intently, and joining in the refrain:

> *All flesh is as grass, its beauty will pass*
> *As in a field the flowers do.*

135

The grasses grow pale and the flowers fail,
Frail as the flowers are you.

John's voice again caressed the night:

A voice in the desert cries, Make straight the way,
The hill roads must look like the plain.
The Lord will be here on his chosen Day,
You die – but his Word will remain.

Simon could be heard above all the rest with the refrain:

All flesh is as grass, its beauty will pass
As in a field the flowers do.
The grasses grow pale and the flowers fail,
Frail as the flowers are you.

The song spoke to the fishermen about the oppression they were having to endure and the deprivation. It could not last for ever. All over the holy land, a feeling was developing into a mood and from this mood strange movements had already come.

Cranks and holy men walked alone into the desert. Zealots or Knife-men – a group of pious Jewish assassins with daggers under their tunics – hoped to restore Israel by taking up arms against the strongest, most disciplined army of occupation the world had ever seen.

The fishermen, to a man, were against such extremes. Yet none of them doubted that the times were decisive. Soon God would step in and end Israel's bondage. He would send his Messiah.

Firelight and starlight. A good time for dreaming and scheming.

The Messiah was a movement, someone suggested. A social or political movement. Others, most of them, said the Messiah would be a person, a great warrior like David, who would restore Israel's fortunes as of old.

Present that evening was a fisherman who had returned to Galilee after living in a religious community in the region of the Dead Sea.

It was quite the fashion for young men like Thomas to

prepare themselves in groups for 'the last days', when the heavens would be rolled up like a scroll and sinners fall as leaves from the vines. Satan was marshalling all the dark forces; the righteous had to organise, too.

Thomas, a sharp-faced, mystical-looking youth told how he had tried to escape the wrath to come: he had joined the community known as Qumran and stayed there for two years.

What was it like, they asked him.

He explained how the community shared all work and property. Meals, preceded by lustrations, were taken together and in silence. They did not marry. They pored over the Scriptures, longing for the day when God would renew his covenant with the elect and complete Israel once and for all.

The fishermen were impressed and questioned Thomas for an hour. John said, 'I don't like all this so-called religious silence. I'm waiting for a warrior-Messiah and when he comes I'll follow him to the death.'

'Shush,' Simon said, 'not so loud.'

Sound travels at night. Antipas had his informers everywhere and the Romans their spies.

'I don't care,' John said, in the zealous, piping tones of youth.

Jesus squeezed his arm and whispered, 'All the trees in Lebanon would not fuel a wrath like yours, John.'

Someone noticed that Jesus had not commented on what Thomas had said.

'Qumran is not Israel's way,' he said simply. 'We Jews believe in enjoyment, surely. Besides, the chosen are for the sake of everyone not for themselves.'

'But it *was* enjoyable,' Thomas said, 'to be alone in the desert, thinking, praying.'

Simon said, to a chorus of agreement, 'There are times when I'd like to get away from it all, I can tell you.'

'God made the world,' Jesus said, impishly, 'and it is not a scroll a mouse has walked on. It is holy.'

'Not always,' someone objected.

'True. But the world, where *people are*, is the place to look for God.'

Some said yes and some no.

'God's kingly rule is to be found here and now among those who live their ordinary daily lives in his presence, with its joys and sorrows. All that is needed is a change of heart, so we serve God humbly and respectfully, and love everyone as we love ourselves.'

Simon looked across the flickering firelight to where Jesus was seated. It was like listening to a voice out of the burning bush.

'Is there nothing decisive about *now*?' James wanted to know. 'Are all these hopes and longings we have for the Messiah nothing but a dream?'

'Now *is* the decisive moment,' Jesus said. 'All our nows are decisive.'

Someone called out, 'That's too glib.'

'Is that so?' Jesus said. 'God comes all the time, as secretly and as openly as sunrise. He is here but he is not always seen because he is too obvious.'

Simon was beginning to pass the cup around as John asked, 'Is there to be no thunder and lightning?'

'God's Kingdom,' Jesus replied, 'comes even in our sharing a cup of wine. Why look for something noisier, brighter?'

He raised the cup that had reached him and gave a kind of toast: 'God's Kingdom, here and now.'

He made them all feel that this simple gesture was somehow momentous. They drank, and never had wine tasted so good to them.

The talk went on for an hour longer. By this time, John had fallen asleep, with his head in Jesus's lap.

'Of such,' Jesus whispered to James, 'is the kingdom of sleep.'

The night turned chill. It was time to turn in.

'Lazy-bones,' James said, prodding John awake.

'Where am I?' John said, yawning.

'You are safe,' Jesus said.

Chapter 24

The time came for Jesus to leave Capernaum. He had been happy there. He had enjoyed the green gardens, the fresh running water, and, lately, the relaxation. He felt at home.

He had made friends not just with Simon, that oak of righteousness, that lion who could eat straw, but with Simon's wife and mother-in-law, with Salome, mother of James and John, with Joanna, the wife of one of Antipas's stewards, and a devout lady named Susannah.

He would miss them all, miss even Simon's snoring that threatened to saw clean through the rafters.

His one regret was that Mary of Magdala had not come back. She was a fine young woman in the making. She needed help. He had asked after her, but no one could tell him anything. She must have left the district.

Jesus made an early start.

Before he left, Simon held him in his considerable embrace.

'Goodbye, Carpenter.'

'Goodbye, Fisherman.'

I feel homesick, Simon was thinking. *It's crazy, I'm not the one who's leaving. But I do.*

He watched Jesus on the upward path, his bag of tools slung from his shoulder. On the crest of the hill, Jesus turned back. The sun was peeping over the eastern mountains and he was the first thing it hit. He seemed to catch sunrise and reflect it down to Simon. Jesus up there looked like the trembling of liquid gold, his hand waving was like water, so brightly it shone. Then he was gone and, with him, for the time being, the sunrise.

For days afterwards, Simon lived as in a dream, so that

Timna kept saying, 'What's come over you? You're quieter than Andrew.'

Why did he have to go away? If he had said, 'Come with me,' I'd have followed him to the ends of the earth. Even walked on water for him.

From the first moment he gave me his hand it was as if he knew me, for all my bluff and bluster, better than I know myself. I tried to put him off, didn't I? Did my prickly cactus act, snatched the oar from him. A little hint that I didn't want to know him. All the time I was big-bullying him, he was playing with me, as a cat plays with a feather. He held on to the oar, fortunately, and so held on to ME. As if he knew I did want him, needed him badly.

Now I know he'd stand by me, come what may. He'd never let me down. He's the only person I ever met who sets no limits to forgiveness or friendship. If you want him, when you want him, whatever you want him for, he'll be there, Odd, when you feel your own limits are as narrow as a sandal round a foot.

What was it he told me about his trip here? He came across a viper swallowing a full-grown hare. That's how I feel. I've swallowed something awfully big and it'll take some digesting.

'Eat up,' Timna pleaded. 'You haven't touched your food. I don't know why I bother.'

How did I come to crack his hand with that mallet? An accident? Even accidents need an explanation. Did I, without thinking, MEAN to hurt him? Why? To keep him here longer? Or because, at a deeper level – dare I say it? – because I hate him? How HATE him? Maybe because he is so good he is a danger to me? Because he might make me in some ways like he is? Yes, maybe I love AND hate him.

'Don't expect me to heat it up again.'

After all, I noticed early on, he was always first for the jobs that needed doing and last for handouts. It showed in simple ways. He immediately gave up his seat around the fire on the beach to newcomers. He always offered to cook food for everyone, serving himself last, naturally, and sometimes going without when food was short, though he hid it well.

This irritated me at first, as if there was something shameful in it. I snapped at him, I remember, 'Carpenter, must you always take the last place?' He blushed. 'If someone else wants it,' he said, 'he's welcome to it. Otherwise, I don't mind.' I said to him, like the idiot I am, 'That's better. There's no need to be greedy!' He bit his lip, poor chap, said sorry. I tried to make it up to him and only made things worse, trust me. I said, 'Do you like pain or something?' 'Not if someone else wants it,' he said. I think he was joking to let me off the hook. 'SERIOUSLY, Carpenter.' He shook his head really hard and said, 'I avoid suffering whenever I can.' I said, 'I'm glad to hear it,' hoping that would be the end of the matter. But he wasn't quite finished. He touched my arm and said, with a twinkle, 'You will be sure to tell suffering to avoid me.'

'What's the matter with the big fellow?'

'I don't know, Mum. Maybe he's sickening for something.'

'Anyone would think *he's* having the baby.'

'Leave me be, will you, the pair of you!'

'Then don't go around moaning like a dove,' Timna said to him.

Next Sabbath, in the synagogue, Simon was for the first time dissatisfied with the Rabbi's teaching. Heartless, empty. His prayers were not like Jesus's; they didn't go the full distance. Blind watchman, dumb dog.

The President made a long, eloquent plea for subscriptions to buy a new scroll. Simon got to his feet. He had never behaved like this before. Andrew thought he was having a brainstorm, tried to make him sit down.

'Are you wanting to make a contribution, friend?' the Rabbi said, gratefully.

'There was nothing wrong with the other scroll,' Simon said. 'There was something wrong with us, that's all.'

The new *hassan* stepped forward, indignant, anxious to prove his worth.

'Maybe you were not here when the Rabbi declared the old scroll unclean.'

'I was here,' Simon said. 'The Rabbi was wrong.'

He sat down.

No contributions were pledged that day. Simon's intervention may have been responsible. Or it might have been John calling out, mischievously, 'We'd be wasting our money, Rabbi, if that mouse came back.'

So many memories to choose from. There was the time Jesus went to supper at Levi's place. When he came home I said, 'Can't you see how odious he is?' He said, 'I really can't. Hate can spot a splinter; love is blind to logs.' I felt properly put in my place. Then he said, 'People like Levi are hurt already, why hurt them more? Respect them and there's a chance they will respect themselves. Until they do, they cannot possibly change. Despise them and you make them despicable. I can't do that.'

I remember how good it felt putting that fish in Levi's hand, and looking at his face. He really thought I was going to lay into him.

Levi looked up from his accounts. 'Yes?'

Simon said, 'Five baskets, sir.'

Poor fellow, Levi thought, so there's something in the rumour. He's not himself. *Sir*, indeed.

'I used to give you false figures,' Simon said.

Levi did not know what to make of this. Tax-men can get to be suspicious.

Simon suddenly produced two enormous fishes out of his tunic, gave them to Levi, wiped his hands on his beard and squeezed Levi's hand. Nearly broke it but, for a change, he didn't mean to. He had this faraway look in his eyes.

'Any news?' Levi said.

'News?'

'About ...?'

'No,' Simon said. 'You?'

Levi shook his head.

'Well, goodbye, Levi.'

'Well,' Levi said. 'Um, I suppose, er, goodbye, Simon.'

Carpenter, Carpenter. Oh, Carpenter.

He's got this concern for everyone even for ... well, for people like Levi. Loves everyone. No exceptions, it's uncanny. A puzzling mixture of content and discontent, if you ask me. He's a man of passionate emotions, everybody says that, but none of them destructive. I know how to lash out, he doesn't. He's incapable of making anyone feel small. He lifts every conversation to a level that makes what the rest of us say seem trivial by comparison. He makes good things seem somehow permanent. He makes 'here' seem everywhere and 'now' everlasting. He ties beginnings to ends so you see they are one and they are beautiful.

142

'What's that, Simon. I'm beautiful, am I? First time you've noticed me in days.'

'Oh, yes, you're very beautiful, Timna.'

'You might at least look at me when you say it.'

He doesn't care a tittle what happens to himself. He's like a pitcher with all the water emptied out, so there's no room for himself, only for God and other people. He can put up with anything but touch someone else, make someone else suffer and you can see what it does to him. As if he has pains in everybody else's bodies. It's odd, really.

A healing man, a man who kissed the lips of peace. How does he do it? Obvious. He's centred on God. That's why he can go out to everyone, make everyone and everything seem important. He makes God present when he holds you, when he shares a cup of wine with you. He shows you no one need be without hope. Not even me.

'After the fire on the beach, Timna, I'm going fishing.'

'About time you got down to something useful. Don't I get a kiss?'

Maybe he intended going fishing, maybe he didn't. When the others had left, he stayed by the fire.

Why doesn't this fire warm you any more?

He sat where once he had seen *him* sit at night, under the stars. Timna had said, 'He's not come in. Where is he?' Simon had gone to look. He found him cross-legged by the remains of the fire, looking out to sea. But not looking. Sleeping. Yet not sleeping, either. Lost somewhere. Lost somewhere far away, where Simon had never been, somewhere beyond anywhere. Simon didn't interrupt him, never asked him what he was doing. He couldn't have told, anyway. Words don't do everything.

So now Simon was spending the night on the strand. Thinking. Once John almost stumbled over him. John had said something. He remembered only because it echoed his own thoughts: 'Why did he have to go away?'

What was young John doing walking along the strand at night? Was he finding sleep difficult, too?

Is this what the Carpenter has done for us, turned all the local fishermen into insomniacs?

Simon shook his head and John walked on. Left Simon thinking.

A fisherman thinking. A monstrosity. Like a dog talking.

HE has done this, with his big ideas. Yet he seemed reluctant to spread them, all the same. Not that he was afraid of them, or was himself unready for them. But because the time wasn't ripe for them. Because he was waiting. But for what?

And who WAS this man who just appeared? Who came out of the hills around Capernaum and turned lives upside down?

A woodworker from the back of beyond who earned only a pittance in his own village and, lately, not even that. A man of set purpose and he pursued it as straight as if he were walking a plank – but what purpose? A man who felt – insanely? – responsible for everything, so that I had to say to him, 'Take it easy, Carpenter. You can't take on the whole world.' And yet everything WAS his business. A man you never tired of – and to be honest, you tired of everyone in time, your wife included and yourself – because he never tires of you. He finds joy in strange places.

When he spoke of God – oh, so simply, no clumsiness there – it was like watching a bird take flight from the top of a mulberry-tree. When he was mending my boat, it was as if, in some sense, he was fixing up a world.

How else can I sum up this man in whom God's Spirit is bubbling up like a spring of water, except by saying, 'God came to the Lake of Galilee?' Thank God for it.

Morning. Simon found himself by the ash-grey fire, with cocks crowing and dogs sneezing, looking out on an ash-grey dawn.

'Catch anything?'

'Nothing, Timna.'

'Simon, you haven't been yourself since the Carpenter left. He didn't steal anything from you, by any chance?'

Everything.

'Nothing,' he said. 'Of course not.'

The night before he left, he said to me, 'I'm lucky.' 'How, Carpenter?' He touched my hand. 'Even before summer, see, I've got my hand on a first-ripe fig.' 'Where are you going?' 'Back to Nazareth,' he said. 'What will you be doing there?' He smiled that enigmatic smile of his and said, 'I am waiting.'

That's what I'll be doing, waiting till we meet again. If we ever do. Such an unpossessive man ...

144

Exactly how unpossessive, he was to discover two weeks after Jesus left. That was when Simon realised, to his horror, that Jesus had left Capernaum without being paid.

Chapter 25

His mother was delighted to have him back. She had been worried, had expected him back sooner.

'Look at your hand,' she said. 'What happened?'

'I had an argument with a hammer.'

'You lost,' she said. And wrinkling her nose, 'You smell of fish.'

When sne enquired if he had made his fortune, he had to admit that he had returned with less than he had taken.

He spent a long time telling her about Capernaum, about his new friends, and his feeling for the place. She enjoyed his enthusiasm.

'You didn't talk to the heathen, I hope.'

'It couldn't be avoided,' he said. He had even picked up quite a bit of Greek.

'It's a wonder your tongue doesn't drop off,' she said, in a mildly scolding voice. 'I thought only slaves and Gentiles learned foreign languages.'

Outwardly at least, Nazareth was almost its old self. There were signs that trees and stalks were bending again with plenty. White rain clouds crossed the sky. Nature had repented.

For Jesus, it was work as usual. Only he could not help noticing that he was being treated, since his return, with a certain coolness. There was no small-talk when he was around; people avoided his company.

Most significantly, when he gave farmers a bill, they paid up at once *as if he was bad luck.*

No children came to his workshop. Well, almost none.

'Sp-sp-sp.'

'Yes, Shimon?' He smiled with relief. 'Have you another message for me?'

'No. My sister doesn't like you any more.'

'Ah.' He could not very well say he was pleased or sorry.

'I think she still likes you, Jesus, but my daddy says she mustn't.'

'*Mustn't?* Why?'

'I dunno.'

'Where are all your friends?'

'They can't come.'

'Why not?'

'Their daddies say not.'

'Why didn't yours?'

'He did.'

After that, Shimon did not come any more, either.

On the day Ezra asked him to help fell trees, Jesus was pleased to have company.

The Rabbi was an alarming sight. He wore a shawl over his shoulders in spite of the heat. He was thin, his hands and arms were knobbly like flowers gone to seed, his face was black-lined like a cobweb, he was puffy-eyed as if he had not slept in days.

'A dry, blasted tree, that's what I am,' Ezra puffed. 'Old age isn't the nicest thing.'

'Thanks for warning me, Rabbi. I'll avoid it if I can.'

Jesus was laughing until he saw the angry boils on Ezra's neck.

No wonder Ezra was not in a contented mood.

His wife hadn't changed, he grumbled. Keep a mite from her and she was like a bear robbed of her cubs.

'Each coin I give her, my son, sprouts wings and flies away.'

His Rib still opposed him, especially on matters of religion. With the Sadducees, she disapproved of 'these newfangled ideas like resurrection'.

146

'Know what she said to me yesterday? "What a terrible thing if, when we've done with this life, we have to start all over again. God can't be as cruel as that."'

Jesus found it hard to keep himself from laughing.

'"What is life," my Rib says to me, "but breath in the nose? When breathing stops, whew"' – Ezra blew on the palm of his hand – '"and goodbye, Ezra, my dear." Why did I marry the witch?'

'Maybe you loved her, Rabbi.'

'That is no excuse.'

He went on about how Sarah had the soul of a goat, treated him like dirt from Babylon. He looked forward to heaven so he could tell his Rib for ever and ever that he had been right all along.

'If you are right, she will not mind too much, Rabbi.'

'"What," I ask her, "do you have against God?" "*You*," she says.'

Jesus shook his head, as a method of controlling himself. 'At least, she believes in God, Rabbi.'

Ezra doubted it. 'I reckon she still worships the gods of the High Places. Only one God is too hard for her to make sense of. According to her, it's like having one splendid tooth in your head, you can't do anything with it. Besides, she says, one God is boring. Like having nothing but plums every day of the week.' He arched his eyebrows. 'She tells this to me, the village Rabbi? I want to stone her, but she cooks my supper.'

Ezra paused to enquire. 'Why are you laughing?'

'Not laughing, Rabbi. Something caught in ... my throat.'

He took a sip of water to ease his discomfort.

'Ah,' Ezra sighed, relenting, 'in spite of all, she has stuck to me over the years like a tail when others wouldn't.'

He took a moment to set a snare for a bird. Since the drought, he was finding it hard to make ends meet.

He came back, only to set about Nebat, his son-in-law. He drank too much, like his father, and slept too long in the mornings.

'And the marriage, Rabbi?'

Ezra snorted in disgust. 'Like the coupling of a hind

147

and a goat. I should have been kind to her and fed her to the lions.'

'Jedidah?'

'Not blameless, my son. Still no sign of my grandson coming so my soul –' He made an eloquent gesture, his hand waving over a void. 'Also, she is becoming like her mother, chatters like a swift. Soon her tongue too will crack walnuts and knock stones out of the wall.'

All through Ezra's tirades, Jesus felt it was only the build-up to something else.

Over lunch, Ezra said, 'And you, my son?'

'I enjoyed my trip to Capernaum.'

'Ah, yes,' Ezra said, sucking his honeycomb. 'I was – '

'Speak, Rabbi.'

The Rabbi's shaky hand was proof that he was approaching the real issue at last.

'One word, my son, goes deeper into a wise man than a hundred arrows into a fool.'

'Ye-es?'

'Rumours, my son. People in this stinking village swallow them like tasty morsels. Finger-pointers!'

'About?'

'About the company you kept in Capernaum.'

'They were fine people, Rabbi.'

'A tax-collector, was he one of these fine people?'

'He needed me.'

'Maybe so,' the Rabbi conceded. 'And the little floozy from Magdala you spent the night with?' Ezra waited. 'I did not believe a word of it, of course.'

Jesus bowed his head. Ezra waited, to no purpose.

'Is your mouth full of nails, my son,' he pleaded, 'that you have no word for *me*?'

The young man had a big door to his heart, but even doors to the heart need to be closed to some comers. It was a torment for Ezra to continue but he felt obliged.

'There is no point in chasing a snake after it has bitten you, my son.'

'I was not bitten, Rabbi.'

The Rabbi closed his one and a half eyes. 'You do know people are saying, "Jesus, son of Mary, is hiring a harlot for a loaf of bread"?'

'I guessed at something.'

'Nebat mentioned ... I mean, it's said you boasted about it round the bonfires in Capernaum. Even here in Nazareth, old Anna swears you spend nights away from home, only return with dawn, sometimes.' He distanced himself from these allegations. 'So she says.'

Jesus bit his lip but still did not defend himself, could not. It was a habit with him.

Ezra tugged the shawl about him like an extra skin to stop himself falling to bits. By that gesture, Jesus knew the old man had brought the shawl to warm his thin blood for its icy task. The very boils on his neck were a testimony of his love and pain.

Jesus spoke, not to defend himself, for it was not his way, but to defend Ezra, to comfort this little Rabbi who had prayed and gone sleepless to find the courage for this.

'She needed me, this woman you speak of.'

'Are you so different,' Ezra said, 'that you will not be corrupted by Satan?'

'I tread as wisely as I can.'

'Aha,' Ezra cried, but without conviction. 'When the world was only a speck of dust, Jesus of Nazareth already had wisdom, is that it? The Glory rests on Jesus of Nazareth. The sun stands still for this new Joshua, Jesus of Nazareth.'

Jesus would have found it less hard to take from anyone else, but this man loved him. It was hard and, in another way, easier. He could see Ezra simply feared to lose something precious.

Jesus was not angry. More sad and hurt.

'I did what I had to do.'

'During the drought, when you went down to the plain,' Ezra said, lashing himself like a stubborn mule. 'You profaned the Sabbath.'

Jesus was jolted by this. 'I broke the Sabbath, Rabbi, because I had to. I did not profane it.'

'I know,' Ezra conceded, his head wobbling on his shoulders. 'It was wrong of me to put it like that. I meant, maybe' – he was hesitant – 'you *enjoyed* breaking it.' His voice dropped to a whisper. 'Could it be you liked to oppose God?'

'No, no, Rabbi,' Jesus burst out, his eyes full of compassion for his teacher who had forced himself to this. 'I *suffered* because of it and never more than now.'

'And you did not enjoy – ?'

'I did not oppose God. I am his servant, Rabbi. I bring him no profit but his servant.'

Ezra met Jesus's candid brown eyes. They were unflinching. There was not a shadow of deceit in him; no half-truth, not even the slightest dilution of truth, that undetectable drop of water in the wine.

The whisperers in this cross-eyed village had invented a second Jesus, a Jesus who never existed.

Ezra shook all over with remorse. How could he have spoken so to Jesus with his pine-straight soul? How foul his tongue by repeating vile rumours about him who had remembered his Creator from the days of his youth?

He reached out and touched Jesus's hand. Age and youth met, past and future, dried feather-light bone met smooth rich flesh. And their ageless hearts were one.

The tension between them was broken by the twittering of a bird. Jesus helped Ezra to his feet and they went to examine the net together. Ezra was hoping for a fat quail or a wood-pigeon.

It was a sparrow.

Gently, Jesus extricated it from the net.

'Its wings?' Ezra asked.

'Not broken.' Jesus was stroking the bird, calming it.

'Not a mouthful there,' Ezra said, in no mood for destroying things. 'What shall we do with it?'

The bird was quiet in Jesus's hands. 'Leave it to me,' he said. He kissed the top of the bird's head and, calling out with the joy of reconciliation, 'The poor man's dove, Rabbi,' he threw it on the wing.

As the bird climbed a jagged path to freedom, Jesus said, 'Peace be always between you and me, Rabbi.'

Ezra said, haltingly, 'I hope I did not hurt you, my son. Not too much?'

'Better a wound from a friend than a kiss from a foe.'

'Oh, I never intended to wound you,' Ezra said, tears falling down his black, ribbed cheeks. 'Take no notice of me. I'm just a bent old nail of a man.'

He opened his arms and pressed Jesus to him, sobbing like David for Absalom:

'My son, Jesus, my son. Oh, my son.'

Yet it was Ezra who felt like a child in the Man's strong arms.

Chapter 26

Quiet months followed. Ezra put the word round that Jesus was innocent of all charges made against him. Farmers deferred payments again. Children came for instruction in his workshop.

Jesus thought nothing more of the incident. It was his share in the pain of his village.

One day, when the winter's rains were diminishing, Shimon put his head in the workshop. 'A visitor, Jesus. He's at your house.'

Jesus went home to find that John, son of Zebedee, was being entertained by his mother. He embraced him warmly, congratulated him on having grown at least an inch since last they met.

John had brought the wages Simon owed Jesus. 'He apologises for the slight delay,' John said, handing over the money.

Jesus laughed. 'Thank him for me. How is he?'

'His wife died giving birth,' John said.

'The baby?'

'The baby, too. A boy it would have been.'

Mary, who had never met Simon or his wife, started to cry and Jesus said how sorry he was, deeply sorry.

'Simon sobbed for three days,' John said. 'It was like watching a rock slowly splitting down the middle.'

'May the God of all comfort comfort him,' Jesus said, 'and turn his mourning into joy.'

'He gave me a message for you.'

'Yes?'

'I don't understand it, he said you would. Made me repeat it a dozen times. Here goes: "Now that my beloved Timna has escaped my net, I am free to walk on water."'

Jesus smiled his gratitude for the warmth of the message and the confidence Simon had placed in him.

John was going by the roundabout route to Jerusalem. He had business to do there, negotiating a new contract to deliver fish to some of the bigger houses.

He stayed with Jesus and Mary for a week. He spent hours with Jesus in his workshop – 'his new apprentice', he called himself – travelled with him to the outlying hamlets. All the time, talking, asking questions.

Mary doted on him. 'He's such a nice boy,' she said. 'Like one of the family.'

When, finally, John tore himself away, Jesus said to him, 'Tell Simon I hold him, his wife and son in my heart. Also, that I am waiting.'

Before spring came, there was another far less welcome visitor to Nazareth.

Mary rushed into Jesus's workshop where he was making a yoke for a pair of oxen. 'Quickly,' she said. 'Anna is being thrown out.'

Jesus hurried to Anna's place. Ezra was outside it, cursing 'that locust of a landlord'.

The landlord was Laban, a Pharisee from Jerusalem, a stout man with huge convex eyes. He was watching his two servants throwing Anna's few possessions into the street.

Anna was screaming, 'I've a brother somewhere in the south, he'll help me.' She ran around the crowd that had gathered, reaching out hopelessly for a hand to defend her. 'Help me, someone, help me.'

Villagers stood around, stolid, silent apart from grimly talking to themselves.

'The day had to come ... These rich folk, they have it their own way ... No point in trying to stop it ...'

They had problems of their own.

As the Pharisee emerged from a brief inspection of the

152

vacated house, Jesus stepped in his path. 'Why are you doing this?'

'Isn't it obvious?' Laban said irritably. 'Would I be here if this woman hadn't consistently refused to pay her rent?'

'She has not refused, as you put it, she hasn't the means.'

Laban gave a quick, empty laugh. 'That's what they all say.'

'In her case, it is true. She is a widow. She has no one.'

'Then she's the fourth widow of that sort I've come across this week.'

'And you threw the other three out as well, I don't doubt.'

The Pharisee, smelling trouble, signalled to his two sturdy assistants. They stood on either side of him.

'Go on,' the landlord said, reinforced, 'make *me* out to be the culprit. The Book says we should pay what we owe.'

'It also says, God help those who wrong and oppress widows.'

'What *are* you talking about?' the landlord said over his shoulder, as he headed for his horse. 'Look at this lot.' He paused to indicate the crowd, with a scornful sweep of his hand. 'What have *they* done to help her? They left it to my good nature.'

'They, too, have suffered,' Jesus said.

'That widow,' the landlord said, 'has not paid one penny in two years.' He spoke louder, addressing the crowd. 'You should go on your knees and thank me for giving her free lodging for that long.'

He mounted his horse. With difficulty. He had a big belly. It was like a boy scrambling over a wall after stealing peaches.

Jesus snatched the horse's bridle, so that Laban raised his whip, expecting violence.

'I will pay.'

The landlord grinned, wolfishly. 'A promise?' Jesus nodded. 'One of my men will give you the document to sign. If you can't write your name, put a cross.'

Jesus nodded and let the bridle go.

Anna turned to Mary and sobbed on her shoulder.

153

'Mary, oh, Mary. Didn't I always say your sweet, darling first born is a lovely boy. He's the Messiah to me, oh he is.'

As he put his name to the parchment, Jesus resolved to work even harder in future.

That evening, his mother asked why he had done this for Anna.

'Never could turn down the request of a widow,' he grinned.

'Oh, good,' she said. 'Would you now eat your supper, then?'

Jesus's happy time continued. The countryside around Nazareth was as beautiful as ever, full of flowers and animals.

A new spring came, lambing time. Ezra suggested that the two of them should go to Jerusalem for Passover. He had friends outside the city, they could stay with them.

'It may be my last chance,' he pleaded, 'before the Lord cuts me off the loom.'

Jesus was afraid the Rabbi's health would not stand up to the journey but the Rabbi's Rib said, 'Let the fool go. If he dies there he'll be happy. We both will.'

Before sun-up they saddled the donkey and set off, thrilled at the prospect of travelling in spring across hills and vales and flower-strewn plains.

Ezra had no surplus baggage. He was equipped for nothing more perilous than death. He had a prayer-shawl and the little boxes he fixed to his arm and forehead.

They had not gone far downhill when the Rabbi turned to look back on the village where he had spent his entire life.

'How can people live anywhere else?' he sighed.

Jesus smiled. 'They manage.'

'Only because they have to,' Ezra said.

In spite of protests, Jesus lifted Ezra on to the donkey. 'Otherwise,' he said, 'we might make Passover next year but not this.'

For Ezra, it was a journey of thanksgiving to God for allowing him to be rabbi for so many years. Also, though he kept it a secret, it was a pilgrimage of atonement, for daring to question Jesus's integrity after he had returned from the Lake.

The first landmark was Mount Gilboa, a mere hill rising two hundred feet above the plain.

A peaceful spot, it was for ever consecrated by the memory of Jonathan, whom the Philistines slew there, and of Saul who, badly wounded by arrows, fell upon his sword. The Philistines had stripped Saul's corpse and cut off his head. They put his body on the wall of Bethshan from where some of his brave followers stole it and buried it at Jabesh in the shade of a tamarisk tree.

It was under a tamarisk-tree that Jesus and Ezra sat and recited together David's famous lament:

> Slain, O Israel, is thy glory on these heights,
> Thy mighty are fallen.
> Tell it not in Gath,
> Nor proclaim it in the streets of Ashkelon ...
> Ye mountains of Gilboa, may there be no rain,
> Nor any dew on you for ever more ...
> O Saul and Jonathan, my beloved and so lovely.
> In life and in death they were inseparable...
> My heart is breaking for you, my brother Jonathan;
> Oh, the joy you gave me.
> More marvellous to me has your love been
> Than all the love of women.

They ate and journeyed on, south to Samaria, once the royal capital of Israel, the northern kingdom. They felt uncomfortable in this land of schism.

Jesus could remember how, as a boy of twelve, he had made his first pilgrimage to Jerusalem. The talk then was of how some Samaritans had sprinkled dead men's bones in the Temple court, defiling it. The deed was done at midnight during the Feast of Passover. What outrage that senseless act had caused.

They hurried through the beautiful pass between Ginaea and Shechem, hurried even past the glorious sanctuaries of Shiloh and Bethel. In defiance, they chanted a Song of Ascents so loudly that the hills rang with it.

My heart sang for joy when they said to me,
'Let us go to God's House'.
These feet of ours are standing
At your gates, O Jerusalem!

It was to Jerusalem not to Mount Gerizim that all the tribes of Israel still went up.

Ezra was coping well with the journey, so was the cross-eyed beast that carried him.

They camped out under the stars in a mild, sweet-smelling spring. Some days they travelled over fifteen miles from well to well. They had to reach Jerusalem by 8th Nisan if they were to participate in the whole week of the festival.

Nearer the capital, the landscape changed dramatically. The mountains towered above them, the valleys narrowed. Water was scarce and the soil was stony. Shades of green gave way to browns and purples.

They camped on the final night with a host of pilgrims in a dark, narrow valley. A stream came out of a rock bank that was pitted with tombs.

Excitement was in the air. Men talked in gravelly voices around camp-fires till late and the children could not get to sleep. Neither could Ezra. Many times had he made this pilgrimage and still he was as keen as any lad at the prospect of revisiting the city he loved.

All the pilgrims were up before the sun, their donkeys loaded, awaiting the signal to begin.

Then, at the sound of a tuneless bugle, they gave a loud cheer and were off, jostling each other merrily, making light of the rugged paths and daunting slopes before them. They sang as they went.

I lift up my eyes to the hills.
From where does help come?
It comes from the Lord
Who made heaven and earth.

In a short while, there – suddenly – high, very high on a hill, was Jerusalem.

Ezra, *both* eyes shining, swung down from the donkey,

noisily sucked in air as if it were the most delicious honeycomb, and, throwing his arms wide, kissed Jesus on both cheeks.

'Peace be with you, my son.'

And Jesus said, 'Peace.'

Chapter 27

Their peace was soon marred. At a bend in the road, the pilgrims came to a silent halt. Men seethed, most women cried, children gaped.

In front of them, on the first straight stretch of road after the junction with the road from the sea, were two lines of what looked like dead and leafless trees. The trees in this avenue of fear, planted at intervals of twenty-five yards, soared upwards for a mile.

This was a warning from the Romans. Any Jew who misbehaved during the festival would carry his own cross beam and be crucified here on any one of a hundred sites.

Each of the pilgrims could see it with the inward eye, even the children. A Jew like them, stripped like a slave, clad only in the oldest garment of the race, rope-readied for a slow and dirty death. Then lifted up in a disgrace most hurtful for being most public, in which the victim is able to savour his own humiliation mirrored in the faces of the watchers. The very manner of the death – a Roman death – a proof that the Jew had nothing left him in his own land, not even the right to be executed in his own Jewish way.

The pilgrims stirred themselves, but hardly had the procession recommenced when there were sounds of commotion in their rear. A large contingent of soldiers was marching towards the city on the coastal road from Caesarea.

An advance party was pressing the pilgrims to move to the side of the road. The Procurator was approaching.

Jesus pulled Ezra up and they took their stand on a hillock under a 'tree'. From there, they had a good view of Pontius Pilate as he rode by, surrounded by soldiers, on a superb black stallion. He was on his way to the fortress of Antonia in Jerusalem from where he would keep an eye on the city throughout the festival.

Pilate's dedication to himself could not be faulted. He hated his enemies as duty demanded and his friends by personal preference. Compassion was a weakness of which he was guiltless.

He sat his steed well. The cold, disinterested set of his head was a sign of the contempt in which he held the race he ruled – a nation born for slavery, as old Cicero had put it. Not the job, not the air he breathed was worthy of him.

He had seen a Jew once, he jokingly told an acquaintance in Rome when he was last home on leave, and there was no point or pleasure to be had from seeing another. They were, to a man, garbage.

The Procurator had a square head, on which was pressed a light ceremonial helmet. His nose was fleshily prominent, his skin sallow, and he had a square, black, droopy jaw. A soldier of no distinction, an administrator devoid of diplomatic sense, he was frozen in provincial boredom.

Every line of his body showed the humiliation he felt at having to rule this universally odious people. He had set his heart on Gaul; if not Gaul, then at least Syria. Instead, he had landed Judaea. Even the capital, Jerusalem, was located in the most preposterous place. It had no water to speak of, no irrigation system; it wasn't even on the main highway to important places like Egypt or Damascus. It was far too easy to lay siege to, as Pompey discovered, and to starve out. Only a military leader with no strategic sense could have chosen it as his chief city. The perfect dream capital of a nation of dreamers. A madman's folly hailed by the local madmen as the most sacred spot on earth.

By day, there was no respite to Pilate's misery.

Nothing ever happened in Judaea. You would not get in the history books by ruling Judaea. Decisions about destiny were taken in the Senate, in the imperial court. Here, what was there here? Sedition, pettiness of mind, sectarianism, hatred of the human race, a people without art – art was a 'sin' – without science, sculpture, learning of any sort, a people too proud and stupid to subject themselves to the improvement of Roman law. Most ironically of all, a people who had contempt for *him*.

No wonder that, at night, he turned nostalgically in his mind to the columns, baths, forum, palaces, vineyards of Rome, to the sparkling talk of the men and commerce with gracious women.

On today's march, Pilate was particularly riled. Not only was he sorry to be leaving behind the beaches of Caesarea, he was going to Jerusalem without his military insignia. He had agreed to dispense with his standards and cover up the silver busts of the Emperor on his ensigns.

It had come about like this.

A group of Jewish elders had recently been to Caesarea to seek an audience with him. His soldiers, they whined, were bearing banners with 'graven images' on them, through the capital. Was Pilate annoyed! He had rounded them up and ordered his men to advance on them with naked swords. Instead of begging for mercy, these old fanatics had actually bowed their heads and taunted the legionaries with, 'Strike us down. But take your graven images out of our city.'

He had called his soldiers off. He had no scruples about killing Jews, but he refused to grant them the satisfaction of dying on their own terms, in their ferocious and frivolous lust for martyrdom. As if their lives were worth *anything*. Imagine, corrupt old men thinking themselves incorruptible!

And why were they literally dead-set against images? They did not allow images of their god. Not even in their Temple. Herod had built them this fantastic Temple, better than any in Rome itself, and the priests wouldn't allow anything in it. You couldn't get much crazier than that.

159

They were atheists, their god was a nothing. Whoever heard of a god who could not be seen or heard or touched?

The Emperor, in his generosity, had offered to house their god – such as it was – in the pantheon with the gods of all other defeated peoples. They had refused. Their god, they said, is not a scarecrow in a cucumber field. We can't pick him up and put him down. They would die first, they said. By Jove, Pilate said ruefully to himself, even a real god is not worth taking as seriously as that!

The real trouble with these Jews, he concluded, was they *thought* too much. They were a nation of thinkers. Now, he was a soldier. He did not like *thought*, even in wise men, very much; but thought in the rabble ... Discipline, order, success in war, depended on not thinking, on letting not-thinking become the source of doing, the well-spring of doing. Thought among the masses destroys armies, ravages civilisation. As if every petty, talentless person, race or nation were free to think its own despicable little thoughts ...

Ah, the crosses had been put up, *as ordered*. It gave him a comfortable feeling to see them. A whole legion of crosses. They will put the fear of the gods of the Romans into even Jewish hearts.

But see the wretches grovel, though. Strange, uncanny almost, in spite of their thoughts and their 'beliefs', they always bowed whenever he passed.

They bowed in fear or awe or hatred, or because they were a peasant people who instinctively made obeisance to those above them, or so they could whisper better into each other's ears without detection obscenities about the Roman governor.

But, whatever the motive, bow they did. Like grass before the wind.

He did not turn his head to right or left, on principle, but out of the corners of his eyes he could see them bowing today as always.

Except ... One Jew, damn him, was *not* bowing. The local idiot? There, on that hill. A young man, is he not? Upright, next to that vertical beam.

Setting aside his principle, as he drew near the young

man Pilate turned his head. It was momentary, like a shadow flitting over the sun. Good. Had he seen rebelliousness on that atheist's face, even a glimmer, he would – such was his mood – have had him crucified on the spot.

But there was none. That Jew would never know how fortunate he was. There was a strange look on the fellow's face. Not rebelliousness, or fear, or hatred, or awe. What was it? He couldn't place it. Why bother?

Pilate rode on.

Jesus looked at Pilate. No wonder Pilate did not recognise what he saw on the young man's face. He had never seen it before. It was love.

Jesus loved him and pitied him his wearisome isolation, his ridiculous pride. And in his love and pity, Pilate was transformed into his beloved Ezra. It was Ezra riding by, not a tyrant, not a military murderer. Only a man who needed saving. Like all men.

As soon as Pilate and his retinue had passed, the pilgrims bubbled over. They were furious yet secretly elated at having seen the Procurator in the flesh.

Ezra, sensing the mood, sat astride the donkey. He might have been reading Jesus's thoughts. For he rode upright, imperious, his head leaning neither to right nor to left.

'Bow down,' he squawked, in an effort to make himself heard. He nudged his donkey into jerky motion. 'Bow down before Pontius Pilate, your beloved Procurator of Judaea.'

Several men bowed in mockery and took up the refrain, 'Pilate, Pontius Pilate'. The rest roared their acclamation, laughing and shouting their delight at this ragged little rabbi who was aping Satan himself.

In this way, they hoped to forget their misery and the sight of all those crosses.

But in Jesus's mind, Pilate was Ezra; Ezra was Pilate. Yes, he told himself, Ezra and Pilate are *one*.

Chapter 28

Jerusalem. City of multicoloured limestone: white, honey-hued, gold, yellow, grey-green. Surrounded by tier upon tier of olive-groves.

Narrow, smelly, bustling streets, stalked by lean cats and mangy dogs with mad-looking eyes. The houses leaned on one another like old women chatting; the courtyards tiny and hidden, too shadowed for trees or shrubs or flowers to flourish there.

Everywhere beggars. Unlike the beggars at home. These were professionals. They were vicious, haughty, clamorous. They begged not in order to survive but as a means of making a lucrative living. Those with sores displayed them like trophies. They were as proud of their wounds as if they had inflicted them on themselves for this very purpose. In speech, they were almost as eloquent as rabbis.

Ezra was not to be browbeaten. Instead of giving alms, he demanded alms from them. He went on and on, in his loud crow's voice, until they were scared he would drive their custom away.

One of them, supposedly blind, pressed a coin into Ezra's hand, with, 'Now get going, old man, and for God's sake leave us in peace.'

Jesus persuaded Ezra to continue. They went on, overcome by the scale of everything. The city, only one square mile in size, seemed to them an endless warren of ways and byways in which to get lost. They held on tightly to each other.

From the northern gate they picked their way past open-air stalls and crowds busily buying anything from a horse to a cucumber, past men arguing, gesturing and slapping hands to conclude a bargain, until they found their way into the grounds of the Temple.

Immediately, Ezra went on his knees, kissed the paving and said, *This is my resting place for ever. Here will I dwell. For here and nowhere else is my heart's desire.*

Jesus stooped to lift him up but there was no need; and they went exploring.

The enclosure rose northward, court upon court, shored up by underground arches and edged by deep, cool colonnades. Around the central shrine was a cloister of sacred buildings and, crowning the summit, the Holy of Holies. It stood on Mount Moriah, part of the threshing-floor King David had purchased for fifty shekels of silver. The Temple rose majestically above the valley floor, a marble and limestone mountain topped by the gold of the sanctuary now shining in the sun.

A group of pilgrims filed past, led by a Levite in brocaded robes. They were chanting a psalm and their singing impressed by its innocence. Jesus and Ezra paused to listen:

> *Thy dwelling-place, O Lord of Hosts,*
> *How beautiful, how beautiful.*
> *The deepest longing of my soul*
> *Is for thy gracious courts, O Lord.*
> *My heart, my flesh must sing for joy*
> *To God, my God, the living God.*

'I,' Ezra said, sighing, 'would like to live here for ever.'

'Tut, tut,' Jesus said. 'What about that loyalty to Nazareth?'

'You could look after it for me. For a while?'

Ezra took Jesus by the arm and led him to the Court of the Gentiles. It was more like a market than a place of prayer. The Levites had set up stalls for the sale of flour, wine, oil and incense. Vast numbers of sheep were allowed to mingle with the worshippers.

'I want you,' Ezra said, 'to see a wonderful Pharisee. He eats nothing but bread and salt, drinks only water and sleeps on the ground.'

Jesus followed apprehensively. He had been brought

163

up by his mother and father to believe that life is meant to be enjoyed. 'Why insult God,' his mother used to say, 'by making yourself miserable when there is no need? Rejoice, rejoice in the Lord.'

'There,' Ezra said. 'The Rabbi Samuel.'

Seated in the shade of the portico where swallows nested and pigeons cooed, surrounded by a dozen or so pilgrims was a crumpled-looking little man. Only five feet in height, the Rabbi seemed even smaller as he crouched slightly hunchbacked, against a pillar. His tunic was a sack, green, once black. He wore no sandals. His round face was the colour of clay but his most striking feature was his eyes. They were round and mellow like a seal's.

Jesus and Ezra were enthralled by his teaching. He spoke of God's love for Israel and for all mankind. He spoke of obedience to God's will. They nudged each other when he repeated what Hillel had said to a prospective convert: The whole law is contained in, 'Do not unto others what you would hate them to do unto you.'

Jesus grinned. 'I've heard that somewhere before.'

Ezra shook his head and whispered back. 'Not from the mouth of the convert himself.'

So this was the man to whom Rabbi Hillel had originally said that wonderful thing: Rabbi Samuel.

Someone asked Samuel about the traditions which had grown up over the years, so many of them stifling. 'What should be our attitude to them?'

Rabbi Samuel held up his bony hands in mock horror. 'Who am I to tell you, my friend, what your attitude should be to anything? Am I the blessed God that I can see into your heart?'

'But, Rabbi,' the pilgrim insisted, 'it is hard to find God sometimes, with so many rules to keep.'

The Rabbi cocked his head. 'Go on.'

'Our Rabbi says we mustn't even kill fleas on the Sabbath.'

Someone else said, 'Ours lets us squeeze fleas. Gently.' Another said, 'Ours says we can nip the legs off them and that helps.'

Rabbi Samuel smiled and said:

'Listen, my brothers. There was once a beautiful green meadow in which' – he paused to put his arm round a stray sheep – 'a flock of sheep just like this one here used to graze. They were so happy there, this flock of sheep. But the shepherd – he was such a fine shepherd – was afraid for the safety of his flock. Wolves might come from the hills, he thought, devour the sheep and what would my master say to me then? So, being a good shepherd, he built a hedge round the green meadow, a fine stout hedge it was, too. The wolves tried hard but they couldn't squeeze through. *But* the occasional fox and badger did. The shepherd was very upset, he so loved his sheep, as well as feared his master, which goes without saying. The shepherd said to himself, I've got to reinforce my hedge. So he planted a thicker hedge and, my, how it grew. Still this fine shepherd was concerned for his flock. I *do* want them to graze in safety, he said. So he planted a hedge inside the hedge. The following year, another hedge inside that. Marvellous hedges, I can tell you, the best in all the land. People used to come for miles around and just stand in front of them crying, What wonderful hedges! Not a wolf or a fox or a badger was able to get anywhere near a sheep or a lamb of his. They were safe at last, and so was he. The only thing was, my brothers, the hedges now filled the meadow. It was, you might say, a meadow of hedges. And the sheep, in perfect safety ... starved.'

Everybody laughed and Ezra slapped Jesus on the back. 'What do you think of him, then?'

Jesus was thinking, If only I could teach as simply and as memorably as that!

When the laughter had finished, the original questioner said, 'So, Rabbi, we *can* kill fleas on the Sabbath, after all?'

Once more, those bony hands were raised. 'Am I the blessed God, brother, that I can see into your heart?'

He patted the sheep which had stayed beside him throughout his story and sent it on its way to nuzzle someone else.

Before another question could be put, more money-changers arrived. Passover was their busiest time of the year.

'Move on, old fellow,' one of them said, officiously. 'We've got work to do.'

Their work was to change ordinary 'secular' coins into the half-shekel silver coins, the only legal tender in the Temple.

As they started putting up their tables, Samuel sprang to his feet with surprising agility. He blessed the money-changers and moved on to somewhere quieter. A small crowd followed him, including several children.

The Rabbi put a purse at his feet. A boy of about eight, with long curly earlocks and thick pouty lips, thinking it was a begging purse, dropped a coin in it. The original instinct of the race: to give to someone in need.

The Rabbi noticed and was delighted. But when he picked the purse up there was no bottom to it. Underneath it was the coin. He handed it back to the lad.

'God bless you, my son,' he said. 'Look how quickly God has given you back the money you loaned him.'

The boy was confused. 'But, Rabbi, your purse holds nothing.'

'On the contrary, my son, it holds *everything*. However much you put in it, there is always room for more. This purse' – he held it up – 'holds all the riches of the world.'

The boy, won over, accepted the Rabbi's invitation to sit next to him.

'My lucky day,' the Rabbi sang. 'First a sheep and now a spring lamb.'

'Our Rabbi at home,' the boy said, 'wears long, flowing robes.'

'Does he, now?' Samuel said wide-eyed. 'Maybe he couldn't find a sack to fit him.'

'Mamma says he could hide the summer's harvest underneath his robe.'

The growing crowd laughed but in a restrained way so as not to discourage the boy.

'Our Rabbi wears amulets, too, around here' – the lad touched his forehead. 'Why don't you?'

'Oh,' Samuel said, 'I wear mine on the inside of my forehead, where only God can see them.'

'Why not let *me* see them?'

166

'Because,' Samuel said, conspiratorially, 'you *might* think I was a holy man when I'm not, you see.'

'I think you're a holy man,' the boy said, graciously.

Samuel's face shone. 'I am flattered, my son. So I didn't need to wear an amulet, after all. I saved myself some money.'

'But you don't have any money.'

'Would you like to hear a story?'

Of course he would.

'Well, my son, it's all about a little fox. We'll call him Sammy.'

'After you, Rabbi?'

'I never thought of that, but yes, after me. In fact, Sammy the fox was as skinny as I am. Very hungry, too. One day, Sammy came across a beautiful vineyard. Sad to say, it had a high wall around it. However hard he tried to jump over the wall or scramble over it he just couldn't manage it. And, oh, he did so like the look of those delicious grapes.'

'Wasn't there a hole in the wall?' asked the boy. 'There usually is.'

'You should have been a fox,' Samuel said. 'That's exactly what Sammy thought. He looked and he looked until he found a hole.'

'I told you,' the boy said.

'But I'm afraid it was only a narrow hole and he was too fat to get through. So he went without food for three days. Still he couldn't make it. He fasted like it was the Day of Atonement another three days. Until he was just skinny enough to squeeze his way through. And did Sammy eat.'

'He needed to,' the boy said.

'Yes, he did. He gorged himself on one big bunch of grapes after another. Soon his belly was bigger than the fattest belly you ever saw.'

One or two fat men in the crowd went red.

'But now,' Samuel said, 'the fox had a problem – '

'He couldn't get out again,' the boy said, squirming with the fun of it.

'My goodness, you are *sharp*,' Samuel said, congratulating him. 'You are bound to be a rabbi yourself some day. Correct, the fox could not get out. So what did he do?'

'Stopped eating.'

Samuel paused. 'You have heard it before.'

The boy giggled at the implied praise.

'Yes,' Samuel went on, with mock sadness, 'the fox had to go without for several days. Until he was skinny enough to squeeze through the hole again. And outside the wall, he said to himself, What a waste of time. I gorged myself and gorged myself. And at the end I'm just as skinny and hungry as when I started.'

The boy smiled his pleasure at the outcome of the story.

'So you see, my son. This Sammy here is old now. I squeezed my way into life at the beginning. Soon I'm going to have to squeeze my way out. I will only be able to take out what I brought in.'

'Nothing, Rabbi?'

The Rabbi held up his little purse with a hole in. 'Nothing,' he said.

Samuel taught for another hour, then, one by one or in family groups, the pilgrims went up to him, whispered in his ear, seeking advice or consolation. He had a smile and a blessing for everyone. Children especially came away from him with shining faces.

At length, only Jesus and Ezra were left. Ezra said, 'My turn.' He knelt shakily in front of Samuel and begged his blessing.

Jesus overheard Samuel say, 'I know you, brother. You are from, let me see, Nazareth.'

'I am Rabbi there.' Ezra beat his breast, causing the dust to fly and doves to look for a quieter place. 'May God be merciful.'

'I remember,' Samuel said, his voice more husky now. 'You and I are grown old together, friend. Between us it is a close race to God, isn't that so?'

He agreed to bless Ezra, provided Ezra blessed him in his turn.

Jesus was deeply moved as he watched these two old men bless and embrace each other. They stood for everything that was best in his religion, something that

168

had never been wholly lost, nor ever could be.

Samuel finally released Ezra and helped him up.

Jesus, last – where, he said jokingly, there is never a scramble for places – stepped forward. He knelt in front of Samuel and bowed his head. 'Rabbi, your blessing upon me.'

Rabbi Samuel drew back, startled. His round, watery eyes were a mixture of awe and terror. He shook all over.

Jesus said again, 'Rabbi, please, I ask your blessing.'

Samuel turned his head away, almost savagely. He stumbled to his feet, bowed and scuttled off like a frightened rabbit.

Ezra joined Jesus who had remained rooted to the spot.

'Why did he leave in such a hurry?' Ezra said. 'In forty years I have never known him withhold his blessing.'

'I do not understand,' Jesus murmured.

Ezra was perturbed. 'He is the holiest, my son. Search your heart. Is there a flaw in you that I have missed?'

Chapter 29

Ezra's friends lived in Bethany, a hamlet surrounded by date-palms. Lazarus, a delicate young man, was the head of a household that consisted of himself and his two sisters, Martha and Mary. They welcomed Ezra and Jesus with open hearts.

Lazarus was thin, consumptive. He coughed a lot, especially at night; sometimes he found it hard to breathe.

Martha, by contrast, was the picture of health, sturdy without being obese, tidy, matter-of-fact, industrious, a fast-mover.

Mary, two years younger at fifteen, was shy, introspective, with black searching eyes as big as plates.

169

She did not say much – she spoke with a slight lisp – preferring to observe and listen. When she herself was looked at by strangers, her eyelids fluttered like the wings of baby birds.

Jesus soon decided that the girls complemented each other beautifully. Martha was concerned with people's needs; Mary with people. Different people would, therefore, react differently to each of them. Sometimes, it would depend on whether you were hungry or not. Jesus appreciated Martha at present because he was famished!

Ezra had known the parents; he had seen the children grow up over the years and deeply loved all three. They owned a few fields on which they grazed sheep and grew the fruit and vegetables they needed. They were comfortably off.

The house was a good house, Jesus noticed. Like all houses, it took on the character of those who lived in it. It had inner space, peace with vitality, companionship with solitude. Had no one been in when he entered, he might have guessed at the kind of people who lived there.

Martha bustled about, preparing the meal. From time to time, she thrust a dish or a plate in Mary's hand. It took Mary some time to work out what this strange thing was, then she put it down where she imagined Martha wanted it to be. Minutes later, Martha reappeared and put it where it *should* be.

Ezra was telling Lazarus of the years of locust and drought in Nazareth. He followed this up with a hilarious account of their journey to Jerusalem.

Jesus was mostly quiet, except when he was called on to confirm what Ezra said or added a detail or two of his own. He was aware that Mary was watching him out of the corner of her eyes. He could tell she had taken a liking to him. Young people, he was discovering, were most in tune with him, best understood him. But then, the young are like the poor in having little or nothing to lose. They can afford to take risks.

Next morning, while Ezra rested, Jesus and Mary walked together to Jerusalem to catch the sunrise.

She led him first to a fragrant garden on the western slope of Mount Olivet called Gethsemane. In the garden were young olive-trees, as well as almond-trees covered with pink blossom, and a host of wild flowers.

Cocks were setting up a chorus from Mount Scopus in the north to Mount Ophel in the south. Ophel, the original Jerusalem, was but a wasteland of scrub and scruffy pines. Somewhere out of sight was the spring of Gihon. A thousand years before, David's men had climbed up the shaft of the watercourse to take the city and install the Ark containing the tablets of the Law. Near to it was Siloam, whose waters softly flow.

Swifts were already cutting the air, darting down into the Kidron valley over the tombs and up above the eastern wall.

After praying for a while, they climbed higher up Olivet for a better view of the city.

As soon as the sun cleared Olivet, a priest stood on the eighty-foot-high pinnacle of the Temple to their left and cried: 'Is the sky lit up as far as Hebron?' To which a Levite chanted the response: 'It is lit up.' A blast of silver trumpets announced that the day's first sacrifice could be offered on the altar of burnt offerings. The blast was magical, it seemed to bring the walls of darkness tumbling down.

The sun, like a benediction, was above the rim of the Mount they were on, gilding the far side of the city. Bright rays speared the triple-towered fortress of Antonia, where Pilate was installed, with its pools, statues and dove-filled arbours and trees. Not long after that, the sun touched the white and gold mass of the Temple and the near eastern wall, and sunrise was complete.

Jesus and Mary stood in silence, almost touching but hardly aware of it.

Jesus was thinking how much this city had suffered over the ages. The irony was that a heathen, Herod the Great, had begun rebuilding the present Temple over forty years ago. He had modelled it on Solomon's. He had even trained a thousand Levites as masons and carpenters so that consecrated hands could finish the

171

Holy of Holies within eighteen months.

'What are you thinking?' Mary asked him shyly.

He told her his thoughts on Herod.

'I've often wondered about that myself,' she said. 'God uses the strangest instruments to achieve his purposes.'

'He does, Mary,' Jesus said. 'He really does.'

Ezra and Jesus went to all the Temple ceremonies. Ezra, conscious that this was his last Passover in the Holy City, was keen not to miss a thing.

One evening, they went up to the Temple to pray. Ezra's old face was a sight to behold at the privilege of praying in this hallowed place.

The ceremony was very long. Afterwards, the assembly filed out exhausted. Jesus, tired too and with a slight headache, waited patiently beside the boundlessly energetic Ezra. The Temple was almost empty.

Ezra suddenly took Jesus's arm in a painful grip. 'Look who's here,' he hissed.

Walking up the very centre was Laban, the Pharisee who had tried to evict Anna. No doubt about it. Jesus could hardly mistake that proud walk, that arrogant way of holding the head.

Laban stood out front, facing the Holy of Holies. His head was partly veiled by his prayer-shawl; he was wearing all the usual frills and phylacteries. He was well prepared for the ritual flattery to come.

Laban prayed aloud in a hoarse whisper that carried like a trumpet-blast, bowing and scraping.

Ezra moved to get a better view of this phenomenon. 'Look at that belly-ache face,' he said softly.

'Mayest thou be praised, O God eternal,' the Pharisee sighed breathlessly, 'who hast made me holy among sinners and set me apart from the rest of men like the tax-gatherer behind me.'

Jesus turned away from this grey dribble of words, knowing by a kind of instinct he would recognise the man referred to. Yes, it was Levi, his friend from Capernaum!

Levi had stationed himself as far from the altar as he

172

could, as if he were not worthy to be in the Temple at all. Not once while Jesus watched did he lift his head or his eyes towards heaven where God dwelt. He was a man who had come for only one thing: to beg forgiveness.

'I fast twice a week on Sundays and Thursdays,' the Pharisee went on, in a high-pitched, mosquito-like whine, the professional holy man, counterpart of the professional beggars who littered the streets. 'I give tithes of all I possess. I tithe the things that have been tithed already so as to give you, God, the service you deserve.'

Ezra was biting his nails in wonderment at this spectacular show of humility. The Pharisee had done his best to pretend he was imperfect but had failed dismally. Ezra would never have suspected that he led so unblemished a life.

Ezra winked at Jesus and they left, waiting at the bottom of the sanctuary steps.

'That hypocrite won't be long,' Ezra predicted. 'Not now his audience has gone.'

Sure enough, within seconds, down the steps tripped Laban. Ezra surprised Jesus again by going to meet him.

'Good sir,' he said, bowing reverently, 'I could not help noticing you at your prayers.'

'Is that so, old man?' the Pharisee said, removing his prayer-shawl. His fat face was bursting with contentment, his little black eyes were shining like the tops of new nails that have been banged in too far.

'Did I hear you say you tithe *everything*?'

'You *heard* me? Oh dear. I am so sorry. I did not realise . . .'

'*Everything?*' Ezra repeated.

'Of *course*,' the Pharisee said. 'But I am sure you do, too.'

'Your prayers,' Ezra said sweetly, 'are as crooked as rams' horns.'

'I beg your pardon,' Laban spluttered, 'did I hear . . . ?'

'You *heard*,' Ezra said. 'You open your mouth wide in the Temple so you can better swallow widows' houses.'

The words 'widows' houses' gave Laban the clue to where he had seen these people before.

'You are a crazy old man,' he said viciously. 'Leave me.'

He walked briskly away but not so briskly that Ezra was left behind.

'Don't you know,' Ezra called out for all the passers-by to hear, 'that landlords who are deaf to the poor are praying to a deaf God?'

'I'll shout in a minute,' Laban said, shouting. 'Be *silent* before I shake you like a bloody melon till the pips pop out.'

'How do you manage to hide your heart from the vultures, tell me that, eh?'

Jesus caught Ezra up, intending to soothe him. But now that the Pharisee had vanished, so had Ezra's scorn. He was muttering, 'God go with you, my friend, my brother Pharisee.'

Not for the first time, Jesus marvelled at the spiritual somersaults of which his teacher was capable.

'I am happy to repent of what I said,' Ezra remarked, cheerfully, 'but I would not be so happy if I had not said it.'

Repentance, he assumed, is only as sweet as the sin you repent of.

Jesus waited half an hour for Levi to come out of the Temple before giving up. Ezra was tired and hungry. He had to take him back to Bethany.

Chapter 30

Jesus was standing alone on his favourite spot, the Garden of Gethsemane. Prayer, he found, was easier there than in the Temple itself. Afterwards, according to a pattern, he climbed Olivet from where it seemed he could stretch out his hand across the Kidron valley and touch the honey-coloured walls of Jerusalem.

The festival was over. He had enjoyed it, especially the Passover meal, held in a hired room in the city, with Lazarus and his friends. Tomorrow, he was taking Ezra home to Nazareth.

It was a moment to take stock.

> *Thy dwelling place, O Lord of hosts,*
> *How beautiful, how beautiful.*

The words sprang to his lips, as did others equally dear, as he looked at this great walled city encircled by hills.

> *Those who put their trust in God are like Mount Zion*
> *That stands unshakable for ever.*
> *Like the mountains around Jerusalem*
> *So stands the Lord around his people*
> *Shielding them.*

In his mind's eye, he saw the Temple rising and falling like a tide. Rising first in Solomon's time in gold and glory. Falling under Nebuchadnezzar when King Zedekiah, his eyes put out, was sent in bonds to Babylon. Rising again when the remnant returned from exile, but so ordinary was that Temple the people groaned, remembering the graciousness of Solomon's. Falling again when, after a horrendous siege, Pompey marched in, slaughtering the priests as they went on sacrificing to the end. Rising again under the Idumean Arab, Herod. This Temple was his, its limestone rock hewn into huge and seemingly everlasting blocks. Yes, it *was* beautiful.

For all that, Jesus could not hide from himself the doubts that were forming, unbidden, within him. He had changed. He did not react as he had reacted when he first saw it as a twelve-year-old.

Uncle Zechariah, a priest of the House of Abijah, had shown Jesus and his own son, John, around the entire sanctuary. Jesus was so proud that day; he was, at *last*, a fully-fledged Jew.

He could remember still the smell of incense and animal blood; there was dust in the air from unfinished projects. Never before had he seen buildings of gold and

175

marble, and they made his spirit soar.

Now he was beginning to feel as he had felt in the synagogue in Capernaum. The building was dictating to the human soul and burdening it; the sense of the holy was in danger of taking second place to a cheap thrill at the grandeur of mere monuments.

It was typified in the Pharisee's meaningless pageant of prayer and Rabbi Samuel, a saint of God, being moved on by money-changers!

From the heights of Olivet, Jesus peered down into the valley. Over the ages, how much blood had flown down into it from the channel in the altar of sacrifice. The stench of blood and burning flesh, the squeals and bleats of a thousand animals, the clouds of flies, the sheer questionableness of it all, worried him deeply. Was God really pleased with animal sacrifice? With the prescribed and presumably well-paid ritual of Levites plucking harps and clashing cymbals?

He was struck by the ultimate irony of the Temple. Not that a pagan had built it. But that the Holy of Holies, the holiest spot in this holy land, was a bare, dark room. There God dwelt in silence, inscrutable and unseen. In a flash of genius, someone had grasped that the God of nomads, the God who had lived in the dark of a storm-cloud, was most 'at ease' behind a thick curtain in a dark and empty chamber. At the heart of Israel, there was a sacred hollow, a holy void, a nothingness where God, the creator of everything, had his home. No place so suited him; nowhere was his glory more eloquently proclaimed.

Jesus wanted to see Jerusalem changed. Not destroyed, as Nebuchadnezzar and Pompey had destroyed it. But transformed, purified, fulfilled. Jerusalem and all Israel had suffered far too much in keeping God's name alive for anything to be destroyed.

One last thought weighed on him. When his long wait was over, when God said to him, 'The time is *now*,' he would have to go into this city, not as a warrior, not even as a pilgrim, but as . . . a quiet, ruthless challenger. As one who must, in God's name, fulfil his own and his people's destiny.

*

176

He had only an hour left to buy provisions for the next day's journey.

He was in the market, picking up salt meat, dried fruit, a few flagons of wine, when a stranger took him firmly by the arm.

'You are paying far too much.'

The stranger was about twenty-two, handsome, with curly hair escaping his mantle in all directions and bright, fierce intelligent eyes that sparkled with mischief and good humour.

'I am?' Jesus said.

'Don't you know, man, when you're being cheated?'

'Not always. It is a fault in me, I know.'

'Come, I'll help you find your way around.'

The young man took him in tow and made sure that none of the stall-holders swindled this quiet, simple provincial.

Afterwards, Jesus thanked him and asked him what he could do for him in return.

'Learn a bit of sense in future,' the stranger laughed, 'and I'll be satisfied.'

Jesus was charmed by the young man's outgoing personality and generous nature. He chatted with him for several minutes.

'I was in the Temple the other day,' the stranger admitted. 'I saw your rabbi friend send that old hypocrite packing with a flea in his ear. It was great!'

It came out that the young man was himself training to be a scribe. He, too, was in the Pharisaic tradition like most scribes. He hated war, all forms of violence, any idea of national aggrandisement. He believed that God was the God of all mankind and of every individual soul. He believed God's Law was paramount and he loved it, or tried to, with all his heart. When the Messiah came, God would use the Law alone to drive the Romans from their land. Then and only then would Israel be worth saving.

All this came out in a torrent within a few minutes and Jesus's heart glowed as he listened to him.

The young man had a beautiful smile and Jesus envied him his learning, his poise, his drive, his cleverness.

Once the young man recognised in Jesus a kindred

soul, he said, 'How I would like to do one great thing for God in my lifetime, something to be remembered by.'

'What sort of thing?'

'Anything. So long as it is huge and heroic.'

It was youth speaking and Jesus found his enthusiasm infectious.

'Where are you from, by the way?' Jesus said, as they were about to part.

'Me?' the young man said. 'I'm from the far south, a day's journey even beyond Hebron.'

'I'm from Galilee. Nazareth, to be precise.'

'As if I didn't know,' the stranger said, with a big, friendly smile. 'You're out of your depth in this wicked place. Why do you think I helped you out?'

'I'm most grateful,' Jesus said.

'Northerner and southerner, opposite extremes. We're worlds apart, wouldn't you say?'

Jesus did not agree. He felt this meeting, apparently so fortuitous, might be providential. He thought, What if, when my waiting is over, this young man were to help me fulfil my destiny?

He took in a final warm embrace the arm of this stranger who was a stranger no longer. It was as if Jesus had always known him.

He said, 'I'm Jesus.'

The young man gripped Jesus equally firmly. 'Judas Iscariot,' he said.

Chapter 31

Two years of routine passed. Two years more of working, praying, waiting.

From Jerusalem came ugly stories. The Procurator was insulting the people of Judaea at every opportunity. Once more, his legionaries were parading the city

178

bearing banners with the Imperial Eagle on; they had plundered stones, meant for the Temple, to build an aqueduct. The crucifixion of objectors was now a common sight on every highway.

There were stories too of happenings down by the Jordan River. On the harsh desert approach, among the reeds and scrub, an awesome hermit had appeared, protesting against the ungodliness of town and city dwellers.

The masses, feeling the oppression of Roman occupation as never before, were leaving Jericho, even making a special journey from Jerusalem to go and hear him. Israel had been too long without the word of prophecy. God was pledged to fulfil his promises some day. Why not *now*?

The hermit was, by all accounts, a strange but impressive man. He dressed in camel's skin held together by a leather belt. He lived, it was said, on nothing but locusts and wild honey.

His peculiar garb, the fact that he operated where Elijah smote and parted the Jordan with the cry, 'Where is the Lord God of Elijah?' gave rise to the rumour that Elijah had come to earth again.

Some said, when the hermit was hungry, he was fed with bread and meat, as Elijah was. One man, passing through Nazareth, reported he had seen huge black birds that flew over the Jordan valley day and night, blotting out the sky.

When Ezra heard of it, he groaned aloud. 'Not another Messiah, surely. God himself has lost count of the Messiahs he has sent already.'

He was even more irritated when his son-in-law claimed to have met this hermit and was thrilled by him.

'Nebat couldn't tell a prophet from a mess of pottage,' he complained to Jesus.

Jesus, not giving it much thought, asked, 'Is Nebat changed?'

'Oh, yes,' Ezra said caustically, 'he's changed all right. This hermit dipped him in the Jordan and my precious son-in-law expects to become rich and powerful as a result.'

179

In spite of Nebat's mercenary reaction, Jesus was mildly interested for the first time.

Ezra went on, 'It would take more than the waters of the Jordan to wash that one clean.' But Jesus was thinking: Not since Elisha made the Jordan a source of healing and holiness has anyone used it to show people the path of repentance.

He asked around but most of what he heard was foolishness.

A minstrel, so it was said, had played his lyre and, in a trance, the hermit was able to foresee the future of anyone who touched his arm.

His body, some said, never cast a shadow. Others: he had two shadows, one in front and one behind. Still others: he ordered his shadow about like a dog. 'Stay,' he commanded, and his shadow remained motionless when he walked away. 'Come,' he bade, and his shadow rejoined him.

So many stories.

The hermit plucked the head off a flower and put it back on so it grew again. He lit a fire by saying a word over it. A woodcutter's axe-head flew off its handle into the river; the hermit tossed the handle in after it, whereupon axe-head and handle came together again and floated ashore.

The hermit, many people swore, travelled everywhere on a whirlwind faster than any chariot. In one version, he descended from heaven in a chariot of fire. When he landed beside the Jordan, a big hawk, till then hovering over him, changed into a mantle for his head, the mantle of Elijah. No wonder the hermit was never wet when he stepped out of the Jordan. Like Elijah, he was able to make his own fords and walk dry-shod across rushing streams.

At Nazareth, when these matters were discussed in the synagogue on the Sabbath, it was agreed this was another false dawn.

The desert was responsible for all this madness. The desert had recently conjured up far too many mirages and crazed dreams which simply disappeared in the cool, sober air of Nazareth.

Then, one day, Jesus was visiting a near-by hamlet when a young reliable farmer, Jacob, gave him a truer picture of the one they were now calling 'John the Baptist'. He was preaching at a ford in the Jordan named Bethabara. He worked no miracles of any sort. He simply told people to behave and plunged them in the water as a sign of repentance.

'This Baptist,' Jesus enquired, 'who is he?'

Jacob's reply stunned him. 'His father, I believe, is Zechariah, of the House of Abijah.'

The Baptist was John, his own blood relative.

Jesus experienced a deep thrill in his soul. John was the son of a priest. Why had he not chosen to follow the vocation of his father? Why had he turned his back on the Temple and its ritual, preferring to live and work in the desert?

Among the masses of rumours, more credible stories started to filter through. John was warning people to die to the old ways. They had to begin a new life if they were to escape the wrath to come. For a new age was upon them; God's Kingdom was drawing near.

The Baptist only accepted those who grieved for their sins and pledged themselves not to sin again. After baptising them, he sent them out of the desert, back to their homes and their jobs where, he told them, they should *wait*.

Asked about himself, he answered in Isaiah's words:

> *I am the voice of one howling in the wilderness.*
> *Make ready the way of the Lord,*
> *Straighten out his paths.*

Pharisees and Sadducees turned out in force to look him over. John called them 'a nest of vipers' and refused to have anything to do with them. They had no future. When a farmer, he said, sets fire to the stubble in his field, the snakes are flushed out of hiding, they try wriggling to safety. His advice to those 'snakes' from Jerusalem was, 'Wriggle away from the wrath that is coming. Wriggle.'

When these important folk said, 'Do you know who you are talking to? Our father is Abraham,' John bent down and picked up a handful of stones from the river-bed. 'Abraham your father?' he cried, throwing the stones in the air. 'I tell you, even from these stones, God can raise up better sons to Abraham.'

A poor woman called out, 'When, John, when will it be?'

'Soon,' he said, 'soon. Already the axe is laid to the tree's roots. Watch. If the tree has no fruit on it, it will be cut down for the fire.'

Still more stories were reported.

An official deputation of priests and Levites, John's own class, was sent to enquire into his credentials.

'Are you the Messiah,' they asked him, 'the Lord's Anointed?'

'No.'

'Are you or are you not Elijah?'

'Not.'

'Who, then, are you?'

The Baptist repeated Isaiah's words. *I am the voice of one howling in the wilderness.*

Pressed by a woman in the crowd, the Baptist said, 'I baptise with water for repentance. But One is coming – oh, he is mightier than I. I am not worthy to untie his sandals. He will baptise you with the Holy Spirit and with fire.'

In a kind of vision, the Baptist saw the Coming One. 'His winnowing fork is in his hand,' he cried, 'to cleanse his threshing-floor and to gather wheat into his barn. As to the chaff' – he glared at the priests and Levites – 'he will throw them in a fire that never goes out.'

One morning, after he had spent a cold, damp night on the slopes above Nazareth, Jesus announced to his mother in a cracked voice:

'I must go to meet John the Baptist.'

Mary was not surprised. She had read the words on his face before he uttered them.

Chapter 32

Jesus completed his trip to Jerusalem in three days. For some reason, he had felt compelled to visit the capital before the long descent to Bethabara.

High on Olivet, he waited in the chill of morning for sunrise. A drizzle had ceased, the air was cleansed, the sky clear. He heard the Levite call the city to prayer and sacrifice. The Judaean hills under the wintry light twinkled like the embers of a vast fire stroked by a light wind into flame.

The cocks were crowing; there were bell-like sounds of people greeting the new day; cold sheep were clattering over stones, their breath smoky as incense.

Inside Jesus there was silence.

He had visited his mother's cousin, Elizabeth. She lived by herself in a big house in a small village to the southwest of Jerusalem. He was hoping she would help clarify his mind. But she did not. She was very old, widowed, wrinkled, bleary-eyed. When he saw her and said his name, she had burst into tears. When he spoke to her, she simply nodded or shook her head. She had nothing to tell him except that she held him in love and awe.

No matter.

As he stood on Olivet, there was, to his surprise, no need for a decision; a spiritual crisis had resolved itself.

For centuries, there had been two great traditions in Israel, the priestly and the prophetic, sometimes in harmony, sometimes opposed. The Baptist, though of a priestly family, had opted not for the cult but for the word as the source and ground of holiness.

Jesus was with him; the word of God spoke to the heart. True, Jesus was not of the hereditary priestly line.

More important than that, the cult did not suit his spirit. He preferred bareness, simplicity, a direct approach to God, *mercy not sacrifice*. Priesthood, as embodied in the Temple and its worship, was too ornate, too respectable, too prone to slide into the marginal, the superfluous. Besides, the cult was too local; it was as limited to a particular spot as the old Canaanite gods of the high places.

Sooner or later, he would have to confront this city and this Temple which he half-loved and half-feared. Even now he shuddered at the prospect of the confrontation. He would either conquer – or be broken. It was in the balance.

It was without regret that he took the path over the southern slope of Olivet towards Bethany.

He was relieved to see a party from Jerusalem travelling to Bethabara. He did not fancy walking the Red Road alone, the road of blood and brigands.

Already the path looked fearsome. Down and down it went like a dun-coloured snake, twisting and turning through the wilderness of rocks forced into terrible antique shapes.

At Bethany, he left the group, intending to say hello to his friends and catch the group up again. But Lazarus was alone and sick. Martha and Mary had left for Bethabara the day before. Lazarus had been well then, but now he was spitting blood. Jesus could not leave him.

Jesus stayed there two days until he was sure Lazarus could cope. As a parting gift, Lazarus gave him a flask of water and a dry-skinned pomegranate to quench his thirst on the road.

Beyond Bethany was Devastation, that long, steep decline into an abyss. Down there, monks and prophets, bandits and escaped prisoners rushed in search of God or mammon.

The first half of the journey was without incident. He disturbed lizards, glimpsed above him the odd black goat and, perhaps, a wolf. Some unseen animal on the heights dislodged a stone and started a tiny, tinkling avalanche.

Jesus was not really worried. What did he possess that

a thief might want? His biggest enemy was the heat. Though wintry in Jerusalem, here it was already warmer than a Galilean spring.

Then he ran into a contingent of Roman soldiers. Six or seven of them were standing around one of their number who was lying prostrate on a rock.

Jesus was as concerned for him as he had been for Lazarus. He asked, in halting Greek, if he could help.

They made way for him – there was something about him that commanded respect. The sick man was a centurion. He was much older than the rest; the sweat was pouring off him. His thick hairy legs were stretched out and on the end of them, like boats, a pair of hobnailed boots.

The soldiers probably thought Jesus was a wandering physician. They were content to let him get on with it.

The centurion had passed out in the heat. Jesus put his water-bottle to the man's lips and made a damp cool bandage to mop his brow. He soon came round.

He looked startled. His first reaction was that he had fallen into the hands of brigands. Realising the truth, he let out an oath, followed by a dry, throaty chuckle.

'Who are you?' he wanted to know.

'A Jew.'

'Hello, Jew. I'm a bit of a disgrace, eh?'

Jesus shook his head, smiling.

'I've been at it too long,' the soldier said. 'Wanted to retire years ago. Before I was drafted to this god-forsaken hole.' He stopped, gulped painfully. 'Sorry, Jew.'

Jesus was non-committal. He offered the centurion more water. There was nothing much wrong with him. A case of a middle-aged soldier, out of condition, dehydrated. The soldiers had underestimated their need for water and one of their flasks had burst.

One by one, without thinking anything of it, they took a swig of Jesus's water container until it was empty.

The centurion did not notice until it was too late. He was furious with his men and showed it. They stood aside, looking sullen. They did not take kindly to being reprimanded in the presence of a Jew.

The centurion explained to Jesus that they were stationed at Jericho. They were on leave for a few days in the capital. He had made a bad start, eh?

After half an hour, he was ready to continue the uphill march. He gave Jesus a silver coin which he tried to refuse.

'Go on, Jew,' the centurion urged, 'don't worry about the Emperor's head on it. Money's the only power in the world that has no enemies.'

One of his men said, 'Silver smells sweeter than a rose,' and the rest laughed. The sound of it echoed and re-echoed in the hills.

'One day,' the centurion said, as he and Jesus parted friends, 'maybe I'll be able to do the same for you.'

Half a mile farther on, Jesus had threaded his way through a narrow defile when he saw five men approaching him on foot. He was relieved to see they hadn't the dark skin of the Bedouins. They were his fellow-countrymen.

He held up his right hand and gave the traditional salutation, 'Peace.'

He began to be afraid only when it was not returned. With grim, angry faces they bore down on him and, bringing staves from under their cloaks, surrounded him.

Jesus raised both hands in the air. 'Friends, I have nothing, truly.'

His throat had contracted, the words came out haltingly.

The leader of the group, a man with a grey beard and a sword-scar on his cheek, snatched his purse, took out the Roman coin and spat on it.

'Nothing?' he snarled, and threw the coin down a ravine.

Jesus was struck from behind – it made a sound like wood on wood – and his skull glowed inside with a pure white light. There was no pain, only shock and discomfort.

'Pig-lover,' someone growled. Another said, 'Are you a Jew?'

Jesus nodded.

'Then why did you help those devils who defile our land and torment our people?'

Before Jesus could answer, he was struck a second time. The stick bounced off his head on to his shoulder, numbing it. The pomegranate he was holding fell to the ground and burst open, and the fleshy seeds scattered silently in the dust. It seemed proof that something terrible was happening to him.

He was thrown to the ground. His legs and shoulders were pinned down. The leader drew out a long, curled knife.

That was when he realised who they were: Zealots. Pious assassins who, in God's name, were pledged to kill or die to rid the country of the Romans.

As he lay there, he was kicked repeatedly, each time they cursed him. As far as they were concerned, he was in league with Pilate, he abetted an administration that was guilty of theft, violence and legalised murder.

Grey-beard, the chief, lifted Jesus's head.

'His brother' – he indicated a younger man – 'was crucified last week.'

'I am a Jew,' Jesus managed to say, through split and bleeding lips, 'like you.'

'You approve of what they did?' spat out the young man whose brother had died.

'No. I do not approve of violence.'

Grey-beard yelled, 'You're one of those weak-knees who would appease them are you? You'd let them ride rough-shod over us.'

'I would try to change them,' Jesus whispered.

'Change them!' The entire gang took it up as a kind of ludicrous refrain. One of them punched him in the stomach. Another brought his sandal down on Jesus's nose, crunching it. Jesus gulped as blood poured in a torrent down his throat.

For Jesus time stood in its track, rooted like a tree to this moment. There was a silence inside his head, more absolute than the silence of the desert or the mountaintop. This, he was thinking, *this* is what it is like to be at the mercy of people with no love for you.

No other experience in his life had prepared him for this. He was hated without cause. He was gripped and tugged *like a thing,* as he himself had often taken hold of a piece of wood, wondering how to shape it or cut it.

He was helpless; no one in all creation was able to come to his aid. Utterly alone. Like the aloneness of death?

Yes, that was it: death. He saw it. He smelled it.

When that old man was murdered in their village, Ezra went to his house. The whole place, he said, smelled of death. The stench was on the roof, the walls, the furniture. But the most astonishing thing was, according to Ezra, *none of it was coming from the corpse.*

The men surrounding Jesus, kicking and pummelling him, exuded death. It streamed out of their clothes and the pores of their skin. It was on the point of this dagger pressed against his throat.

Not death, then, through slow starvation or a still slower old age. But swift death, nimble death, with the thrust of a knife.

Another blow struck him. It might have come from an alien world. It was not fear he felt so much as a quiet horror of something dreadful. He was resigned to it like a small animal in the grip of a bigger predator. And with resignation, for all the confusing action of which he was the centre, came a lucidity which put monumental order into his thoughts.

What soothed him was a Presence stronger and sweeter than death, so that with every beat of his racing pulse his soul cried, Abba, Abba, Abba.

He made out the figure of the chief again. Saw him raise his cudgel and watched the arc of it, the entire free fall of it, until it struck him on the head. Blood spurted out, running down his forehead, into his eyes.

'Simon,' the chief growled, 'the filth murdered your brother. You finish him off. Be quick about it.'

Seeing Jesus was semi-conscious, the group marched off, leaving the young man with the knife.

Jesus could distinguish the young man's face, the unblinking eyes, the hatred, the lust for revenge; and pitied him for feeling so.

Simon was still watching his brother hanging on his

188

cross. Had watched him for days, without respite. Hour after hour, his brother had cursed the Romans and cried out, 'Freedom for the Jews' and 'Let my people go'. No one took any notice. Only a few friends agonised with him, witnessed the mass of flies, the odour of sweat, the shame of incontinence, the slow strangulation.

Simon had killed men before but this killing would give him a special pleasure.

'A last word, traitor,' he said, through gritted teeth.

Jesus, fighting to keep his head clear, whispered, 'I am sorry for your brother.'

Simon turned his head away as if he had received a blow. He was bitter. What right had this scum ... ? Until he grasped this stranger really meant it. *He's not sorry for himself; he's sorry for my brother.*

His victim stretched his hand out. Simon thought, at first, it was a last despairing effort to wrest the knife from him. Instead, the victim gently stroked the hand with the knife in, and smiled.

'I forgive you, Simon.'

Then he fell back, exhausted, the throat beneath the beard white and exposed.

What was that? Did he say ... ?

Simon refused to contemplate that his victim had spoken his name, forgiven him. He put the dagger to the throat again. One lunge and it was done.

But, to his horror, this man's face turned into his brother's face. *This stranger is a Jew, too, isn't he? With no one able or willing to help him.*

I forgive you. Did he really say that? Or did I imagine it?

The victim had no right to say to his killer, I forgive you. It blurred lines. It made a heroic thing somehow ... sordid.

Sweat was pouring off Simon's face like water from a jug. *How can I kill my own brother?*

To his relief, the victim had his own face back.

The smile was still there, though. Was it love? Lunacy? Was this idiot not afraid?

Something else struck Simon so forcibly that the breath escaped him in a painful gasp.

None of his hatred was coming back at him. In the

victim – he knew this from experience – there was always a counter-image of the assassin's hatred, however impotent it might be. For the first time, his own hatred did not clash with his victim's. *There is no hatred in him.*

Simon grasped that his own ferocity was being absorbed by his victim, like water in burning sand. So that when he examined his feelings he found that he, too, was drained. Not a trace of hatred left. *If I don't hate him, how can I kill him?*

'Hurry, Simon.' The gang higher up the Jerusalem road were getting anxious. 'We'll be late for the Temple service.'

'Coming.'

The cries reverberated around the stony hills. 'Coming. Coming. Coming.'

It was a lie, then. This was no secret deed, after all. The entire world was watching him, listening to him ... *Coming* ...

In that moment, Simon knew he could not kill this stranger, nor ever again. In his hands, was something sacred, like the scroll of the Law.

He dragged Jesus by the shoulders into a narrow gully off the road. Then he reddened the blade of his knife with the blood oozing from the stranger's head.

Next, he went, on a staggering run, to catch up his companions. And as he ran, he held the bloodstained knife at arm's length in front of him, trying desperately to escape the face of this man who had become his brother.

Chapter 33

How long he lay between the rocks he did not know. Unconscious for the most part, he came to from time to time, only to relapse into an unquiet sleep.

Once, on waking, he had attempted to rise. No good. Something was twisted in his back. His head ached, he was thirsty. One eye was completely closed, the other puffy so that when he looked out of it, it seemed as if it were covered with feathers.

On the road, he saw the remains of the pomegranate. If only he could crawl out there he would be able to ease his thirst.

The sun, at its zenith, shone directly down on him. He shielded his face as best he could. It was the worst time of day but this was a busy road. Help was bound to come.

He listened. Someone was approaching. He sat up. From his position he was able to look back fifty yards in the direction of Jerusalem.

Into view came a middle-aged priest and his attendant, both on stallions. Jesus laughed painfully, he was in luck. Many Sadducees lived in Jericho, they preferred it to the capital with all its recent disturbances. The priest was most likely returning from his spell of duty in the Temple.

Jesus held up his hands. He did not try to call out, there was no need. His plight was plain enough.

The priest, however, did not halt, did not turn his head, even momentarily. He rode straight by.

The servant looked and looked again. He shrugged, dug his heels into his horse's flanks and galloped after his master.

Jesus had not expected this.

Had the priest not seen him? Impossible. Maybe he had not realised he was hurt. But should he not have made sure? It could be Jesus looked ill enough to die, in which case the priest would not want to be defiled. No, it must have been fear. If one traveller had been assaulted, why not a couple more?

For Jesus, that day was hurt upon hurt.

Disappointed, he leaned back and dropped off to sleep.

Some time in the afternoon, he opened his eyes again. How many others had passed by he had no means of knowing.

191

His lips were split and swollen, his body was dried out. He had lost a lot of blood from a head wound; it stained the sand around him. His back no longer hurt, but he was still unable to move.

The ground was vibrating. He shot up. From the direction of Jerusalem, a Levite appeared on a donkey. Over the saddle in front of him was his robe of office. He, too, was going home to Jericho.

Jesus wanted to make sure this time. He called out. A cracked sound emerged from his lips, like a whip.

Thank God, the Levite was stopping. A young man. He reined in his ass, alighted and went to examine the stranger lying in a cleft in the rocks.

'For the love of God,' Jesus managed to say, 'help me.'

He had spoken the words distinctly, he was certain. But the Levite gave no sign of having heard. He was sniffing the air like a suspicious animal.

Is he drunk? He spoke with a strange accent, he's not from around here. God! Could this be a trap? Is he in league with Bedouins hiding up in those rocks?

The Levite backed away, his eyes switching in all directions like a fly. He scrambled on to his ass and whipped it into motion.

Jesus was left feeling terribly alone. Dusk came on rapidly. He could hear hyenas crying in the hills and above him, silhouetted against a copper-coloured sky, big birds were circling. With a silent prayer, he fell backwards into unconsciousness.

A dream? Someone lifting his head? He knew it was his because of the pain in it, because it was torn apart like a pomegranate.

A flask to his lips. Pressed gently but it hurt. Water? Ah, so *good*. His tongue was swollen, it nearly filled his mouth but he managed to swallow a few drops, then coughed for over a minute.

His rescuer did not speak, not once. He cleansed the wounds in his head, face, hands, with oil and wine. With a big green leaf he covered the head wound and wrapped it round with a scarf to keep the leaf in place.

Next, Jesus was lifted up. He was placed, face down,

across a donkey like a rolled carpet or a dead sheep. He glimpsed his rescuer's robe. It *was* a dream, for the man was dressed as Samaritans dress. He was being saved by a foe, a heretic?

The day's heat was hours past. His body, apart from his lips and tongue, was frozen. Or, rather, was cold and hot at once.

His rescuer, sensing his confusion, was murmuring, 'Be still. You are safe. I will take care of you.'

Jesus felt entirely safe with this Samaritan. Long before they reached the inn, he was sleeping peacefully.

It was dark when he came round. He was in a small room. He could tell from the sound of someone moving near his bed. He felt for his eyes and found they were bandaged.

'Lie still.'

Jesus recognised that voice, that accent.

The Samaritan explained that he had hired a room in a roadside inn. He had examined Jesus's injuries on arrival. He was badly bruised but nothing was broken, as far as he could tell. A cracked rib or two, perhaps, he did not know.

Jesus stretched out his hands. For some reason, the Samaritan did not take them.

'Friend?' Jesus said. 'Are you still there?'

'I am here,' the man said. 'But I am not your friend.'

'Whoever saves my life must be my friend.'

There was a silence. Jesus withdrew his hands because it was too painful to hold them up for long.

'I am a Samaritan,' the man said.

Jesus stretched his hands out again as a visibly deliberate act. 'I know that, friend.'

The Samaritan still did not move from the other side of the room.

Jesus said, 'A man has as many friends as he has a heart for.'

He held his hands out for three minutes. It was a superhuman effort, like being crucified.

The Samaritan did not stir.

When Jesus's arms fell on his chest it was because he was asleep.

The bandages covering his eyes were unwound. Afterwards, pitch darkness was replaced by a thick, pink haze. He still could not see, the fleshy parts around his eyes were swollen.

The Samaritan brought him food: flour and raisins mixed with milk into balls, a cup of honeyed water. In silence, the Samaritan fed him and left.

Jesus could feel the heat pounding on the flat roof. He heard animals stirring and smelt them in the stable at the back of the inn. There was the occasional tramp of feet on the road near by.

He fingered the garment he was wearing. It was not his own, it was in the Samaritan style. Yesterday, it might have bothered him, not today.

He had no means of judging the passage of time.

It was the next day, perhaps, when he heard the familiar sounds of someone praying. At first, he thought the Samaritan had left and been replaced by a priest or Levite and he felt angry.

But it was the Samaritan. He was reciting the ages-long commandments as set down in Deuteronomy. They were as much the Samaritan's creed as they were his own.

I am the Lord thy God, who brought you out of the land of Egypt and out of the house of bondage.

Jesus joined in, softly, in a chesty voice. *You shall have no other gods before me.*

Jesus had said only a few words when he became aware that he was praying on his own. The Samaritan had left the room.

For two days more, the Samaritan fed him and changed his dressings. They did not exchange a single word. After the Samaritan had fed him, Jesus did not say 'Thank you', though his heart ached to say it. He wanted to go down on his knees and kiss the man's feet.

When Jesus awoke the following morning, he found sunlight streaming in through the narrow aperture of a window. The swelling round his eyes had gone down; for the first time he was able to see more than outlines.

The Samaritan had been attending to his donkeys. He

194

came into the room carrying food and drink. A head-
scarf completely covered the lower part of his face.

'Peace,' Jesus said.

The Samaritan noticed that Jesus was looking directly
at him. Instinctively, he turned to go out.

What has happened to him, to US, Jesus wondered, *to make
him such a mixture of loving and loathing?*

'Friend,' Jesus called out. The word was spoken with so
much authority and affection that the Samaritan paused
at the door. 'My name is Jesus. I come from Nazareth.
Near where you must live.'

The Samaritan shuffled over to the pallet where Jesus
lay, put the food down beside him.

'Eat,' he said, his breath billowing the scarf. 'We live
far, *far* away.'

He had brought bread, fruit, goat's milk.

Jesus picked up the bread and broke it and offered half
to the Samaritan, the immemorial gesture of love and
brotherhood.

The Samaritan stood there, transfixed. His head began
to twitch, slowly at first, and then he shook it in a fierce
gesture of refusal.

Jesus nodded slowly but firmly, in a battle of wills. He
was still nodding when the Samaritan's head stopped
moving.

Once more, without words, Jesus held out the bread.
The Samaritan regarded it for a long moment as if it
were a snake, then took it. Turning on his heel, he made
for the door.

'Friend,' Jesus called, 'here with me. Eat with *me*.'

The Samaritan came back, unsteady, his hands
shaking. Jesus was reminded of a curious incident when
the locusts swamped the village. Every cat had climbed a
tree to paw them and could not get down. No one
bothered about them so they had to stay where they
were all night. The Samaritan looked to him at this
moment like a cat stranded up a tree. He had got himself
into a position where he did not want to be but could not
get down by himself.

'I cannot,' the Samaritan said, the fruit of struggle.

'You can, you must.'

The Samaritan had lost confidence entirely. 'I eat alone,' he said brokenly. 'It is *always* so.'

'Not always. Not now.'

'But,' the Samaritan said. 'I am ... not good to look at.'

'Come.' Jesus beckoned to him.

The Samaritan knelt beside the bed and Jesus unwound the head-scarf. Under it was half a face. The man had one good eye, the other was like a stone. Most of his nose had been eaten away so that in the centre of his face was one big hole. The left cheek looked as if it had collapsed and the skin over it was white as snow.

He had suffered once from leprosy but the disease had been halted.

The Samaritan had all this while searched Jesus's face for some sign of abhorrence – and found none.

'I am sorry,' he sighed.

Jesus smiled, gratefully. 'The face of an angel,' he said. 'More beautiful to me than the most beautiful of women.'

The Samaritan was quite unprepared for what happened next. Jesus leaned forward, pulled the Samaritan to him and kissed him on the lips.

The Samaritan sprang back, awed and horror-stricken.

'We are enemies, you and I,' he whispered. 'It is so, now and for ever.'

'From the moment you took pity on me,' Jesus said. 'I became your brother. Now and for ever. There is nothing you can do to alter that.'

He gestured to the Samaritan to return. He did so. And they ate – together.

Jesus told the Samaritan about his life at Nazareth. Ammiel spoke of his frequent journeys between Jericho and his home town, Sychar. He was a merchant, and dealt mainly in cloth and balsam.

He spoke, diffidently at first, then with pride, of the Scroll of the Law, 'the first of all scrolls in the world,' he said. 'Given us by God himself.' He spoke fondly too of Gerizim, the Mount of Blessing, and the deep cool waters of Jacob's well.

He expected every moment that Jesus would interrupt him, check him, contradict him. He was almost angry that Jesus did not react in any way, whether to agree or disagree. He only listened.

'Are you not a loyal Jew?' he said.

'Oh, yes, Ammiel.'

'Then why do you not fight with me?'

'You are a loyal Samaritan,' Jesus countered, 'why did you not leave me to die on the roadside?'

'I have sinned,' Ammiel said.

Jesus shook his head. 'It is no sin to love enemies. We *must* love them and do good to them.'

'If we do that, we will have no enemies left,' Ammiel said, confused. 'We will not be Samaritans any more, nor will you be Jews. There will be no real difference.'

Jesus signalled partial agreement. 'One man can be a loyal Jew, another a loyal Samaritan, and still be brothers.'

'How?'

'By worshipping God in spirit and truth. Only if we Jews and you Samaritans are disloyal will we hate each other.'

'My own people,' Ammiel admitted, 'hate me. Why? Because of my affliction. And'–he hesitated–'because of my marriage.'

He explained that he was married to a woman who had already been married, so to speak, four times.

'I was an outcast. She, too,' he said grimly. 'We were made for each other.'

'You love each other?'

'We fight, we spit, we love. We need and understand each other.'

'I can see,' Jesus said simply, 'why she loves you.'

'No one will speak to her, like she was a Jew,' Ammiel said with bitterness. 'She even has to draw water when no other women are at the well. Else they would stone her.'

'Because,' Jesus said, 'they are loyal Samaritans?'

For the first time, Ammiel smiled. It was wonderful what a smile could do to that ravaged face. Jesus guessed he had not smiled in a long time.

'I know why I saved you,' Ammiel said. 'It was because of your sense of humour.' More seriously: 'No, I picked you up because you looked as I felt.'

Jesus knew how hurt and wounded that was.

'Also,' Ammiel said, grasping Jesus's arm in a fond embrace, 'I badly needed a neighbour.'

Chapter 34

Ammiel had to leave. He was already five days late. His wife would be worried.

Jesus said, 'I am sorry. I cannot repay you.'

'Are you my enemy you talk to me like that?' Ammiel said cheerfully. 'No, my friend, we rescued each other.

He was a regular client of the inn. He gave the innkeeper two silver coins, enough to keep a guest for two to three weeks.

Jesus, in his room, heard Ammiel say, 'Look after him for me. If he's not better when the money runs out, I'll pay you next time round.'

Jesus was expecting Ammiel to return for a final farewell, but he must have saddled his asses earlier, for the next thing he heard was the departing clip-clop of the donkeys' hooves.

Maybe Ammiel was shy of being thanked. Or was this his way of saying that between them there was no goodbye?

Jesus made rapid progress. Within a week, his back was better and his ribs were aching less and less.

He spent the days resting, walking in the hills, preparing, praying.

When he left the inn finally, he was wearing his white Sabbath robe which Ammiel must have rescued for him. He went on his way towards Jericho refreshed and in the best of spirits.

The road continued on, serpentine, shadeless, through a thousand hills. The heights in the distance were lilac-coloured and, near by, bluish grey.

Though the heat and humidity clogged his lungs, he did not mind. Down there, whence Elijah emerged from time to time to make and unmake kings, something momentous was about to happen.

Round a bend, he had a clear view of Jericho in the distance, circled by mud walls and its edges softened by innumerable trees. Behind it, a steep mountain. Beyond, seemingly near but really many miles away, were the blue waters of the Salt Sea. And beyond the sea, to the east, were the mauve-streaked flanks of the Mountains of Moab.

At the foot of the Judaean mountains he began his march across the wilderness towards Jericho. His heart was beating fast.

Jericho was a green oasis in the middle of the plain. Herod's winter palace was still standing; there were many big houses. He passed herds of goats, countless chickens and turkeys, burbling camels, and blind beggars whom he could oblige with nothing but a prayer.

A rich patch of countryside. The heat and humidity brought everything to fruition: corn, fruit, vegetables, bushes of multi-petalled oleanders, balsam trees that were the envy of the world. He could smell for a mile out of town spices, perfumes and scented oils that were on sale in the market-place.

Soon, his excitement growing, he came to a small hamlet with tamarisk trees and a small stream with running water. Gilgal.

It was here in Gilgal that the Israelites pitched their first camp after crossing the Jordan. Here, the Ark first came to rest in the Holy Land. Here, twelve stones, representing the twelve tribes, were gathered from the river-bed and built into a memorial of God's power and providence. The first Passover was celebrated here and here circumcision, the rite of initiation into the Jewish people and the sign of the covenant in the flesh, was reintroduced. It was here that his namesake Joshua made his camp and waged war against the Canaanites.

Jesus was thrilled. Was he not a circumcised Jew, a lover of the Law and Passover, a worshipper of the God who brought his people out of bondage? Was he not one with them in their joys and tribulations? One with them even in their guilt?

He prayed a long while in Gilgal. When he stood up, the heat was shimmering, water-like.

He increased his pace over the last few miles. While he could not see the river, he could pick out the thickets beside it. Up to the Jordan's banks grew Euphrates poplars and tamarisks with their slender scaly branches. It was winter, though it felt hot and steamy, and the trees were all bare.

The Baptist paused in his labours. He was tall, thin as bamboo, wiry. His skin was black as ebony, his hair was burned to a crisp. He might have been sixty but was only half that age.

From where he stood in the middle of the ford, he could see a shape in the desert. It attracted him by its solitariness. It refused to crystallise.

On came the shape, floating above the ground and beneath a puff of white cloud. Slowly, slowly it came nearer, down the long final slope to the water.·

The Baptist was not a man of distractions; he wanted to continue his work. The crowds were chanting and many were crying out to be baptised. But he went on peering into the distance.

Jesus stretched his arms wide and the shape John saw was the shape of a dove flying low over the wilderness. Was this, could this be Israel, God's faithful dove? John felt the fierceness of his soul abate, he was awash with peace.

He stepped out of the water in anticipation. His peace turned to longing, and longing was a nail being driven into the heart.

People were pressing him on all sides, asking him questions. He pushed them aside roughly and they let him pass.

Silence came over them when they saw him staring into the desert.

The dove became a man, tall, stately, moving with dignity.

The Baptist heard a cry, so loud he clasped his head in his hands. '*This ... This ... This ...* '

He scrambled up the bank, went running to meet this Man from the desert and fell down before him, shuddering, full of awe. The Man helped him up and embraced him. John's tears fell on the Man's shoulders.

'You have come at last.'

'Yes, cousin. You have done well.'

A cry went round the crowd. 'He has come ... Who has come? ... Who is he?'

Those at the back were angry. Something was happening but they could not see or hear.

Jesus laid his outer tunic aside and the crowds parted as he walked towards the water.

John leaped after him, cutting him off. 'No, Master, it is not right. My turn to be baptised. By you.'

Jesus shook his head. 'This way all things will be fulfilled.'

'But, Master,' John said, yielding, but beginning to whimper.

Jesus gently silenced him. '*All* Israel must be purified. It is ordained.'

He waded into the water, knowing that this was death. Not his own death which he had sipped on the Jerusalem road but the death of death.

John splashed after him. He who up till this moment had seen things so clearly was bewildered, frightened. Was the Saviour of Israel also to be purified – and humiliated?

There was a hint here of something terrible.

Must I? Only the Baptist's eyes asked it. And only Jesus's eyes answered, *You must.*

Jesus leaned back like a lamb about to be slaughtered and John, trembling, took him and plunged him under the water.

Jesus stayed there a long while, still as death, until his

lungs were bursting. Then up again with a rush and a breath like a baby's first breath, painful and glorious.

Jesus walked ashore, the water streaming from his body, his face shining like the sun. He picked up his tunic and walked away into a quiet place.

The Baptist watched him go. So much had happened and so little. Was everything changed – or anything? What would God do now? What more had he to do for God?

Many people were asking him on all sides, 'What is this all about? ... Who is he? ... Why did you go on your knees to him?'

John did not hear them for a long time. Eventually he roused himself. His voice had lost its wild, croaky sound. Softly, he said, 'I have seen something wonderful.'

'Wonderful,' those around him echoed, excitedly. 'Wonderful.'

'I have seen a Light come into the world.'

Again his words were repeated and repeated.

'God's Spirit is on this man. I tell you, I heard the voice of God out of a cloud, telling me, "This is my beloved Son. Listen to him."'

Chapter 35

Jesus made himself a booth of reeds, similar to the huts they put up for the Feast of Tabernacles.

Like the Baptist, he too was uncertain of the way ahead. He still had to pray. And wait.

Next day, he had been to the river, bathed and was resting under a tree when two shadows appeared in front of him. He looked up and recognised immediately his fishermen friends, John and Andrew.

He smiled a welcome and leaped up to embrace them.

Their attitude had changed. Andrew was shifting from one foot to another like a lizard trying to keep cool and John, in a stilted way, said, 'Where are you staying?'

'Why not come and see?'

He led them to the hut. It was late afternoon and the sun was relaxing its grip on the land. They stayed for several hours.

When they were relaxed, they told him that they had asked the Baptist who Jesus was.

'And he said?'

'The Lamb of God.'

Jesus was still thinking of the Baptist's enigmatic words an hour after his friends had left. He heard a loud, unmistakable cough.

'Hello, Fisherman,' Jesus said, delighted. 'I was expecting you.'

Simon was on his knees, trembling, overcome. He said, 'Master.'

With that one word, he had made his covenant. He might waver at times but he would never retract his will to be faithful to death.

'Have you brought me a fish?'

Simon lowered his head. 'Only myself,' he said.

Jesus put his index finger under Simon's chin and raised it until their eyes met.

'It is enough.'

'I knew God sent you,' Simon said in a rush. 'I always knew.'

He had understood something that still puzzled the Baptist: why Jesus had allowed himself to be baptised. It was because he felt responsible for everyone and everything. For all sinners and all sins. Because he wanted to take the blame for everyone. *And he could, because he was innocent.*

'Simon, son of Jonah, from now on, I am going to call you Peter.'

'*Peter,*' Simon echoed. 'Am I so rock-like?'

'Stubborn, deaf, unyielding, immovable,' Jesus laughed. 'Yes, you are a rock.'

'Ah,' Simon said, winking. 'But can a rock walk on water?'

Jesus thumped him on the back. 'This rock will have to learn,' he said.

On the following morning, by the Jordan, Jesus was surrounded by friends. Peter and Andrew were there, James and John. Jesus introduced them to Judas Iscariot, down from Jerusalem. He too had witnessed the baptism. Jesus could not help noticing that the Galileans were a bit stiff in the presence of this southerner.

He felt someone tugging at his arm. He turned to find himself looking into the face of the man who had wanted to kill him.

They walked apart from the rest.

Simon the Zealot said, 'I nearly did a dreadful thing.'

Jesus nodded understandingly. 'You were walking on a wrong path, that was all.'

'I know. I just wanted to say thank you.'

He was walking away when Jesus called his name.

Simon turned to face Jesus again. He looked incredulous. 'I can stay?'

Jesus nodded.

Simon went up close to Jesus and placed something in his hand. Without looking at it, Jesus threw the knife into the middle of the Jordan. The assassin's knife, also, needed to be baptised.

He had introduced Simon to the others when Judas held up a jar of ointment.

'For you, Master.'

The word 'Master' came easiest of all to Judas.

'For me?'

'It smells good,' Judas said. 'A young woman asked me to give it to you. Thin, long-haired, a small scar on her left cheek. A northerner.'

'She is a friend of mine,' Jesus said. He scanned the crowd in the hope she was still there.

'She left in a hurry an hour ago,' Judas said. 'She was heavy with child.'

Jesus's eyes creased with pity for the plight of Mary of Magdala.

Jesus spent a restless night and at the end of it he was not refreshed. It was as if a caged bird was inside him, flapping its wings in a bid to get free. But his apprenticeship, he knew, was not yet over.

The Baptist had acknowledged him and he had the makings of a bold little following. But some part of him was clearly not yet ready for the fray. He had still to be tested. He would have to go where he had no wish to go. Something was out there waiting for him and God's Spirit was impelling him to advance bravely to meet it.

He left his booth at sunrise and went to the river where his friends were breakfasting.

'Peter,' he said, for the rest to hear, 'I am going into the desert.'

'For how long, Master?'

'Until my task is done. Wait for me here.'

Peter's jaw jutted out. 'We will wait,' he said.

Chapter 36

Jesus walked prayerfully from the Jordan through a waste-land to the Salt Sea. The air was stark and strangely odourless. At midday, a flat white light brooded over everything, casting not a single shadow.

He passed a few Bedouins with the faces of hawks. For shade, they had pitched their goatskin tents or thrown black blankets over a few sticks in a dry river-bed. They did not deign to look his way.

The land was sterile, vivid, with nothing compromised or fudged. His people had been fashioned in such a terrain as this. In centuries to come Jews might live in great cities but they would always bear the marks of having been born in a land like this. If nothing else, their Writings would remind them.

He saw a wild boar with her young and a few long-eared goats. Sand was everywhere: sand in heaps, sand furrowed by a now dead wind. His feet sank into it and, heavier than water, it held him back.

He reached the Dead Sea. The water was pale green with a mist rising from it. He could scarcely see across. There were no ripples on the water, which gave off a sulphurous smell. The only vegetation was wild caper-bearing shrubs and other shrubs, tall with red berries, which he wanted to taste but did not.

He had not expected birds, but at the mouth of the Sea there were many of them. Huge shoals of fish were borne southward by the river. A few yards into the Salt Sea and they perished. As they turned over, cormorants and kingfishers speared their bellies and flew off to gorge themselves or their young. Above the banks ravens, and vultures, descending from immense heights, fell on the carcasses of fishes washed ashore.

He saw with more contentment palm turtle-doves, an Egyptian goose, even a stray lapwing. He came across a noisy band of hopping thrushes. With tails jerking, they followed one another up a bush, fed greedily, then dropped down again and, in single file, hopped away.

For a long time, Jesus stood gazing at Mount Nebo from where a dying Moses was given a parting glimpse of the promised land. Those eastern hills were scabby, all right. Scratch them, he felt, and blood and water would stream out. He felt sorry for Moses.

This was the end of his pilgrimage.

From there, he changed direction, travelling north-westward over a land as featureless as the sea. The heat immobilised everything, holding it tightly as in a wrestler's arms.

He came across a flock of black storks and a beautiful little sand-partridge which had laid its eggs in the fissure of a rock. Finally, he came to what he had been looking for: a cave at the foot of a rocky slope. This was to be his refuge.

He was very thirsty. Near by, was a dried-up water-hole. Just below its almost transparent crust he saw the lumpy outlines of frogs. His mind went back to his boyhood days. Whenever he was thirsty and there was nothing else, he dug up frogs like these. They had burrowed and drunk their fill of water while there was something to drink. He squeezed their gorged bellies and drank the sweet water stored up in them. He wanted to do that now, but he did not.

From early afternoon, a wind had been blowing from the east, a dry, rustling wind off the bare heights of the wilderness. He was not used to anything as scorching as this. In Nazareth, the rare east wind was a discomfort not a torment.

The bone-dry sand found its way into every fold of his garments, into every crevice of his body. It was an irritant to eyes, nose, ears; it stung worse than sawdust. It even wedged itself into the gaps between his teeth. He longed to wash his body clean and anoint it with oil.

The sun went down sharply. But before it disappeared, it lay momentarily shimmering in mist on the western hills. It seemed at the last to change its shape, to flatten itself like a container whose bottom had dropped out and was discharging its ruby contents prodigally over the edge of the world.

Suddenly, from unbearable heat, the air turned cold, then very cold. He jumped at the mysterious noises in the still air – it was like the cracking of thousands of finger-joints or walnuts – as the land chased away the daylight heat.

It was a red clear night; stars were roses coming into bloom as he watched.

He huddled up, a hibernating animal. He retreated into himself. Not into himself so much as into God. Soon came that barely perceptible breathing and he went into a night far darker and yet more luminous than the desert's.

Sunrise. This was no gentle wooing of a sleepy world. A warrior sun rose, fully armed, aggressive, triple-sized. And hot. From the first, sharp. Within the hour, it was a great gong smitten by some cataclysmic force from over the horizon; the waves of sound metamorphosed into waves of shimmering light.

Under that sun, nothing stirred and nothing was still. Even the solitary eagle, a speck in the sky, was as still as a star, turned black, left over from night.

Ah, but life was good, all the same, so good. The Man had always liked simple things and here everything was reduced to its simplest. Rock, light, sand, wind; at night, moon and stars.

He was hungry and thirsty. But he remembered the children of his village, how they hungered and thirsted during the drought. He thought of other starving children in other droughts throughout the world. There was nothing that chased hunger and thirst away like the sight of a hungry child.

He endured. For days and nights, he endured.

Days and nights fused into one another, so he could not tell how long he had been there. He only knew he was happy.

Sometimes a rock-badger inspected him; he first heard the shuffling sound, a few stones disturbed. Next, he was looking into a pair of fiery eyes. Moments later, nothing.

He heard a screech-owl and once the *kiu-kiu* of a scops owl. A bird flew by, anxious, a fluffy arrow off target. Jackals yelped. Tree frogs on a leguminous plant set up a terrific din, then they stopped as if all of them together had run out of breath.

Most desert things were elusive. Something flashed in the sky – a hawk? Something moved at his feet – a viper or lizard?

They did not want to be observed. In this, they were like the deep thoughts of men, better hidden, best buried.

Sunset followed sunset. The same grape-press, trodden by angels' feet, squirted red juices over distant hills. Sometimes, in the night, black clouds came ploughing in the stars like seeds. He, too, was a seed, buried and dying, waiting to fructify, to bring forth a life that was new.

This was the hope that sustained him.

Back at the Jordan his disciples were growing uneasy.

'What shall we do?' John asked.

Judas suggested they go look for him and, if need be, bury him.

Peter took charge. 'He said wait, so we wait.'

'But by now,' Simon objected, 'even a camel would be dead out there.'

Peter said, '*Wait*.'

In the desert, Jesus had found ultimate peace. He was touching God as easily as he could lift his hand at night and pluck the stars. In stillness, he had travelled far.

Outwardly, he was thickly caked with sand, the desert mud; he had assumed the dessicated shape of all things that manage to survive there. His eyes had shrivelled and sunk into his face. His hair was coiled like snakes. Had he walked away from the rocks, he would have seemed a cactus plant, sculpted by a roguish wind.

Inwardly, he had found the Fountain of Life. His senses sharpened, his mind like a sword, he was impregnably happy. Or he thought he was.

In the desert by day, an excess of light makes for unreality. In such a light, things are seen that are not there. The cruellest trick of light is to turn moistureless air into water – and good into evil, evil into good?

One second, the Man was bursting with felicity; the next, dread filled him and foreboding.

As when a dagger was pressed against his throat, he smelled the vile odour of death. He twisted and turned in agony, expecting this more than human wickedness to take shape before his eyes. He could feel it come from the four corners of the world, coalescing.

But it did not materialise. It simply invaded him, body and spirit. Threatened to overwhelm him.

How was this possible? Had he not been cleansed in the River? Was he, Israel's Saviour, to be separated from his God?

'God,' he cried, 'where are you, God? What are you doing?'

The sun was blazing in the sky, yet he was cold and shivering.

Then spoke the Voice. Quiet, soothing, immeasurably hideous. A Voice at once familiar and never heard before.

The foundations were tottering. He looked up sharply in case the rocks over his head should split and a thousand jagged fragments rain upon his head.

'Who are you?' he screamed.

'Your friend,' the Voice said. 'Your dearest friend.'

Chapter 37

THE FIRST TEMPTATION

'You are my enemy.' The first panic had passed. Jesus was in command of himself.

'Surely,' the Voice said, 'you do not share with the masses that silly notion of me. I am no enemy. I have simply come to claim your allegiance.'

'I owe you no allegiance.'

There was a loud chuckle. 'Of course not. How could I hope for that? I have witnessed with admiration your life-long fidelity to God. No, no, no. I have come to ... beg your allegiance to mankind.'

Jesus was silent, trying to fathom what this meant.

'You *are* the Christ, the Anointed of God, is that not so?'

Jesus did not answer.

'Never mind. You are hungry, Son of Man?'

After the first few days of fasting, Jesus had given no thought to food. Now, one word of reminder sent a pang right through him.

'I am,' he admitted.

Hunger was a presence that suddenly filled the horizon of all his senses. And he was hungry with more than his own hunger. He hungered on behalf of the world.

'These stones,' the Tempter said, urbanely, 'why not turn them into bread?'

Jesus regarded the stones near his feet. Lime-covered, like bread out of a kiln.

Bread. The word sounded so good. He could smell loaves, crisp, warm, freshly baked. Like his mother made.

A man might give his soul for bread ...

'It is wrong,' Jesus muttered to himself, 'I must not.'

'How *wrong*?' the Voice of Satan enquired. 'Moses whom you so admire gave his people bread from heaven. Was that *wrong*?'

Jesus considered it deeply. Without manna, without bread from above, there would have been no Israel. Bread kept the covenant alive. Could not he himself serve God, as Moses did, by giving his people bread in life's wilderness?

Besides, he had already suffered and starved in the drought a few years previously. He was entitled to bread. It was wicked to be without the staff of life, the most basic of necessities, without which a man is not a man.

Bread for himself, first of all. His life was precious. He needed it to be strong for his mission.

Bread for others, so they would believe in him and in God.

Was it so bad a thing for God's Kingdom to come in bread? The people would follow him to the ends of the earth. If only he guaranteed them bread – whether from heaven or from these desert stones.

'Your village,' the Tempter said, interrupting his thoughts, 'a nice, quiet, pleasant village. No different from most others. No better but no worse.'

'A fine village,' Jesus said proudly.

'Oh, yes,' the Voice agreed. 'Until the bread ran out. Then life fell apart. Virtue, their holy religion even, turned out to be a sham. The most pious of the villagers became ravening wolves.'

The Tempter hastened to add, 'I do not criticise them, you understand. I feel for them, they touched my ... heart. My point is, they reacted exactly as others would have acted, as peoples have always reacted in those

211

dreadful circumstances.'

'They were starving.'

'Of course, they were. You should pity them.'

'I did what I could.'

'You did what you could *then*,' Satan said, with more precision. 'The question is what to do *now*.'

Jesus shook his head, not knowing.

'When the pressure was on them, your nice, quiet, pleasant villagers showed what they were really like, under their masks. Base. Unredeemable. They will never be any different, whatever you say or do, while they are not assured of enough to eat.'

'I do not believe – '

'Hunger,' the Tempter went on relentlessly, 'shows the world its own cruel, rapacious, ugly self. You are honest, how can you deny it? You *saw* it. You saw the crop of lies, extortion, greed, hatred, bitterness, superstition of the grossest sort, suicide, murder – in your own village. And all of it, even harlotry, was *justified*, because of hunger. They sinned without remorse, because of hunger. For there was no sin, or so they reasoned, as vile as hunger, and God, not they, should apologise.

'The most heroic of men like Rabbi Ezra, blessings on him, cursed the God who made him, because of hunger. My ears winced, believe me. I have never achieved anything so surprising before, nor wish to again. Hunger did this, it stripped the people you love of all their dignity.'

Jesus put his fingers in his ears, but it did no good.

'Hunger is God's great enemy, Son of Man. In the desert in days of old, your people Israel grumbled against God because they were hungry. And God knew they were *justified*. Why else did he feed them? He made them his people by feeding them, for, grasp this well, he who does not feed his people is no god to them.'

For a long time in that timeless time of temptation, Jesus pondered these things in his heart.

'Save them from hunger, I beg you,' Satan pleaded, and they will be saved for ever. Your villagers who have done their best to forget that they were wolves, that they *are* wolves, will be saved from their guilt and egotism only if you give them bread, plenty of bread. If you do not save them from hunger, you know as well as I that they will never be changed, not *under* the masks.'

'I am fasting for them,' Jesus hissed. '*With* them.'

'Indeed you are and I both admire and am puzzled by it. For is not this the *real fast: to share your bread with the hungry and not to hide yourself from your own flesh?*'

Jesus bowed his head, since a rebuke is a rebuke, even if it comes from Satan.

'I counsel you, Son of Man, forget your antipathy to me. Think of mankind. Do not pass through this world and leave a single belly empty. For with one empty belly you will leave trouble, disillusion, unbelief. Fulfil the beautiful prophecy – it is in the power of God's Anointed: end the obscenity of a baby's dying a few days old from hunger.'

'A-ah,' Jesus passionately sighed, remembering Deborah dead in his mother's arms.

'The child should die at a hundred, so Isaiah said. The days of your people should be as the days of a tree. It really is up to you.'

Tears sprang into Jesus's eyes at such a prospect, but he forced himself to say, 'I have come into the world to make it free.'

The Tempter greeted this with a polite laugh as though it were a slogan from a has-been politician.

'The world is free already, Son of Man. If it were not, would you be here! No, your role, correct me if I am wrong, is to make the world as free as it can possibly be; to make it *free to be free*. Without bread, people will always be slaves of their lower appetites and make slaves of one another.'

A throb came into the Tempter's voice:

'Give them bread *and* freedom, Son of Man. Do not ask them to choose between the two things they cannot do without. They will not thank you for that. Better ask a loving mother to choose between her husband and her child. No, a starving man is as free to love and serve God as a legless man is free to walk from Dan to Beersheba.'

Jesus thought this through in long, anguished moments. He was remembering the misery, the sheer

213

unsightliness of hunger. The cruelty of it. The bloated bellies of children who once crowded his workshop.

'You are a man,' the Voice broke in, mercilessly. 'You have known hunger, so there is no excuse. You have felt its tragedies, first-hand. You know how it drives out the good and brings every evil in its wake. Is it too much to ask that a poor man should be able to stretch out his hand and find bread? Make it so, I beg you. Become the Servant of Man.'

Jesus still had before his eyes the disintegration of his lovely village. It still hurt beyond words that he had been forced to infringe the Sabbath on the plea that the Sabbath is for the free *and starving men are never free.*

Yes, he had said it. Satan *knew* he had said it.

'Why are you hesitating, Servant of Man, in face of the obvious? You broke bread with a Samaritan a few days ago and you and he are brothers for ever. You did not discuss freedom with him or truth or honour. It was bread that made you one, made your body grow with his, your spirit grow into his. Break bread with mankind. Create a new and everlasting brotherhood in bread.'

Jesus did not move, did not breathe.

'You still do not say yes. Perhaps, no surely not, perhaps you harbour the forlorn hope that mankind will *feed off you.* A great risk for you and what of those whom you think you love? Will they be satisfied with the bargain you struck on their behalf? Will they not rather curse you, knowing you could have chosen *real* bread for them and yet chose ... something else?'

'Peace,' Jesus murmured, 'love, generosity. These are important, these come first.'

'Give them bread,' the Voice said sternly, 'and peace, love, generosity, selflessness, truth, contentment with God, hope – as well. Bread is the universal remedy; even babes and lunatics understand it. The starving cannot eat truth. Give them an endless supply of bread and it will make them one, it will consolidate religion. For religion as it is at present cannot make men one; religion divides. Men know there is only communion in bread. Give them bread and all things will be added unto them.'

'Will it end war?' Jesus demanded, challengingly.

'Of course,' came the smooth reply. 'There would be nothing to go to war *for*. Become the bread-man of the world and you will end tyranny for ever. There will be no more Egypts, Assyrias, Babylons, Romes. Empires arise out of the need and greed for bread. They steal land for the sake of bread. Jews will never drive the Romans from this land. But if at home the Romans had an abundance of bread, Tiberius would summon Pilate home tomorrow. Why would he stay if their land, like all other lands, is a land of undying plenty? Why are there wars, invasions, massacres, except there is not enough bread to go round, or there might not be? You must see this.'

Jesus saw it only too clearly. His people hated the capitation tax imposed by Rome because it was a sign of slavery. But far more crippling was the land tax. It sometimes amounted to a quarter of the harvest. What point would there be in Rome's taxing the produce of Jewish soil if their own soil produced more than they needed?

Satan was saying, 'God is responsible for all wars, Son of Man, and men know this in their hearts. Which is why, in crises, even the most religious rebel. God just did not make enough bread. All I am asking is that you persuade God to be more generous to mankind. Does it really need ... me' – he did not name himself – 'to tell you that? It is really so simple. If only God would finish making the world, do a proper job – through you. Do not make your ideal the salvation of men. That is painful and you stand for joy. Besides, it is not necessary. Ask God to let *you* complete his creation *so that men do not need to be saved*. Afterwards, mankind will remember that it was a Son of Israel who gave the world bread, and with bread dignity and with dignity an appreciation of the spiritual things of God.

'For this, Son of Man, you were chosen. For this, you were chosen out of the chosen. Bread is life and love – as locusts, drought, famine are death and sin. Adam was cursed and made to earn his bread by the sweat of his brow and it is never enough. You have it in you to undo that curse which divides people and nations, to bring back Paradise and lasting peace on earth. Then all men

215

will live in harmony in an abundant land and even the animals, tamed once more, will bless you for ever and ever.'

For ages, Jesus strove within himself. Sweat poured from him. The gnawing pain in his belly made him feel like a starved animal. And with this feeling came a sense that God was betraying him. His belly spoke to him with the accents of the Tempter. It was *shameful* to be so hungry. *It should not be.*

Of course man needed redeeming but that was due to his hunger. That was why men hated, were envious, fought one another. If he fed them they would not need saving.

Yes, this was a way, a better way; not to share men's misery, as he had till then imagined, but to end it. How, he argued, will one more wretched man on earth prove or *improve* anything? If there was bread, he would eat, too. He would have a wife and children – how he adored children – and a blessed old age, like Abraham and Moses. Did not Jacob in the desert rest his head on such a stone as this and look up at the pulsing stars and see in them a pledge of numberless offspring? Why should he be different from his father Jacob?

With a huge effort, he stood and lifted up one of the heavy flat stones. One word and this would become .... life. His lips were straining, as a dog strains on a leash when it smells food, to speak that word.

But at the last moment, he began to doubt his doubts. He saw, as through water at first, then clearly, the real face of man.

It occurred to him that man had everything in the beginning. Was there not an abundance of every kind of food in Paradise? Did he not find a way of being a miserable sinner in the midst of bliss? Would he not always? Would not man starve himself on purpose *in order to rebel*, so he could express his sinfulness somehow? Would he not even destroy his neighbour's bread to starve him into submission?

No, bread would not make man holy. On the contrary,

man would *invent ways of profaning bread*. He would always need redemption.

Jesus threw the stone away with a loud cry:

'*Man does not live by bread alone but by every word that proceeds from the mouth of God.*'

He listened. The Voice was not speaking any more. When he looked, he saw to his horror that the stone at his feet had turned, unbidden by him, into a white, flat, appetising loaf.

He tried to spit on it in derision, but when he opened his mouth there emerged nothing but a puff of dust.

Chapter 38

THE SECOND TEMPTATION

When the Voice spoke to him a second time it was less shrill, less self-assured. It remained the familiar unfamiliar Voice, attractive and horrible. But now it was mellower, more civilised.

'You are right, Son of Man, I should have known. Bread is not immediately spiritual enough to appeal to you. I suppose I am so much in love with mankind, so keen to eliminate their misery, I underestimated you and them. By all means, let them starve, provided you make them holier in the end.' Satan paused. 'You are listening, my friend?'

'You are my enemy.'

'No!' Satan sounded offended. 'Not your adversary, but your adviser. You do not have to take my advice, but I give it for what it is worth.'

'I am listening.'

'Come with me.'

In an instant, Jesus found himself standing on the pinnacle of the Temple. It was the morning of a great festival. The sun was not yet risen.

Familiar sights were visible to him. Olivet and Gethsemane to the east, Mount Scopus to the north. To the south was Gehenna, a desolate, smoky scrub-land with wilting terraces and ancient groves; there, some centuries before, children had been sacrificed by fire inside the huge bronze belly of Moloch, the god.

'Look down, Son of Man.'

From the dizzy height, where soon the Levite would announce morning and the day's first sacrifice, Jesus gazed down on the sanctuary.

The worshippers were the size of ants. In their millions, they scurried here and there, moving in lines and touching each other, just like ants.

'Religion,' the Voice said. 'The little black ants of religion.'

'This place is holy,' Jesus returned.

'Indeed.' The Voice was reverent. 'Otherwise you and I would not fear it as we do. And yet it is holy *in spite of religion.*'

Jesus plugged his ears but still heard, for the Voice was within him. He knew it and it worried him. *The Tempter knows his way round my heart.*

'You do fear it, do you not?'

'Yes.'

'In the long nights you spent on the hills round your home and here on Olivet, you felt about the Temple a certain... apprehension?'

'Yes.'

'You did say that too often the Jewish religion tried to make people safe and secure, and ended up in smugness.'

'Not merely the Jewish religion.'

'True, but it is no exception?'

'No.'

'And you object because God is a fire, unpredictable and wild and lovely?'

'Yes.'

'See those flagstones.' Jesus looked. 'Why not take off from this platform you are standing on and float down there? Like a bird. Like the Dove of Peace.'

'I am a man,' Jesus said, 'made of flesh and bone. I would die.'

There was a chuckle in the Voice. 'Not if you are the Christ-Messiah. Is it not written: *God will give you into his angels' charge* and *They will hold you up lest you even hurt your foot on a stone?*'

'What purpose would that serve?'

'The ants will listen to you, Son of Man. You will rid this place of all the things that anger you.'

'Such as?'

'You *know*. Hypocrisy. Heartlessness. The irreligion of men who give a pittance and have the nerve to call it "alms for the love of God". The senselessness of giving without self-giving, so the giver can feel better afterwards without any abiding concern for the one to whom he gives. Look down there.'

Jesus looked and the tiny black ants were peering skyward. Every one of them had the face of Laban, the Pharisee whom Ezra had mocked in the sanctuary.

'Get rid of it all, Son of Man. It is in your power. Get rid of these everlasting prayers, this false godliness that enables men to pray, with a quiet mind, while they eject widows and orphans from their houses and leave their fellows to die, bruised and broken, on the road-side.'

A Levite in magnificent brocade appeared beside Jesus. It was the young Levite who had passed him by on the Jerusalem road. The sky turned pitch-black at the very moment the Levite called out, 'The sky is lit up as far as Hebron.' He blew on a small silver trumpet and, instead of a blast, out came a noise like an animal stampede. Cows, bullocks, sheep – lowing, bellowing, bleating – as they raced across an echoing courtyard. Below, only the faces of the ants were illuminated. Eyes closed, lips moving like a weaver's shuttle in prayer, heads swaying from side to side.

The light returned, the Levite disappeared.

'You can put an end to this, Son of Man. Send away these priests in their purple and fine linen, religious leaders who betray God's name. Stop this incessant lust for animals' blood. Help poor wounded mankind to acquire a heart of flesh.'

Jesus was more disturbed by this than he had so far been. The Tempter was putting into words ideas that had insinuated themselves into his own spirit. He remembered how he had stood on Olivet and marvelled not at the Temple and its services but at the holy hollow at the heart of the sanctuary.

'Make God the centre of all centres,' the Voice went on in honeyed tones. 'Rid religion of its trivialities, its long spiritual decay.'

'What if I purify them,' Jesus asked, 'and they go back to the old ways?'

'Then come down again, Son of Man. With a sword of fire. They will understand you in the end. Think on it.'

'I am thinking.'

'What did the kings and patriarchs demand and the prophets? What was the true Israel created for? For this empty ritual of the ants? For this lip-service, this duck-like head-wagging? Or was it for steadfast love and the knowledge of God?'

For the first time, the Voice became imperious:

'Cast yourself *down*.'

Jesus did not budge.

'I beg you,' the Voice said, softening, '*out of love for mankind*, float down and sweetly purify religion. Or is this tawdry, peculiar place still precious to you?'

'I fear it,' Jesus said, in a powdery voice, 'but it is very precious.'

'Pardon me,' the Tempter said with a certain tolerance. 'How can that be? That building below has almost succeeded in making pagans of God's people. Israel was born in the desert; there she grew in innocence, like a young girl growing in the love of the Lord. You yourself came into the desert to discover your roots, is that not so?'

'Yes.'

'With the bloom of innocence upon you, far from the snares of priestly ritual. Alas, Israel forgot its origins. Israel put up a building and God was no longer the God of the heart but of the building.'

Jesus tried to interrupt, but Satan was too quick for him.

'Hear me out. In the beginning, the God of Israel had

no dwelling except his people's heart. He was a wanderer like his people, he shared their exile. He wanted no building made with hands.'

'It is the heart that counts,' Jesus said harshly.

'It is. But God is worshipped here as if he were an idol. As if his people needed to make a special journey to meet him. As if he were not already present everywhere, before they lift a foot, or speak a word, or their hearts awake. Look down on the ants, Son of Man. What are they admiring? God or the building?'

'Both,' Jesus exclaimed.

'Even were I to grant that,' the Tempter said, 'what do they trust in most? Can you not hear the ants chanting, exactly as Jeremiah heard them chant?'

From the sanctuary came the incessant clamour of, 'The Temple, the Temple, the Temple.'

'Oh, yes, Son of Man, it is hard to find God in such a splendid place. That is why David did not build a temple. He wanted to: to assuage his guilt. But no building can do that. Solomon dared to build a Temple and his heart was led astray; *and* his people's hearts. You must concede that the so-called sacredness of this place destroys the sacredness of the rest of God's world?'

Jesus was wrestling with this temptation because the seeds of it were already planted in his heart, flourished there.

'Look again, Son of Man, and tell me what you see.'

'I see gold, silver, fir, cedarwood, pageant, blood, the smoke of incense.'

'You speak honestly, Son of Man.'

'There are no images of God.'

'True,' the Voice returned. 'Or is that so? Are not gold and silver the most perverted of all images of God? As if only glory and splendour befit the Most High. Tell me, what idea of God is conjured up by a place like this? Is it not of an Oriental despot, the kind of heathen who built this Temple for his subjects? Someone who thirsts for gold and glory and domination? God's children should search for him in humility and poverty of spirit, not in a building that takes their breath away.' Satan paused before daring to add, 'If I were God, Son of Man, I should prefer the ants to choose a piece of wood, carve it or leave it shapeless, and say, "This is what God is like," rather than put up this blasphemy which overwhelms without humbling the spirit.'

'What would you have me do?'

'Float down on a cushion of angels' wings. Enter the Holy of Holies before priests and people. Lead them away for ever from this desolate place, this last relic of paganism. Tell the ants you have come to save them from whatever destroys true piety and installs idolatry like this. Never again allow them to seek refuge in religion that bars their way to God.'

'Then?'

'Then, Son of Man, take my hand and come with me into the world of men. No room for religion there, only for God's word. For God is the God of all the world, he loves everyone. Make the world sacred, every inch of it. End finally this blood-letting, this abiding concern with the fabric and upkeep of buildings. End the hypocrisy of soulless ritual. End the costly priest-craft, the flamboyant Levitical ministrations.'

Jesus was muttering, 'If only I *could*.'

'But you *can*, Son of Man. See down there the tables of money-changers, the stalls of the Levites. This is the proof that religion depends on mammon. They are not enemies but allies. Religion cannot exist without mammon; and with mammon comes greed, excesses, the oppression of the poor. After all, who pays for the Temple but the poor? Money is the real incense of religion, you can smell it everywhere.'

'This cannot be,' Jesus said, shaking his head. 'It cannot.'

'It *is*,' the Voice insisted. 'Religion is not good for people. Better the quiet Sabbath at home, meditation, vigils and lonely prayers, the gift of self to God in silence and holiness. You, above all others, Son of Man, were not made for religion.'

'I am a Jew,' Jesus said, defiantly. 'I was made for the religion of my fathers.'

'The religion of your fathers is mercenary, like all the rest. The Temple, what is it but the biggest business in

Israel? Twenty thousand servants to keep it going: dignitaries, priests and Levites, treasurers, porters, musicians. But worse, look again, Son of Man.'

At the entrance to the sanctuary, about to make his annual visit to the Holy of Holies, was a big bloated ant in the vestments of the High Priest.

'Behold, your leaders, Son of Man. The priests, the High Priest himself, all Sadducees. They do not believe in life eternal. That High Priest is supposedly closer to the blessed God than all Israel, yet he believes himself to be nothing but a lump of clay in priestly finery. This is the proof the entire system is perverse. The higher up the ladder, the more faithless they get. Right up to the chief representative of a believing people. He uses Torah to nullify faith in life eternal, the ultimate blasphemy.'

'It is an aberration,' Jesus said, with a gasp.

'It has always been so,' the Voice insisted. 'It is rare to find a priest who believes in God or in mankind. Talk not to me of aberrations. Religion has always given rise to the greatest blasphemies. The sacrifice of infants to the god Moloch is but one instance. Religion is always willing to sacrifice its children to the gods, even to God. Believe me' – the Voice became concerned *and* menacing – 'that High Priest now grovelling in the Holy of Holies would not think twice about sacrificing you *in the name of religion.*'

Jesus said, 'I must walk the path my Father has mapped out for me.'

'I am surprised at you, Son of Man,' the Tempter said. 'What have you in mind?'

'To be loyal.'

'Loyal to what and to whom? To the priests who live off religion or the people who have to endure it? Tell me, why is it the people accept John the Baptist as the greatest of men and the priests reject him? Because priests fear anything new and nothing so much as the word of prophecy, the word of God. Because they, greedy and jealous, cannot tolerate that a holy man, a *genuinely* holy man, should instruct and purify the people *free of charge.* Because he shows there is no need to make a living out of God. Because he offers God without strings, without tying people to himself.'

223

Jesus did not react, whether to agree or disagree.

'You are not a priest, Son of Man. You are a layman, a teacher, a prophet. You are not one to accept bribes, preferment. You do not support the establishment but the poor, the gentle, the lowly. You are apart. I say again, Loyal to whom?'

'To God.'

'God needs you to speak loyally to him. Tell him religion is a paradise for hypocrites, an Eden of self-deception. Tell him plainly, religion is bad for mankind.'

'No!'

'Tell him some men and women, exceptional people, become better in spite of it, but is it fair that only the heroic can survive it for long?'

'Only bad religion is bad for mankind.'

'When was there any other kind?'

Jesus was silent, unable or unwilling to answer.

'In every religion, priests will disparage men like Ezra, try to close him down, preferring Achbors whose holiness is only a bloodless form of lechery.'

'Ezra.' Jesus spoke the name as if there was strength in it, and an answer to his Tempter. 'Ah, Ezra.'

'I can guess now what you have in mind, Son of Man. Your baptism surprised me, I must admit. I thought you were the champion of joy.'

'I am.'

'Yet you are here in training for – how shall I put it? – the wrong things. You wish to conquer by the unarmed word of God. You consider it sinful to float down there in front of those wretched little ants. You prefer to suffer.'

'I do not prefer it. I am prepared.'

'For whose benefit, Son of Man? If you insist on suffering, it will doubtless give you pleasure.'

'What pleasure is there in suffering?'

'The deepest,' Satan said, 'believe *me*, the most satisfying, the most seductive. There is nothing like it to bring a sense of fulfilment to an otherwise wasted life. But if you suffer and die – I say *if* – remember this: your death will be twisted as only religion knows how to twist things. Your followers will use it as a justification for inflicting death on others who do not agree with you –

or, more likely, do not agree with *them*. Why, if you die, even your own race might be put to death in atonement for it.'

Jesus flinched. 'Tell me how.'

'Have you considered the possibility that Israel will reject you?'

'It will not.'

'*If* it does, and if Gentiles say yes to you, who will be to blame when Gentiles slaughter Jews *in your name*?'

Jesus turned his head aside in wrath and incredulity.

'Believe me,' the Tempter said, 'you will never be *loved*, if you go the way of suffering. Someone will have to pay for that. Your followers will make it their sacred duty to see that someone does. They will never forgive you for allowing yourself to suffer, but they will conveniently divert their hatred of you into a hatred of others. They will turn their guilt into destructiveness. And your beloved Israel will say, It would have been better for us if that Man had never been born.'

'Impossible.'

'Far from it. And because no aberrations are as cruel as religion's, they will make a religion out of you.'

'But ... but I have my religion,' Jesus said, hoarsely. 'I have not come to found another.'

'I know it, Son of Man. But who else will believe you? Beware, a new cult will arise around a sacrificed Messiah. You will be worshipped with gold vestments and gold utensils, the entire paraphernalia of incense, bowings and scrapings – special clothes, special people, special rites and places.'

'But ... '

Satan pressed on. 'Your followers will find it hard even to utter your name without adopting a special sanctimonious tone. A new race of ants will say, "Jesus, Jesus, Jesus," just as the old ants repeat, "The Temple, the Temple, the Temple." They will think that merely by repeating your name, without any change of heart, they will dodge divine retribution. It will be a talisman against disease and death, a coin to gain admission into Paradise. Men and women will repeat your name as if it stamped your approval on them, unutterably boring, conventional men and women, I mean, who never *dared* anything in their entire lives. And your prophetic word will be forgotten or, worse, changed into rules and regulations in ever-increasing numbers.'

'Impossible!'

'Impossible, you say. Look what happened to Moses. Ten commandments already multiplied into thousands. Can you guarantee that your followers will be different to those of Moses? No, two tablets will not be nearly enough. They will quarry mountains to write your regulations on. Whole codes of laws. A new breed of lawyer to write them, another to interpret them. They would have to stand on one leg until it was worn away and still they would go on and on interpreting your simple word. For you are not so naive or unjust as to think the excesses of the Pharisees are unique. They are mild compared to what your followers could do.'

'No,' Jesus said, desolately. 'Not possible.'

'I agree,' the Tempter said, 'not *possible*, but *certain*. A religion based on you will be the worst the world has seen because it will be a perversion of the best. The same, only a crueller compulsion: Do this, the priests will say –'

'*Priests?*'

'Oh, yes. Wherever there is religion there are priests. They pop up, you see, like fleas on a dog. You who are no priest will be represented by armies of priests. They may even have the gall to call you, "The Great High Priest". In fact, they will have to do this if their mischief and malice are to triumph. They will put pressure on people in your name to do this, at this time, in this place –'

'But I apply *no* pressure.'

'Do not worry,' the Tempter said, allowing himself a moment of irony, 'they will do it for you. They will be able to read your most secret thoughts, your un-expressed intentions, *unerringly*. They will refine your "prescriptions" until the purpose of them is lost in an antiquity that never existed. Remember, religion always exists – and *your* religion will exist – not to serve God but to serve men. Faith is and will always be confidence in the power and cosiness of a believing community that feels itself safe behind a high, unscalable wall.'

226

'But,' Jesus objected vehemently, 'I am opposed to all these things.'

'That is why I fear for you and why what I fear will come to pass. You are a man who insists on asking, Why, Why, Why? And whoever asks why, him religion destroys. The prophets understood this and accepted this. *Any* attack on religion, however heinous religion is, is judged by religious people to be blasphemy; and blasphemy is an "insult to God". The more you defend God from blasphemy, Son of Man, the more blasphemous you will seem to be and the more certainly you will die. You will be reinstated, certainly, by the very sort of people who put you to death and turned you into the new religion. Being dead, of course, you will no longer oppose it or ask why. Only appear to authorise it.'

'Never!'

'Oh, yes. As part of the new religion of Jesus, huge buildings will be erected in your name out of the pennies of the poor. They will fill these buildings with images of you, busts, sentimental statues – '

'But I am a Jew. I am opposed to images.'

'They will not see the humour of this. They will choose *not* to see you as an image-breaker. Those statues of you will be decorated with royal robes as though you were a pious version of Tiberius. They will put a gold crown on your head – '

'I am a poor carpenter,' Jesus yelled. 'I have never *seen* a gold crown.'

'Your mother will not escape. Spiritually, very touching, very marketable. She will be depicted, let me see, as tall and slender, young and beautiful, with an unblemished complexion, in gowns of silk, with a crown on her head, of course.'

Jesus pictured to himself his dumpy, tired, prematurely aged little mother, with her rough hands and wrinkled eyes, who prayed hard to God for the onions to grow. Who would dare depict her as a king's daughter?

Jesus was incensed. This disrespect to one dear to him was the serrated edge of misery. He would not listen to the Tempter for a long while, thinking he had a sense of humour worse than any Jew he ever knew.

Satan waited patiently before saying, with humility, 'I did not mean to be offensive, truly. My imagination ran riot. Maybe these things could never be. But *you* will not be let off so lightly. There will be jewel-encrusted Jesus-rings for followers of yours with more than a million acres. Special Jesus-brooches for rich ladies who can afford to pin them on their pious bosoms. It is true, Son of Man. Disciples of yours, without a pang of conscience or the glimmer of a smile, will wear images of you which, if sold, would feed a starving child for fifty years.'

Jesus was banging his head in unbelief.

'There will be times, Son of Man, when your most devoted disciples will band together to acquire most of the land in a country. They will feed the poor, it goes without saying. The poor will certainly not have enough to feed themselves. And now for the worst part.'

Jesus lifted his head in anticipation.

'The stage will be set for you, *whether you wish it or not*, to become the greatest tyrant in all history.'

'Tyrant? Me?'

'Your followers will sanction methods you outlaw, kill where you choose to die, kill the body to save a soul and think it a very acceptable bargain. They will massacre entire populations to regain the land you sanctify with your blood, forgetting that you prided yourself on not owning one inch of it. They will place emblems of you and your suffering at the head of processions whose one aim is to persecute those who do not agree with you – or, rather, *them*. And when the tormented ask their torturers who they are, they will reply, "I am Jesus who has come to persecute you." Such are the disciples of yours who will decide with a smooth, infallible certainty truths which you never entertained, and, had you done so, you would have laughed at.'

'My soul despises such things,' Jesus said fiercely. I would repudiate them.'

'Son of Man,' the Tempter pleaded, 'do mankind a favour. Come down from this pinnacle, your hands and feet stretched out like a bird, soft hands, unblemished feet. Do not risk rejection. Do not ask too much of those busy, deaf little ants?

Jesus weighed up the consequences of rejection for a long time until Satan said:

'Consider, too, Son of Man, how every crank, every darkness-loving lunatic will hail you as his leader and guide. The masochists, the self-flagellants will have a stupendous time. "Jesus could have avoided suffering," they will say, justifiedly, "and did not. He must have enjoyed it." You will then be called on to sanction every abuse and contempt of the flesh, the exaltation of pain over joy, of death over life. Every maniac who sits up a pole or digs a hole and squats in it for a lifetime will honour you for showing them the way. They will knock the heads off roses and, with bare hands, grasp the thorns – "Did not Jesus my Lord?"

'Men and women will be put on a pedestal for never in fifty years breathing fresh air or seeing the light of the sun, for never watching buds burst in spring, for never lifting their eyes above their unwashed feet. People less like you it would be hard to imagine, but these will be honoured as the great champions of your cause, the ones credited with soundest insight into your message, the ones who keep that message unsullied from generation to generation.

'And you, the scourge of religion, will be, yes, *you* will be the most world-denying religion the world has ever seen. You will be taken over by the rich and powerful –'

'No,' Jesus cried.

'I say yes. They will tame you. The powerful will argue, "Jesus loved the poor, the hungry, the dispossessed. This is the proof he *wants* them to be poor, hungry, dispossessed." Of course, the poor *will* love you but the rich will have made the best use of you. You will be the unseen power behind the throne of many a tyrant.

'More humbling, in many ways, Son of Man, you the Saviour will become a method of salvation, a *system*. There will be infallible ways of winning Jesus's favour. Millions of books will be written about you, theses, dissertations, even though you yourself might never write a word. The very learned will specialise in you. Senates of old men will expound you, and use you to malign youth and suppress originality. All, *all* will be commentary, Son of Man, but hardly anyone will notice. You will become a piece of merchandise. They will name political parties after you, armies, militia, weapons of war. Every single thing you ever do or say will be scrutinised, agonised over, fought for. A hundred groups, all contradictory, will declare with absolute conviction – they will call it "faith" – that you are their Jesus and no one else's, "the authentic Jesus", though they have invented you. And they will be sure, without a hint of perfidious doubt, that you will justify all the excesses they do in your name.

'Yet, for the last time, Son of Man, who will be to blame but yourself? They will not countenance that you suffered because you hated evil; no, the love of suffering for its own sake will be the new orthodoxy. Whoever suffers most – however bizarre, pointless, self-inflicted – is most like Jesus. Would you wish that on your greatest enemy?'

Jesus wrenched his mind away from Satan's arguments to look down once more from his awesome height. He looked through his own eyes, with love. And in his love, the ants disappeared. In their place were people dear to him. There were his mother and Joseph, with Ezra his teacher, and holy Rabbi Samuel who was even able to love the money-changers, and Simon Peter and James and John and Judas, and a host of other holy men and women.

How much contempt Satan had for people that he depicted them as ants on an ant-heap!

When Jesus broke his silence, it was like the crash of thunder:

'It is written, *You shall not tempt the Lord your God.*'

There was an immediate sound like that of fast retreating footsteps. He listened further. Nothing. The Tempter, he knew, was gone.

And Jesus found himself peering, cold and trembling, into the desolate wilderness.

Chapter 39

THE FINAL TEMPTATION

The third time Jesus heard the Voice it had neither a hectoring tone, nor a worldly suaveness. It was sad, even humble.

'Come with me,' the Voice said.

'What will you show me?' Jesus asked, shaking, for he sensed something momentous.

'Everything,' the Tempter said.

'Everything?'

'Everything in time and space.'

'I will come,' Jesus said, for there was such sorrow in the Tempter's voice that he was unable to resist.

With a whoosh, he was lifted up in a fiery chariot, beyond the realms of Elijah, to a mountain above all mountains from where he witnessed all the kingdoms of the world.

'Look, Son of Man,' the Tempter said, 'there are Egypt, Assyria, Babylon, Greece, Rome. Behind them and in front of them other nameless and unspeakable tyrannies. Your own pleasant village was undermined by petty greed and the need for self-protection; but here is iniquity on an altogether cosmic scale.'

'Why do you show me this?' Jesus asked, recoiling in horror.

'To prove to you how the world was sunk in darkness from the beginning.'

'It was you who did it,' Jesus cried.

'True,' the Tempter said, but without a trace of triumph. 'It was I. I have shown you this lump of wickedness so you will not doubt that the world is mine.

My mark is everywhere upon it: wars, factions, hatred, mindless destruction. You have seen it; it has reached you in your very flesh already.'

'It is horrible what you have done.'

'Ah, yes,' the Tempter said, immeasurably contrite, 'but I have repented, you see.'

Jesus was perplexed. Was Satan really able to regret his wrongdoing and beg pardon of God?

'Where are the signs of your repentance.'

'I am afraid there are none, Son of Man. But that is because I am helpless, unredeemable. I need *you* to assist me.'

'To do what?'

Satan did not answer immediately. He was content to stall. When he spoke, he merely said, 'Be brave, Son of Man, do not turn your eyes away from a wounded world. It had a series of false starts, certainly. It requires you to purify it, to make it a place of harmony and love. I will leave you to choose the rules by which it is to live, you may think me biased, you see. The proud you will crush, and the domineering and the godless. Not in the age to come, either, but now. I want you to be as impatient as I am to see justice *now*.'

'A new creation.' Jesus fondled the idea in his heart. 'Is such a thing possible?'

'It is,' the Tempter said. 'No more wickedness. Good not evil will flourish. It is an infinite burden but you are strong, Son of Man. You will be able to bear it, to make of things what you will. Under you, men will learn to obey – and love to obey – what is good and only good.'

'The price, Tempter, the price?'

Satan was still not forthcoming.

'Wait till you see better, Son of Man, the marvellous thing you are purchasing. A world for you to tidy up, discipline, rejuvenate.'

'You would have me lash men into obedience?'

'Do you think,' Satan said, with a quick laugh, 'that men resent obedience, resent the love and order that obedience brings? No, no, no. Besides, the world was built to be a brotherhood, was it not? You are at the age of Alexander when he died. You can be greater. You can make a Jewish empire of all the world, if that is what you wish, only a spiritual empire. Through you, all men will be chosen to love and serve God.'

'The *price*, Tempter.'

Satan spoke with deliberation, 'Simply acknowledge the fact: the world is mine. And accept it from my hands.'

'No.'

'Then,' the Tempter continued, 'fall down and worship me.'

'Never!'

'You are thinking of yourself again, Son of Man. Am I the only one with pity for mankind?'

'Is it pity to impose justice?'

'Is it pity,' Satan countered, 'to allow injustice to be rampant? To leave the oppressor to rob and maul his victims? Surely it is kindness to impose justice with as stern a will as tyrants impose injustice? Look again, I beg you, Son of Man. Do not blind yourself to all that *misery*. God has bungled, it is plain. He has made the world too easy a prey to my wiles and I am not happy with this. God has, without wanting it, made a monstrous error. He asked men for too much and is disappointed that they give him nothing. Be their guide, their teacher. Be a new Adam at the dawn of a new creation. Be not bashful that you have to learn from me what mercy really is.'

'And how will you "give" me the world?'

'Ah,' the Tempter said, as if at last he was willing to reveal his master-plan. 'I shall simply withdraw from it.'

Jesus was astonished at this answer.

'You would withdraw?'

'I would slip away, Son of Man, like a Bedouin who folds up his tent in the night. In the morning, no trace. Look for him and you might as well look for the wind that blew yesterday or smoke from yesterday's fire.'

'But *why*? Why would you renounce your empire and go away?'

'I am not the loathsome monster you take me for,' Satan said, humbly. 'I will go in atonement. To leave the field open for goodness and only goodness. Is not this the aim of your strivings: the Kingdom of God? If I can help, if I can speed the coming of the Kingdom, I should be

233

happy for the first time. It would be – how shall I express this? – the joyful repentance of the sinner. Think of it. You have but to say the word and you will end strife, bloodshed, sorrow – *for ever.*'

'If there is to be no temptation,' Jesus said, suspiciously, 'why are you tempting me now?'

'I tell you, Son of Man, with all the fire and fervour of my being: this is the Last Temptation. If you pity mankind you will have the distinction of being the last man on earth whom I will tempt. I give you my word.'

Jesus was shivering like a dog dreaming. His bones ached. 'Abba,' he kept crying inwardly. 'Abba, my Father.'

The Tempter was softly saying to him:

'Take the entire earth from my hands, Son of Man. Take it and offer it up as a perfect sacrifice to God. Believe me, the Most High has only to stop thinking of the world for a moment for it to turn into rubble, into nothing. I, too, have my little tricks. I can rid the world of evil once and for all, simply by going away. I am prepared to do this because I love mankind. This is *my* sacrifice. Make yours. Take my place. Put goodness where there is now evil, love where there is now hatred. Bring in the Kingdom speedily. It is late for light, peace, love – but not too late. Behold, the whole world is beneath your feet. Manifest yourself in all your shining glory. There! I bequeath it to you. *Pick it up, Son of Man.*'

Will the Tempter really make his peace with God? Is he truly repentant? Is he God's champion, the lover of mankind?

Something was wrong. Something had to be wrong.

Then, to Jesus's needle-sharp brain, there came a massive illumination.

This temptation was itself proof that only through trials and tribulations can God ever be served. When Jesus saw this, the last shreds of plausibility were also torn from the other two temptations he had endured.

God would not be better served if Satan left the world. He would not be served at all. Service of God cannot be had on the cheap. It requires the overcoming of evil; there is no other way.

234

Evil, Jesus saw, will never be banished, but all the while it is being contained and often mastered. The role of good is to suffer and absorb the evil and, by so doing, to redeem it.

For love feeds on hatred, as hatred feeds on love. They need each other as two fighters need each other to make a contest. Without a contest, without a possibility of losing, there is no victory.

A world good through and through, without trials, without temptations, is a milk-sop world. A world of happy children who never grow up. It would have no cowards but no heroes; no sinners but no saints; no failures but no triumphs; no hazards and no ecstasy. It would be boring, tepid, monochrome. Greyly uniform, with no rosy dawns, no blood on sunset hills. There would be nothing to achieve in it. Finished as soon as made. In such a *terrible* world, there would be no way for people to prove their love.

No wonder the Tempter prefers to leave the world. It would then revel in its own mediocrity, whereas now it threatens him. Then he would spit on it. Yes, Satan was ingenious. He would far sooner slip away than fight battles which, however bloody, he could never ultimately win.

To evil, there are no victories. Only if Satan were permitted to leave the world would he triumph over creation. Final victory would be assured him, when he saw goodness unassailable, unthreatened – minuscule.

Jesus finally saw the temptations for what they were: a huge deception, a marvellous piece of effrontery. He let out a loud, cracked laugh. He was laughing at the Tempter for posing as God's rival, as his equal. When really God has no rivals and Satan is *nothing*. Satan has no final victory; he only contributes desolately to the final victory of good.

No wonder Satan saw his best hope was not to haunt the world and make it even messier but to clear out. This he cannot do, though he tried, and he is in agony. His greatest punishment is knowing he is necessary to the glory and greatness of God's world.

'Abba, Abba.'

Jesus worshipped his Father as the God of all creation. Even of the evil within it. *Especially* of the evil within it. For evil, in some curious way, witnesses more vividly to God's glory than the Temple itself. A sinner more genuinely speaks the praises of God than a priest offering sacrifice.

Father, I know you are working until now. You are making the world as you made it at the beginning of time and you will make it unto the end. You do not vary or falter in your purposes. Your Kingdom comes not in spite of evil but through it. For mercy overcomes heartlessness or there is no mercy; humility overcomes pride; purity overcomes impurity. And every tear shed is a seed of glory.

Jesus took a deep breath and cried, 'Go away from me, Satan. For it is written, *You shall worship the Lord your God and serve no one but him.*'

It was suddenly sunrise. Night's spectre was gone. A weight, like the sycamore-tree he had once carried for Ezra, was lifted from his back.

'Where are you, Tempter?' he called in exultation.

In a searing flash, he *knew*. For, finally, he recognised that familiar unfamiliar voice that the Tempter was using. It was his own.

The Tempter resided in his own heart. Jesus carried him around with him, had always done. Should he turn a corner, lift a stone of his heart, he might see him there.

One day in particular, he knew, he would hear that Voice again. He was a man. Like the rest of men, he would never be free of temptation.

Even this realisation could not disturb his peace of mind. He had come through. He knew what he had to do and what it would cost him. His apprenticeship was over.

His Father, he was convinced, would send angels to minister to him. He stood up on limbs of wood. He stretched; tried one leg, then the other; straightened his back.

He was a butterfly, emerged from its chrysalis, unfolding its wings, shaking them to pump blood into its veins in preparation for flight, but already beautiful, already fully-grown.

He started to move. Possessed of ferocious determination. Physically diminished, his new spiritual stature was tremendous. Ready. He was ready.

He stumbled out of the desert. To look at, a root out of a thirsty ground that had sprouted legs.

The sun was a cherub whirling a flaming sword, but there had been a shower in the night. Spring had come to the steppe. Dizzy and blinded at first, he walked on grass and flowers.

So sharp were his deprived senses, he had only to sniff the air and, like a camel or a thirsty ass, he could smell the greenery and the waters of Jordan while still a mile away.

He grew stronger and straighter as he walked, like Elijah on the way to Horeb. But where were his angels?

Yes, his Father had not failed him. There were Peter and Andrew, James and John, Simon and Judas. In spite of his rags, his caked yellow face, his stalk-like figure, they recognised him and cheered.

The Baptist was with them. Jesus heard him say, 'Look, the Lamb of God. He is the One who takes away the sin of the world.'

Peter was running towards him. Breathless, he embraced Jesus and kissed him. Their joy in each other mingled like blood.

Through dry lips, Jesus croaked, 'Thank you.'

'You said, "Wait," Master, so we waited.'

Jesus was flagging. The last drop of energy was spilled. Before collapsing in Peter's arms, he managed to whisper, *'I am waiting no longer.'*

Chapter 40

Jesus rested for several days beside the Jordan.

It was Judas who first noticed the change in him.

237

Something big had happened to him in the desert wastes. Before, Jesus was hesitant; now, decisive. Before, he had made no demands on them; now he demanded everything. Judas was very pleased. God's Kingdom could not come without the total gift of self.

When Jesus had sufficiently recovered, he and his disciples took the Jordan valley route to Galilee.

At the Lake, Jesus surprised them, especially Peter, by saying, 'Go ahead to Capernaum. I have a job to do. I must do it alone.'

No one questioned his authority. They embraced and he turned west in the direction of Nazareth.

His appearance in the village caused a stir. News of what had happened at the Jordan had filtered through in a garbled way, including the Baptist's testimony. But who was the Baptist? Prophet or crank?

His mother was shocked to see how gaunt he was, how he had aged. But she saw, too, that the strength in him, always plain to her, had come to the surface. She did not need telling that his waiting was over. Even when he said, 'Shall I tell you what the Baptist said?' she shook her head as if to say, I do not need to be told.

He ate hungrily but without concentrating on eating. His mind was elsewhere.

Afterwards, he said, 'Ezra, how is he?'

'Not well.'

'Ah,' Jesus said, sorrowing for himself and for Ezra, because he needed something from Ezra, something very special.

'There isn't a meal on him for a maggot,' his mother said.

Jesus went to the Rabbi's house. It was a jumble of stones covered by a flat roof. If a fox jumped on it, it would tumble down.

Sarah was sewing a tunic, using a bone needle and her own thread. Quiet. She had no one to argue with. What was it Ezra always said of her: 'That woman is argumentative. Even when she talks to herself she can't agree.'

Sarah indicated, with a tired gesture, where her

238

husband was. In the next room.

'Is he ill?'

'Sneezing,' she said, in her offhand way. 'Like the little boy Elisha raised from the dead, nothing more.'

At the entrance to Ezra's section of the house, Jesus removed his sandals as a mark of respect. In the dim light, he saw him lying on a straw mat.

His head was on a pillow. His face, with its dust-coloured skin, was as transparent as a bat's wing. So thin the face, the ears and nose seemed bigger than before. His beard stood up like a patch of desert scrub. His eyes were closed.

Jesus stood there as in a hallowed place. This was Nazareth's Holy of Holies. He was intensely aware of how much Ezra meant to him. Of the good wine God had poured into Ezra's soul he had not spilled a drop. He was an example of all the secret forces, humble and terrible, locked up inside a human being.

Ezra had never thought of himself. 'Go on,' he used to say, joking, 'step on my toes. What else did God give me them for?' He had carried everybody's burdens like a donkey. No, like Moses, he had carried the whole people on his back and taught them how to walk before God.

A mouse or some small creature stirred in the corner, but Ezra did not open his eyes. His breathing was harsh, irregular.

Oh, yes, how Jesus loved this unpaid, selfless, poverty-stricken guardian of the Law who always followed his God, limping at times but always following. Religion had never corrupted him and he had sweetened religion. The blessed God was gold to him and eternal wonder. *This*, Jesus told himself, *is a true Pharisee.*

He bent down and kissed the Rabbi's beard. Ezra opened his eyes and, when they adjusted, he saw Jesus near him and smiled. He cleared his throat, sand-clogged by the sound of it, and said, 'Is it you, my Jesus?'

'I came back,' he whispered. 'Especially to see you.'

'Stories, my son. I have heard so many stories. But with your own lips I must hear it.'

'Ask.'

'Are you *Meschiah*, the One whom God is to send?'

239

'What do *you* think, Rabbi?'

Jesus said it earnestly, with a kind of affectionate longing. In all the years of waiting, no moment took as long to pass as this.

The Rabbi did not answer. His eyes had, for a while, lost their focus. He was thinking.

In the mist surrounding him, he saw with a curious clarity. It was God's joke at his expense. As though, at the very end of his lifetime of searching, something precious was being revealed to him which was within a hand's grasp all the while.

This boy, *his* boy, so innocent, so gentle, so different from all others and so unafraid ... Was this a silly case of an old man seeing visions and a young man dreaming dreams?

How he had admired his son's serenity, his ageless wisdom. Jesus had always seemed to him older than he was himself, and so much wiser – effortlessly wise, as if it were second nature to him.

Is my Jesus sent by God? Has the Messiah come out of Nazareth? Is this possible?

Was it possible that this boy who had laughed at his funny ways and chopped wood with him was God's Anointed?

He picked out a couple of memories like the two rosiest peaches on a tree.

Joseph was dying. He, Ezra, had come to the house. Mary and Jesus, then fourteen years old, were holding hands round the bed and Jesus, in a kind of trance, was saying repeatedly, 'Abba.' Ezra had taken it for granted that Jesus was addressing Joseph. But what if he were calling God his 'Father'? What if he had a special right to call God 'Father'?

Then there was the holy Rabbi Samuel in the court of the Temple. He had not blessed Jesus. What if he had been unable to, not because there was a flaw in the boy but because of his overpowering holiness? So that no blessing of his would do any good because God was in the boy already?

Ezra turned his head this way and that, painfully.

What does it mean? Ezra asked himself. *Do I have a place in*

God's plan, as no other Rabbi has? I was the boy's teacher. I instructed him, rebuked him – God help me – corrected him. In this pitiful village, not in the palace of the High Priest.

How could this be?

The strain was too much for Ezra. He felt a blow as if someone had struck him with an axe.

Jesus looked with anguish on him. Ezra's veins popped out in his forehead, purple, rope-like. His eyes glazed. He was twitching at the mouth from the corner of which a viscous liquid, the colour of mother's milk, was dribbling. One side, then his entire body, shook and rattled.

Ezra tried to speak but only a snorting sound emerged. Jesus laid him on his side, soothed him, stroked his forehead until he was quiet.

He stayed with him a long time. There was a big hollow in his heart. Ezra's inability to express faith in him had scooped it out.

'Your husband is ill, very ill.'

Sarah regarded him stupidly. She was practically deaf. It was hard to make her understand.

'Is it any wonder?' she said, at last, continuing to sew. 'He's not been himself since he heard those silly stories.'

'I'm sorry,' Jesus said, faltering.

'If you're who they say you are,' Sarah barked, 'you cure him. All I can say is, if he goes to God, heaven help him.'

'Your husband has nothing to fear.'

'I was thinking of God,' she said.

He smiled briefly. 'God will be pleased any time to continue arguing with Rabbi Ezra.'

Sarah shook her head. 'If that one lives on after death, what's the point in his dying, then? No, if you ask me, death is its own reward.'

In these few moments, Jesus grasped something about Ezra and Sarah that had eluded him before. Love has many languages. When a man hardly understands the language he himself speaks, how can he understand that of others?

They were not hard, but simple people. If she had been ill, Ezra would have acted as she did now. They accepted

241

what they could not change. Any other attitude was madness.

'This is worse,' Jesus said. 'Much worse. He needs you.'

'Needs me?' she echoed, incredulously.

Sarah put down her sewing and, in a totter, went to tend the man she loved.

Next day was the Sabbath. Jesus called in on Ezra on his way to the synagogue. Sarah was still sewing, but there was evidence of tears. The tumbledown house was dense with expectation.

Ezra was nearing the end. Already his tiny body was too big for him. God the Grape-Gatherer was coming soon to pluck his life from him; but what was left on the branch but gleanings?

Ezra's face lit up when Jesus entered. He tried to speak but his words had no edges. They came out glued together.

The Rabbi's head was full of clamour. However loudly Jesus spoke, the words reached Ezra like a still, small voice.

With an effort, the old man lifted himself up and raised his eyebrows questioningly, like little arrow-heads. Words were struggling within him, like a puffed old man climbing a rickety staircase into a loft.

'I must know,' he gurgled. Success, even if it was only a thin string of sound.

'Do you believe, Rabbi Ezra,' Jesus said, solemnly, 'that I am the Holy One of God?'

The Rabbi nodded his head, once, twice, then sank back on his pillow, his eyes guttering like candles, his face creased in a smile.

'I knew.'

He had the impression of always having known. Deep down in the unmuddied places, where words do not interfere with thoughts. Why, when still a little boy, Jesus had protected him, shaded his blind old Ezra better than a fig-tree in the noonday heat.

There was a long silence during which Jesus gripped Ezra's arm as he struggled for breath.

It's strange, Jesus was thinking, *how in solemn moments like*

242

this, it is the humorous incidents that come to mind.

He was remembering the day he and Ezra went into the woods together. A shiny, green day. Day of birdsong inside the heart. Ezra had finally accepted that Jesus would never marry his daughter Jedidah. He was in a wonderful mood, making a big thing, as he did so often, of his bad luck.

'Bad luck,' he said, funnily, 'I have a talent for. I do not have to invite it.'

Jesus nodded, humouring him. Then Ezra launched into one of his monologues, many of which Jesus used to repeat to his mother later word for word.

'Do you think I got all this bad luck, my son, by sheer bad luck? Then you are wrong. It was *planned*. How? you say. Why? I say, it proves the good Lord is thinking of me. He chose bad luck *specially* for me, as a favour. He gives me a head-to-toe look and says, "It's tailored for *you*. There, Ezra," God says, "not just any sort of bad luck for you but this top-class stuff. Oh, smart!" He says it like I was paying for it. "What a fit it is. Like a skin. I tell you, Ezra, if a flea tries to get in with you he will squash his head." I whisper, I always whisper when I want to get his attention. "God," I whisper, "can't I have a bit of good luck for a change?" 'Who said that?" God says. "Ezra? Not *Ezra*! But Ezra, in bad luck you look so well," he says. "If you had good luck, you wouldn't be happy. You'd have nothing to laugh at. Besides, look," and he pulls back a curtain and shows me rows and rows of bad luck *already made up for me*. "What will I do with these," he wants to know, "if you switch to good luck?" I am tempted to say, "Give them to someone else, God", but he will be hurt. So I bite my tongue and *I'm* hurt. My bad luck again. I should have known; I saw it behind the curtain. "All right, God," I say, "but just one favour." "Name it," he says, "but no promises, mind." "I think I'll come back tomorrow, God." "No promises tomorrow, either," he says. "Right, Lord, here goes. I have a daughter." "I know," he says. "My Jedidah, she has a face on her would look bad on a man." "*I know*," he says, "it would look bad on a duck." "Is there nothing you can do for her, Lord?" "I already did," he says. "Something nice, Lord." He says,

243

"You know *your* luck, Ezra." I can take a hint. "Goodbye, Lord," I said. Then God said, "Before you go, Ezra." "Yes, Lord?" He says, "Ezra, you think *you've* got bad luck, but look at me. With all the nations of the world to choose from, I had to choose Israel!"'

When Jesus thought back on these things, he envied his mother her ability to laugh and cry at the same time.

The truth was, Ezra never really believed in his bad luck. Every day of his long life, he had asked God humbly why he, with all his sins, had been numbered among the chosen. Now, he knew.

Calling on his last reserves, and with the joy of a dumb man at last able to speak, Ezra whispered clearly, 'I always loved your Messiah. Remember me, O my God, for good.'

With that, he died.

Tears rolled down Jesus's cheek but he was laughing all the while he held the old man tightly and when he touched his face so it became the face of a sleeping child.

'He believed,' he said softly, without pride. 'Ezra believed in me.'

He gazed at that revered face a long time; they had endured so much together. Then he kissed his beard and the thin lines of his lips. His breath had gone to God. The good and sturdy pitcher was finally broken at the well.

Cradling him, Jesus said, 'I always loved *you*, little father.'

He went to tell Sarah the news.

'God kissed him, Sarah, and he died.'

She nodded, sobbing. 'He waited for you so he could die in peace.'

'If he waits for me now,' Jesus said, stronger than he had ever been, 'he will rise again.'

Sarah did not hear it, so absorbed was she, a one-winged butterfly, at having lost a half of herself.

'He shouldn't have gone away,' she grumbled. 'He never did break the Sabbath before.'

Jesus pointed to the room where Ezra was lying. 'Aren't you going to see him, Sarah?'

She touched her heart. 'No need.'

Jesus smiled sympathetically. 'So the Rabbi Ezra is risen already.'

Sarah dried her eyes and afterwards said, 'How was his dying?'

'Like drawing a hair out of a bowl of milk,' he said.

Chapter 41

Having comforted Sarah, Jesus strode towards the synagogue. There was sorrow in his heart but, with it, an immense pride in Ezra. His old teacher had done him a last, his most generous, service.

The moment had come for him to prove that Satan was wrong about his village. He had waited a long time for this day. A lifetime. His own people had the right to be the first to hear the glad tidings. He had longed to tell them it when the locusts came and the drought, to console and strengthen them in their affliction. Ezra had believed. This was a good omen. The rest of the village had always taken their lead from Ezra.

He took his seat in a lowly place and prayed.

Word whipped round from house to house and crowds streamed into the small building. Ezra was dead. Jesus, it was rumoured, was about to stake his claim to be their rabbi.

They were surprised to find he had not installed himself in Ezra's place. Instead, Achbor was seated there, long and dry as a grasshopper.

The Benedictions droned on interminably. People were chatting, swopping tales of what was supposed to have happened at Bethabara by the Jordan. Jesus tapped his foot impatiently.

Eventually, Achbor, out of malice, called on Jesus to step forward. He knew by a kind of perverse instinct that once Jesus had spoken he himself would be unchallenged as Rabbi of Nazareth.

Mary watched with pride as her son unrolled the scroll and kissed his hand out of reverence for it. He searched until he found this passage in Isaiah:

> The Spirit of the Lord is upon me,
>   For he has anointed me
>   To bring good tidings to the poor and afflicted,
> He has sent me to proclaim
>   Pardon to prisoners and sight to the blind,
>   To free the oppressed,
> To tell the people, this is the year that pleases the Lord.

He closed the Book and gave it back to Achbor. With the eyes of his fellow villagers fixed upon him, he said:

'Today, this scripture has been fulfilled and you are the fortunate ones who have heard it.'

The congregation settled back, waiting with curiosity for his commentary.

There was none. Jesus felt there was no need of commentary. He stood still for a few seconds, then, as briskly as he had come, he left them and walked home.

There was uproar in the synagogue. Had they heard right?

'Are *we* the poor and afflicted he talked about? Are we the prisoners and the blind? ... Is he the one who is sent by God to heal us and help us? ... Who does he think he is?'

Shaphan, the ploughman, called out, 'He is an uncircumcised Jew,' and Nebat his son said, 'Would that his mother had buried him when he was a baby – dead or living.'

The consternation got worse. People were jumping up and down, shouting.

Who was this, they demanded to know, who was claiming to be God's Anointed? The son of Mary, the carpenter, an odd-job man with no outstanding talent even for that? A Messiah who makes boxes and bedsteads? A Messiah with a Galilean accent?

One of Jesus's relatives shouted, 'He's crazy. Take no

246

notice of him. He'll only get crazier.'

They were incensed that this yokel had come unclean from being with a corpse and dared to hold the Book and tell them how to behave.

Someone said, 'He makes images and idols in his workshop when the children are there.' Yet another, 'He has been corrupting our children for years without anyone knowing.'

'Isn't he the one,' Nebat said, hungrily, 'who mixes with tax-collectors and whores?'

A great clamour went up of 'Yes'.

Mary, among the crowd, was frantic. She had always realised that her boy's innocence was both his strength and his weakness, but there was something out of the ordinary here. This was demonic. Why were they saying such things? Why had they turned on him? What had he done to them?

No need to worry, she told herself. *It's just another of these awful nightmares I've been having lately.*

Achbor, lean as a skinned rabbit, now that the damage was done, demanded quiet. He was secretly delighted. Even Ezra in his wildest moments had never made a fool of himself like this.

Just when silence was imminent, old Anna, Mary's friend, shrieked, 'That boy shames his dear mother and rots her bones.'

'Amen,' came from more than a hundred throats.

Mary tried to object but her words were lost in the uproar.

'Poor, kind Mary,' Anna howled, and the congregation took it up as a kind of refrain.

'I have a secret,' Anna hissed, 'that must be told.'

Slowly, but less grudgingly than before, silence descended. Nazareth loved a secret.

'My sin be upon me,' she said, 'that I did not tell it before. But I wanted to be kind, you see.'

'Tell it, Anna,' they yelled, assuring her they never doubted her kindness.

'Very well,' Anna said, her bleary eyes blazing of a sudden. 'I saw that wicked boy break the Sabbath.'

'Break the Sabbath? The Messiah? Never!' They

247

howled with morose glee, while Mary moaned, 'Oh, no.'

'Yes,' Anna continued, her least whisper creating its own segment of silence. 'He worked on the Sabbath *for the heathen.*'

'Heathen?'

The story was getting better and better.

'I did not mention it before for Mary's sake,' Anna said, tearing at her sheepskin coat, taking care not to damage it. 'She did not deserve *him*, oh, no.'

Mary was sobbing into her hands. Her whole life with its quiet, even tenor, its familiar pattern, had suddenly disappeared. She was in a foreign land and did not understand the people or the language. Joseph had always protected her, then Jesus. It was as if a pet animal, which she had always nourished in her bosom, had rounded on her, was tearing her to pieces.

'Yes, my dear,' Anna insisted, as if Mary was trying to gag her, 'it is true, I swear.'

'If that one brings in God's Kingdom,' Nebat said, sarcastically, 'I want no part of it.'

'All along,' Anna declared, 'I knew he was no good.'

Others of the congregation were now allowed to voice their venom. 'If Jesus is the Messiah,' someone said, 'how come we were devoured by locusts?' Another asked, 'How come the drought and famine visited us?'

Shaphan, inspired, settled all scores by calling out, 'His wickedness was the cause of all our troubles. God punished us because of him.'

Mary tried to say her son had done his best to ease their troubles. All that was audible above the din was 'troubles'.

Had they hated her, reviled her, even stoned her, Mary could easily have borne it. But they were doing it to her boy. For the first time in her life, she wondered, agonisingly, if God himself could give her the strength to forgive them.

'Troubles,' the crowd repeated, as if his own mother was blaming Jesus for their woes.

That morning, they had been expecting something fascinating to happen. Instead, they had been grossly insulted by a local nonentity. Having hit on him as a scapegoat, the mood of the synagogue turned even blacker. Behind it, was a genuine grief that Ezra had been taken from them just when he was getting too old to bother them any more.

'Our village is a laughing-stock as it is,' Achbor said, assuming leadership again. 'They will think us even more absurd when they hear of this.'

Shouts of agreement were almost unanimous.

'There is nothing for it,' Achbor said, licking his lips and chortling. 'The blasphemer must be stoned.'

'Stone him,' cried Shaphan, as if it were the last of life's pleasures left to him.

'Stone him' cried Nebat, who wanted to destroy someone who was cleverer at school than he was, whom his wife had wanted to marry, whom Rabbi Ezra always preferred to him.

'Stone him,' cried Anna, who had never forgiven Jesus for feeding her when she was starving and paying her rent – when all she had really wanted was to lie down and die.

'Stone him,' the rest cried, for the service had been shorter than they had expected and time was on their hands. It might even atone for their insults to God in times past.

They stormed out of the synagogue in the direction of Jesus's house. Only deaf old Reuben was left, his eyes closed, beating his breast and calling out, 'Amen, Amen.'

Mary followed the crowd, stumbling, weeping, tearing at her hair, wondering when the nightmare would end.

The stones began to fly. Even the children, including Shimon, joined in. They were the best shots of all.

The cry went up, 'Come out. Come on out,' as the stones rattled on the roof and against the front wall knocking down the hyssop plant.

Mary tried to put her body in front of the throwers but they dragged her aside.

'Come out!'

Slowly, the door opened from within and Jesus appeared. Under a hail of stones, he did not once raise his hands to defend himself.

A stone from Shimon hit the side of his head and blood

flowed, immediately attracting flies. He did not flinch. He went on standing, motionless, his lips moving in prayer.

The crowd, ashamed, stopped throwing and simply looked on in silence. Shimon burst into tears and went looking for his mother. One of the women said, 'It's a sin to throw stones on the Sabbath.'

'True,' Achbor decided, in his most formal manner. 'Anyone who casts another stone will be guilty of breaking the Sabbath like the carpenter.'

Mary struggled through the crowd to her son. With a cloth, she wiped the blood off his face. Proudly she did it. As if her boy had done something wonderful for God.

People were beginning to drift away when Achbor called them back.

'It is wrong to throw stones on the Sabbath,' he said. 'But how far is it to the brow of the hill?'

Nebat answered at once, 'There and back is about the distance the Law allows us to travel on the Sabbath.'

There was a tramp of feet and a crush of bodies as Jesus was separated from his weeping mother and carried up the hill, like a piece of wood on the tide. Their intention was never in doubt. They were going to rid their village of its shame once and for all.

Jesus was pushed and jostled and poked up the narrow path he had taken so often on his nights of prayer. They were chanting a psalm to give them courage for the dreadful deed.

At a bend in the path, he side-stepped smartly into one of the caves he had played in as a boy. He was on home ground.

But, he remembered, so was Nebat.

At the rear of the cave was a narrow passageway into another cave. To his relief he was still able to squeeze through. From there, he crawled as far as he could into the darkness and settled down like a cornered animal.

Minutes later, he was sitting with his back pressed to the cave wall, not daring to breathe, when a Voice, his own and not his own, whispered, '*It has begun, Son of Man.*'

At that moment, Nebat's ugly head was thrust into the entrance, silhouetted against the sky.

'I think I've found him,' Nebat called in triumph behind him.

Above the cries of delight Achbor made himself heard. 'Too late. We have gone as far as the Sabbath allows.'

'Who cares?' Nebat said, peering again into the dark.

'It is the *Law*,' Achbor thundered, revelling in his new authority as the custodian of righteousness.

Nebat cursed and withdrew his head.

Jesus heard their retreating footsteps and the clatter of rolling stones. Then he could hear no more.

Pedantry, he mused painfully, *has its uses, after all.*

An hour before the Sabbath ended, he crept back home. Not that stealth was needed. The villagers were peering through their windows, but he knew they would not break the Sabbath rest. It was against their religion.

His mother had heard the news and was anxiously awaiting him. The lamps were alight. She was praying hard, for she too had been grappling with Satan and had overcome. After the incident in the synagogue, Anna had invited herself to a meal and Mary had fed her.

As soon as he saw his mother, Jesus felt that her love cancelled out all the hurt and disappointment.

'God's will be done,' she said.

He told her not to worry. Everything was in his Father's hands. It was her turn to be comforted.

Having eaten hurriedly, he made ready to set off for Capernaum. As his mother held him in a farewell embrace, she whispered in his ear, 'God go with you, my son. Do not think too badly of our people here. They would have forgiven you anything, except being born and bred among them.'